SOME

STRANGE

UNIVERSE

The moment he saw his body, Morfiks began screaming again . . . the first terror driven out and replaced by—or added to as a higher harmonic—the terror of finding himself in a sexless body.

SMOOTH. PROJECTIONLESS. HAIRLESS. HIS LEGS HAIRLESS, TOO. NO NAVEL. HIS SKIN A DARK BROWN—LIKE AN APACHE'S.

MORFIKS SCREAMED AND SCREAMED, AND HE GRIPPED HIS FACE AND THE TOP OF HIS HEAD. THEN HE SCREAMED HIGHER AND HIGHER. THE FACE WAS NOT THE ONE HE KNEW, AND HIS HEAD WAS SMOOTH AS AN EGG.
 HE FAINTED.

Other SIGNET Science Fiction Titles You Will Enjoy

Down in the Black Gang

and other stories

by
Philip José Farmer

A SIGNET BOOK from
NEW AMERICAN LIBRARY
TIMES MIRROR

For Charles Tanner

COPYRIGHT © 1971 BY PHILIP JOSÉ FARMER

All rights reserved

ACKNOWLEDGMENTS

"A Bowl Bigger Than Earth," *Worlds of If*, © Sept. 1967, Universal Publishing and Distributing Corp.

"The Shadow of Space," *Worlds of If*, Nov. 1967, Universal Publishing and Distributing Corp.

"Prometheus," *Magazine of Fantasy & Science-Fiction*, March 1961, Mercury Press, Inc.

"How Deep the Grooves," *Amazing Stories*, Feb. 1963, Ziff-Davis Publishing Co.

"A Few Miles," *Magazine of Fantasy & Science-Fiction*, Oct. 1960, Mercury Press, Inc.

"Riverworld," *Worlds of Tomorrow*, Jan. 1966, Galaxy Publishing Company.

"The Blasphemers," *Galaxy*, April 1964, Galaxy Publishing Company.

"Down in the Black Gang," *Worlds of If*, March 1969, Universal Publishing and Distributing Corp.

"Down in the Black Gang" was rewritten for this collection. None of the stories in this collection except "Prometheus" has been published in a book.

 SIGNET TRADEMARK REG. U.S. PAT. OFF. AND FOREIGN COUNTRIES
REGISTERED TRADEMARK—MARCA REGISTRADA
HECHO EN CHICAGO, U.S.A.

SIGNET, SIGNET CLASSICS, SIGNETTE, MENTOR and PLUME BOOKS *are published by The New American Library, Inc., 1301 Avenue of the Americas, New York, New York 10019*

First Printing, October, 1971.

PRINTED IN THE UNITED STATES OF AMERICA

Contents

DOWN IN THE BLACK GANG   7

THE SHADOW OF SPACE   28

A BOWL BIGGER THAN EARTH   55

RIVERWORLD   72

A FEW MILES   105

PROMETHEUS   138

THE BLASPHEMERS   184

HOW DEEP THE GROOVE   213

Down in the Black Gang

I'm telling you this because I need your love. Just as you need mine, though you don't know it—yet. And because I can't make love to you as a human makes love to a human.

You'll know why when I've told you the true story. The story I first told was a lie.

You must know I'm not human, even if I do look just like one. Do humans sweat quicksilver?

You must know I can't make love to you. If you were Subsahara Sue, you'd have no trouble. But they'll be watching Sue, so I won't dare go near. No, I didn't mean that I prefer her. It's just . . . I don't want to get into subtleties. Anyway, Sue might turn me in, and if I'm caught, I'll be keelhauled. Let me tell you, keelhauling is no fun.

I need love almost as much as I need a hiding place. That's why I'm telling you. You, the first human to know. I need love. And forgiveness. Only, as you'll see . . . never mind . . . I'll tell you all about me. I have much explaining to do, and you may hate me.

Don't.

I need love.

The Rooster Rowdy had caused the trouble almost 2500 Earth-years ago.

I didn't know anything about it. None of the crew knew anything about it. You see, communication is instantaneous, but perception is no faster than light.

You don't see? Maybe you will as I go along.

The instruments on The Bridge had indicated nothing and would not for I-don't-want-to-tell-you-how-many years. If the Quartermaster—let's call him The Filamentous Wafter—had not been prowling that particular deck, hunting down ratio fixers, nobody would've known about it until it was too late.

As it was, it still might be too late.

The first I knew of the trouble was when the call came from The Bridge. *Directly.*

"Hello, engine room MWST4! Hello, engine room MWST4!"

Five minutes earlier, the call would not have been able to get through. The electric sparks, microwaves, and hot mercury drops—spinning like tops—would have warped transmission. They were flying all over inside our tent. Five hundred years had passed since Subsahara Sue and I had seen each other. Although we both worked in the same continent, my territory was the Berber-Semitic area, and Sue's was all the rest of Africa.

After finally getting permission to have leave together, we'd signed in at a Libyan seaside hotel. We spent most of our time on the beach, inside our tent, which was made of a material to confine the more explosive byproducts of our lovemaking. During half a millennium, we'd dormantized our attraction—notice I say, attraction, not love, if that'll make you feel any better—but even in dormancy attraction accumulates a trickle charge and 500 years builds up a hell of a lot of static. However, there's a large amount of resistance to overcome, and I'd been oscillating and Sue resonating for hours before our nodes touched.

The tourists on the beach must have wondered where the thunder was coming from on that cloudless day.

Afterwards, Sue and I lay quietly to make sure that no one had been alarmed enough to investigate our tent. When we talked, we talked about personal matters first, what we'd been doing, our loneliness, and so on. Then we talked shop. We chattered about philiac thrust/phobiac weight efficiency ratios, toleration tare, grief drag, heliovalves, and so on, and ended up by reminiscing about crewmen.

She said, "Who's in charge of cosmic bleedoff?"

The intercom bleeped.

"Hello, engine room MWST4! Hello, engine room MWST4!"

Groaning, I turned on the intercom, which looked just like a portable TV (for the benefit of humans). The "head" and part of the "shoulders" of The First Mate filled most of the screen, even though the camera must have been several thousand miles away. Behind him was a small part of The Bridge and a piece of abyss-black shadow edged by a peculiar white light. The Captain's tail.

That was all I cared to see of The Captain at any time. I'll never forget having to look at a closeup of his "mouth" when he chewed me—not literally, thank the stars—in A. H. 45. I have to admit that I deserved that savaging. I was lucky not to get keelhauled.

Oh, how I goofed up the Mahomet Follow-up! The black gangs all over The Ship had to sweat and slave, all leaves cancelled, until proper thrust could be generated.

The First Mate, seeing the mercury drip off me, roared, "Mecca Mike! What the bilge have you been doing? You oscillating at a time like this? You sleeping at the post again? You neglecting your duty *again?*"

"Sir, I'm on leave," I said. "So I couldn't be guilty of neglecting my duty. Besides, sir, I don't know what you mean by *again*. I was never courtmartialed, sir, and . . ."

"Silence!" he bellowed. Behind him, the tail of The Captain twitched, and I started to oscillate negatively.

"Why didn't you answer the all-stations alarm?"

"It didn't get through," I said. I added, weakly, "There must have been too much static and stuff."

The First Mate saw Subsahara Sue trying to hide behind me. He yelled, "So *there* you are! Why didn't you answer your phone?"

"Sir, I left it in the hotel," Sue said. "Since we'd be together, we decided we'd just take Mike's phone, and . . ."

"No wonder both of you are still in the black gang! No more excuses, now! Listen, while I tell you loud and clear!"

The Rooster Rowdy was responsible for the emergency.

I was surprised when I heard The First Mate mention him. I'd thought he was dead or had run away so far into the lower decks that he'd never be found until The Ship docked. He was one of the ring-leaders—in fact, he was The First Mate then—in the Great Mutiny 100,000 Earth-years ago. He was the only one to escape alive after The Captain and his faithfuls mopped up on the mutineers. And the Rooster Rowdy had been running, or hiding, ever since. Or so we thought.

He was called Rooster for very good reasons. His mounting lust had driven him out of hiding, and he'd tried to rape The Crystalline Sexapod.

A moment ago, I told you Sue had asked me who was in charge of cosmic bleedoff. I would have told her that The Crystalline Sexapod was in charge if we hadn't been interrupted. The Sexapod had her station at that moment inside a quasar galaxy, where she had just finished setting up the structure of a new heliovalve. The Rooster Rowdy was near enough to sense her, and he came galloping in, galactic light bouncing off the trillion trillion facets of his spinning three-organ body, and he rammed through sextillions of sextillions of stellar masses and gases and just ruined the galaxy, just ruined it.

The Crystalline Sexapod put up a good fight for her virtue, which was the same thing as her life— I haven't time to go into biological-moral details—but in the process she completed the wreckage of the galaxy and so wrecked the heliovalve and wasted a century and a half of time. She took off for the lower decks, where, for all anybody knew, she might still be running with the Rooster Rowdy hot (2500°F) after her.

The wrecked heliovalve meant that there was no bleedoff of phobiac drag in that sector or in a quarter of all of the sectors, since this valve was the master valve in a new setup intended to increase efficiency of bleedoff by 32.7 percent. And that really messed up our velocity.

Fortunately, The Quartermaster happened to be in the lower decks, where he was hunting ratio fixers. A ratio fixer, I'll explain, is a creature that lives in the interstices between ratios. Thus, it's compelled to be moving on, can't stay in one place long, otherwise it'll lose its foothold and fall. If it stands still very long, one of the quotients—analogous to a human foot—dwindles, and the other expands. The ratio fixer, like any form of life, wants security, so it tries to fix ratios (freeze them). Its efforts to keep from falling messes up proportions and causes The Ship's bulkheads and sometimes even the hull to buckle.

The Ship's shape, size, and mass are in a constant state of flux, but generally controlled flux. And if these are changed without The Bridge finding out about them in time, the vectors of velocity, direction, etcetera, are changed.

Using human analogies, ratio fixers might be compared to the rats in a ship. Or, better, to barnacles on a hull. Or maybe to both.

The Quartermaster had caught one and was choking it with its filaments when it caught sight of the wrecked heliovalve and of The Rooster Rowdy chasing The Sexapod through a hatchway into the depths. He notified The Bridge at once, and the all-stations alarm went out.

Now I understood why The First Mate was talking directly to me instead of the message being filtered down through sub-to-the-2nd-power officers and petty officers. With this emergency, it would take a long time for an order from The Captain to reach every engine room if it went through normal procedure.

But I had not, of course, understood completely. Or at all. I just thought I did because I was too awed and stunned to be thinking properly.

The Mate thundered, "In the name of The Port! You better not foul this one up!"

"I'll do my best, sir, as always," I said. Then, "Foul what one up, sir?"

"Idiot! Nincompoop! I'm not speaking directly to you just to give you a pep talk! A Thrust Potential has been detected in your engine room!"

"A Thr-Thr-Thrust Po-Po-Potential! In this area? But—"

"Imbecile! Not in your area, what is it, the Semitic? But it's your specialty! According to the message, it's in the Southern California area, wherever in bilge that is!"

"But what do I have to do with that, sir?"

"Stoker, if we weren't in such a mess, and if the Thrust Potential wasn't so promising, and if I didn't have to contact 10,000 other promising TP areas, I'd have you up here on The Bridge and flay you alive! You don't ask questions while I'm talking! Remember that, Stoker!"

"Yes, sir," I said humbly.

The First Mate then became very businesslike. Aside from a few numbskulls, coprolite-heads, and other terms, he addressed me as one entrusted with a great task and with the abilities to carry it out. That is, if I had learned anything from experience. He did remind me that I had not only screwed up the Mahomet Follow-up, I had blown the whole Ancient Egyptian Monotheist Deal.

(I was called Ikhnaton Ike and Pharaoh Phil by my chief engineer for a long time afterwards.)

The First Mate was, however, kind enough to say that I had shown much skill in the Follow-up to the Burning Bush Business.

Beware The First Mate when he's kind. I said to myself, "What's he working up to?"

I soon found out. It was the last thing I'd expected. It was a transfer to the Southern California area and a promotion to engineer, first class. I was staggered. The chief engineer and several engineer's mates and a number of very competent stokers operated in that area. In fact, there were more black gang members there than in any area of Earth.

"The chief engineer's had a breakdown," The First Mate said, although he did not have to explain anything. "He's on his way to sick bay now. This report says there's something about that area that generates psychic collapse. A distortion of psychomagnetic lines of force. However, as you know, or should know, you ignoramus, this kind of field also compensates by generating thrust-potential impulses. The Northeast section of this—what's it called? U.S.A.—has a similar distortion. Both are danger areas for our engines. But, on the other hand, you don't get anything good from a safe neutral area."

"Thanks for the elementary lecture," I said inside my head, which was a safe, though not neutral, place for my retort.

A few minutes later, I had finished saying a sorrowful good-bye to Sue and was checking out of the hotel.

"Why should you be transferred to Beverly Hills, California?" Sue said. "It may be largely Jewish in population, but the citizens are basically English speakers. They don't think Semitically, like your Arabs, Abyssinians, and Israelis."

"That's not the only puzzling thing," I said. "The Thrust Potential is non-Semitic. That is, it's not even descended from Semitic speakers."

The engineers and stokers in that area must all have become somewhat unstable, too. Otherwise, they surely would have been used. The thinking of The Bridge was, Let's shoot in Mecca Mike. He's fouled up, but he also had some great successes. Perhaps this time he'll come through. He's the best we have, anyway, The Dock preserve us!

The First Mate told me that I had better come through. Or else. . . .

There would be officers watching my work, but they wouldn't interfere unless I was obviously ruining an "engine" beyond repair.

If I came through, if I developed the badly-needed Thrust Potential, I'd be promoted. Probably to chief engineer.

The situation for The Ship was much worse than I'd guessed. Otherwise, they'd have let me take an airliner. But orders were to get me to California with utmost speed. I drove into the Libyan countryside during the daylight. At noon the saucer-shaped vehicle landed, picked me up, and took off at 30 G. It socked into its base fifty miles west of

Phoenix, Arizona, with Air Force jets scrambling from
Luke Field. They neither saw the ship nor the base, of
course, and I drove into Phoenix in what looked like a
1965 Buick and took a plane into Los Angeles.

Coming down over Los Angeles must have been dis-
heartening to the other passengers. They saw the great
greenish-gray tentacles, the exhaled poison, hanging over
the big complex. I had my special "glasses" on, and what I
saw was encouraging, at least momentarily. Down there, in
the blackness which is phobiac drag, were a dozen fairly
large sparks and one huge spark. That big spark, I knew,
must be in Beverly Hills.

There, if all went well—it seldom does—was the potential to develop a thrust which, combined with the
thrusts in existence and with those being developed on
other worlds, would, hopefully, cancel the drag caused by
the wrecking of the bleedoff heliovalve. And so the vitally
needed velocity would be ours.

Can anything good come out of Nazareth?
Can anything good be in Beverly Hills?

History has answered the first question. The future
would answer the second.

I told the taxi driver at the airport to take me to a
street which angled south off of Wilshire between Doheny
Drive and Beverly Drive. This was lined with dry-looking
maples. The block where the taxi let me off was, in a
sense, in the "slums" of Beverly Hills. Relatively speaking,
of course. Both sides of the street in this block were occupied by apartment buildings, some only five years old
and others about 25 to 35 years old. The apartments in
the new buildings rented from $350 to $650 a month and
so were considered low-rent in Beverly Hills. The apartments in the old buildings averaged about $135 a month.

My Thrust Potential, my TP, was in the second story
of an older building. I had the cab park across the street
from it, and I went inside a newer, more expensive apartment building. This had a VACANCY, 1 BDRM, FURN., NO
PETS, NO CHILDREN sign on the lawn. I put down three
months' rent in cash, which upset Mrs. Klugel, the land-
lady. She always dealt in checks. I signed the lease and
then went back to the taxi to get my bags.

My second-story apartment was almost directly across
the street from my TP and almost as high as her apartment. I carried my three bags up to it. One was full of
clothes, the second full of money, and the third crammed
with my equipment. Mrs. Klugel stood in the vestibule.

She was a heavy short woman about 65 with orange-dyed hair, a nose like a cucumber, and a clown's mouth. Her black-rimmed eyes widened as I went lightly up the staircase with a huge bag in each hand and one under my arm.

"So you're a strong man in some act already?" she said.

I replied that I was not a strong man, professionally, that is. I was a writer who intended to write a novel about Hollywood.

"So why don't you live in Hollywood?"

"By Hollywood, I mean this whole area around here," I said, sweeping my hand around.

She was such a lonely old lady, she was difficult to get rid of. I said I had work to do, and I would talk to her later. As soon as she shut the door, I readjusted the anti-grav belt around my waist under my shirt. My two thousand pounds of dense metal-shot protein would have buckled the floor if I hadn't had the belt operating. Then I took out my equipment and set it up.

I was nervous; quicksilver beaded off me and fell onto the floor. I made a mental note to clean up the stuff before I left the apartment. Mrs. Klugel looked as if she'd snoop around during my absences, and it certainly would be difficult to explain mercury drops on the floor.

The set-up for my work was this. Across the street, in the 25-year-old building, were four apartments. My concern was the upper story on the right side, facing the street. But I soon found out that the apartment just below was also to be intimately involved.

The apartment upstairs was reached by climbing a steep series of steps, carpeted with frayed and faded material. A long hall at the top of the stairs ran the length of the building, ending in a bathroom at its far end. Off the hallway, starting next to the bathroom, were doors leading to a bedroom, another bedroom, the doorway to the back entrance, the doorway to a tiny utility room, and the doorway to the living room. The utility room and living room connected to the kitchen.

The back bedroom was occupied by Diana, the 20-year-old divorced mother, and her 20-month-old child, Pam. The grandparents, Tom and Claudia Bonder, slept in the other bedroom. Tom also did his writing in this room. Claudia was 45 and Tom was 49.

When I looked through the spec-analyzers, via the tap-beam, I saw the baby, Pam, as the bright light I had seen coming in over Los Angeles. She was the big Thrust Potential.

Sometimes the light was dimmed. Not because its source was weakened. No. It darkened because of the hatred pouring out of the grandfather.

This black cataract was, seemingly, directed mainly at the people in the apartment below. If hatred were water, it would have drowned the people below. And, if they were what Tom Bonder said they were, they deserved drowning, if not worse.

Tom Bonder's hatred, like most hatreds, was not, however, simple.

None of the hatreds in that building, or in any of the buildings in Beverly Hills, and believe me, there were hatreds in every building, were simple.

I digress. Back to that particular building.

Watching that building was like watching the Northern Lights during a meteor shower on the Fourth of July. I ignored the pyrotechnic displays of the tenants on the other side of the building. They had little to do with the "stoking" and the follow-up.

Tom Bonder, ah, there was a splendid spectacle! Although he had been depressed in his youth, at which time he must have radiated heavy-drag black, like smoke from Vesuvius, he had semi-converted his youthful depression into middle-aged anger. Reversed the usual course of psychic events, you might say. Now he looked like Vesuvius in eruption.

Bonder, the grandfather, was determined not to fail as a grandfather just because he had failed as a father, husband, lover, son, teacher, writer—and you name it.

And truly, he had failed, but not as badly as he thought, or, I should say, desired, since he lusted for defeat. Rage poured out of him day and night, even when, especially when, he was sleeping.

What most infuriated him was the uproar beating upwards day and night from the Festigs downstairs. The Festigs were a father, 40 years old, a mother, 28, and a daughter, Lisa, two. From the time they arose, anywhere from 9:30 to 11:30, until they went to bed, midnight or 1:00, or later, the mother was shouting and bellowing and singing and clapping her hands sharply and the little girl was screaming with glee but usually wailing or screeching with frustration and anger. The father was silent most of the time; but he was like an old sunken Spanish galleon, buried in black silt, with his treasures,

his pieces-of-eight and silver ingots and gold crosses,
spilled out of a breach in the hull and only occasionally
revealed when the currents dredged away some mud.

Oh, he was depressed, depressed, which is to say he
was a very angry man indeed. The black heavy stuff
flowed from Myron Festig like a Niagara fouled with
sewage. But sometimes, out of boredom, as he sat on his
chair in the living room, he groaned mightily, and the
groan went up and out the windows and into the windows
of the apartment upstairs.

And Tom Bonder would jump when he heard the groan
and would quit muttering and raging under his breath. He
would be silent, as one lion may fall silent for a moment
when he hears the roar of another from far away.

The screaming joys and buzzsaw tantrums were enough
for the Bonders (not to mention the next-door neighbors)
to endure. But the child also had the peculiar habit of
stomping her feet if she ran or walked. The sound vibrated
up through the walls and the floors and through the bed
and into the pillow-covered ears of Tom Bonder. Even
if he managed to get to sleep, he would be awakened a
dozen times by the footstompings or by the screams and
the bellows.

He would sit up and curse. Sometimes, he would loosen
his grip on his fear of violence and would shout out of
the window: "Quiet down, down there, you barbarians,
illiterate swine! We have to get up early to go to work!
We're not on relief, you bloodsucking inconsiderate
parasites!"

The reference to relief, if nothing else, should have
turned Myron Festig's depression into rage, because the
Festigs were one of the few people in Beverly Hills living on relief. The relief came from the county welfare
and from money borrowed from Mrs. Festig's mother
and doctor brothers. Occasionally, Myron sold a cartoon
or took a temporary job. But he was very sensitive about
the welfare money, and he would have been astounded to
learn that the Bonders knew about it. The Bonders, however, had been informed about this by the manager's wife.

Rachel Festig, the wife and mother, was revealed in the
analyzer as intermittent flashes of white, which were
philiac thrust, with much yellow, that is, deeply repressed
rage sublimated as sacrificial or martyred love. And there
was the chlorine-gas green of self-poisonous self-worship.

But there was the bright white light of the Bonder baby,
Pam. Now that I was near it, I saw it split into two, as

a star seen by the naked eye will become a double star in the telescope. The lesser star, as it were, radiated from Lisa Festig. All infants, unless they're born psychotic, have this thrust. Lisa's, unfortunately, was waning, and its brightness would be almost entirely gone in a year or so. Her mother's love was extinguishing it in a dozen ways.

But the far brighter white, the almost blinding Thrust Potential, radiated from the Bonder granddaughter. She was a beautiful, strong, healthy, good-humored, intelligent, extremely active, and very loving baby. She was more than enough to cause her grandparents to love her beyond normal grandparental love. But they had reason to especially cherish this baby. The father had dropped out of sight in West Venice, not that anybody was looking for him.

Furthermore, both Claudia and Tom felt that they had been psychically distorted by their parents and that they, in turn, had psychically bent their daughter, Thea. But Pam was not going to be fouled up, neurotic, near-neurotic, unhappy, desolate, and so on. At the moment, both the elder Bonders were going to psychoanalysts to get their psyches hammered out straight on the anvil of the couch.

Neither the daughter nor Mrs. Bonder, though they figured significantly and were to be used by me, were as important in my plans as Tom Bonder.

Why? Because he was an atheist who had never been able to shake himself free of his desire to know a God, a hardheaded pragmatist who lusted for mysticism as an alcoholic lusts for the bottle he has renounced, a scoffer of religions whose eyes became teary whenever he watched the hoakiest, most putridly sentimental religious movies on TV with Bing Crosby, Barry Fitzgerald and Humphrey Bogart as priests. This, plus the tiniest spark of what, for a better term, is called pre-TP, and his rage, made me choose him. As a matter of fact, he was the main tool I had for the only plan I had.

Rachel Festig thought of herself as the Great Mother. Tom Bonder agreed with that to the extent that he thought she was a Big Mother. Rachel's idea of a mother was a woman with enormous breasts dripping the milk of kindness, compassion, and, occasionally, passion. The Great Mother also had a well-rounded belly, wide hips, thick thighs, and hands white with baking flour. The Great Mother spent every waking moment with the child to the exclusion of everything else except cooking and some loving with the husband to keep him contented.

Now there was a Mother!

Myron needed to be dependent, to be, at 40, an invertebrate, a waxingly fat invertebrate. Yet he wanted to be a world-famous cartoonist, a picture-satirist of the modern age, especially in its psychic sicknesses. Recently, in a burst of backbone, he had stayed up all night for several weeks, and completed an entire book of cartoons about group therapy. He knew the subject well, since he was a participant in a group and also had private sessions once a week. Both were paid for by arrangement with the county and his brother-in-law, the doctor.

The cartoon book was published and sold well locally, then the excitement died down and he subsided into a great roll of unbonestiffened protoplasm. Depression blackened him once more. He gained a hunger for food instead of fame, and so he ate and swelled.

Tom Bonder worked daytimes as an electronic technician at a space industry plant in Huntington Beach, and evenings and weekends he wrote fast-action private-eye for paperback publishers and an occasional paperback western.

He loathed his technician job and wanted to go into full-time fiction writing. However, he was having enough trouble writing part-time now because of the uproar downstairs.

I used the tap-beam and sight-beam to listen and look into the apartments and also to eavesdrop on Bonder's sessions with the analyst. I knew he ascribed his problems to a too-early and too-harsh toilet training, to a guilt caused by conflict between his childhood curiosity about sex and his parents' harsh repression of it and so on. His main problem throughout most of his life had been a rigid control over himself. He thought himself a coward because he had always avoided violence, but he was finding out in therapy that he fearerd that he might become too violent and lose his self-control.

Fortunately, he was now getting rid of some of his anger in little daily spurts, but, unfortunately, not swiftly enough.

He was always on the verge of going berserk.

Berserk! That was the key to my "stoking."

The Ship must have been losing speed even worse than we of the crew had been told. About six months after I got into Beverly Hills, I received a call from The First Mate again.

"How's the set-up coming along?"

"As well as can be expected," I said. "You know you can't stoke too fast, sir. The engine might overheat or blow."

"I know that, you cabin-boy reject!" he bellowed so loudly that I turned the volume down. Old Mrs. Klugel quite often kept her ear pressed to the tenants' doors.

I said, "I'll use more pressure, sir, but it'll have to be delicately applied. I sure wouldn't want to wreck this little engine. Her nimbus looks as if she could provide enormous thrust, if she's brought along properly."

"Three hours you get," The First Mate said. "Then we have to have 1,000,000 T units."

Three hours of Ship's time was 30 Earth-years. Even if I got the stoking done quickly, I had a hell of a lot of hard mercury-sweating work in the next 30 years. I promised I'd do my best, and The First Mate said that that had better be better than good enough, and he signed off.

Tom Bonder and Myron Festig were working themselves closer to that condition I'd been working for. The Festig child was stomping her feet and screaming all day and until one in the morning, and the inability to get sleep was putting black circles around Tom Bonder's eyes. And red halos of wrath around him.

Myron Festig was deep in the sludge pit of despond. His latest cartoon had been turned down by *Playboy*. He had just been fired from a job as a cheese salesman. His mother-in-law was threatening to visit them for a long time. His brother-in-law, the doctor, was needling him because he wasn't making a steady income, aside from welfare payments. And Rachel, his wife, when not chewing him out for his inability to hold a job, was crying that they should have another baby. They needed a son; she would deliver him a boy to make him proud.

The last thing Myron wanted was another mouth to stuff, and, though he dared not say it, another noisy mouth and big heavy feet to distract him from his cartooning.

Tom Bonder would have agreed with this. He was, he told his wife, slowly being herded to suicide or homicide. He could not take much more of this. And more frequently, as if in jest, he would open a drawer in the kitchen and take out a hand-axe, which he had brought with him when he moved from the Midwest. And he would say, "One more night of thumping from Little Miss Buffalo Stampede, one more night of bellowing

'Myron!' or 'Rachel!', and I go downstairs and chop up the whole swinish bunch!"

His wife and daughter would grin, nervously, and tell him he shouldn't even joke like that.

"I'm fantasizing!" he'd cry. "My headshrinker says it's good therapy to imagine slaughtering them, very healthy! It relieves the tensions! As long as I can fantasize, I won't take action! But when I can't fantasize, beware! Chop! Chop! Off with their heads! Blood will flow!" And he would swing the axe while he grinned.

Sometimes, exasperated beyond endurance, he would stomp his foot on the floor to advise the Festigs that their uproar was intolerable. Sometimes, the Festigs would quiet down for a while. More often, they ignored the hints from above or even increased the volume. And, once, Myron Festig, enraged that anyone should dare to object to his family's activities (and also taking out against the Bonders the rage he felt against himself and his family), slammed his foot angrily against the floor and cried out.

Mr. Bonder, startled at first, then doubly enraged, slammed his foot back. Both men then waited to see what would happen. Nothing, however, followed.

And this and other events or nonevents are difficult to explain. Why didn't Tom Bonder just go down and have a talk with the Festigs? Why didn't he communicate directly, face to face, with words and expressions?

I've watched human beings for a million years (my body was shaped like a ground ape's then), and I still don't know exactly why they do or don't do certain things.

Bonder's overt problem was communication. Rather, the lack thereof. He kept too rigid a control over himself to talk freely. Which may be why he turned to writing.

He probably did not go down to tell the Festigs how they were disturbing him because, to him, even a little anger meant a greater one would inevitably follow, and he could not endure the thought of this. And so he avoided a direct confrontation.

Yet, he was getting more and more angry every day; his safety valve was stuck, and his boilers were about to blow.

I can tell by your expression what you're thinking. Why don't we build "engines" which will automatically put out the required thrust?

If this were possible, it would have been done long ago. The structure of the universe, that is, of The Ship, requires, for reasons unknown to me, that philiac thrust be generated only by sentient beings with free will. Automatons can't love. If love is built into, or programmed into, the automaton, the love means nothing in terms of thrust. It's a pseudolove, and so a pseudothrust results, and this is no thrust at all.

No. Life has to be created on viable planets, and it must evolve until it brings forth a sentient being. And this being may then be manipulated, pulled and pushed, given suggestions and laws, and so forth. But the blazing white thrust is not easy to come by, and the black drag is always there. It's a hideous problem to solve. And hideous means often have to be used.

And so, obeying my orders, I speeded up the stoking. Far faster than I liked. Fortunately, a number of events occurring about the same time three months later helped me, and everything converged on one day, a Thursday.

The evening before, Myron Festig had gone on the Joseph Beans TV Show to get publicity for his group-therapy cartoon book, although he had been warned not to do so. As a result, he was stingingly insulted by Beans and his doltish audience, was called sick and was told that group therapy was a mess of mumbo-jumbo. Myron was smarting severely from the savage putdown.

On the next day, Tom Bonder was two and a half hours late getting home. The motor of his car had burned out. This was the climax to the increasing, almost unendurable, frustration and nerve-shredding caused by the two-hour five-day-a-week roundtrip from Beverly Hills to Huntington Beach and back on the freeway. In addition, his request for a transfer to the nearby Santa Monica plant was lost somewhere on the great paper highway of interdepartmental affairs of the astronautics company, and the entire request would have to be initiated again in triplicate.

Two days before, Myron Festig had been fired from another job. He'd made several mistakes in giving change to customers because he was thinking of ideas for cartoons.

Tom Bonder found his wife did not want to listen to his tale of trouble with the car. She had had a setback in therapy and was also upset about some slights her employer had given her.

After tapping in on Myron's account to his wife of how he lost his job, I made an anonymous phone call to the welfare office and told them that Myron Festig had been working without reporting the fact to them. They had called Myron to come down and explain himself.

Myron Festig's brother-in-law, the doctor, wanted part of his loan back. But the Festigs were broke.

Tom Bonder, on coming home, was received with a letter of rejection. The editor to whom he had sent his latest private-eye thriller had turned it down with a number of nasty remarks. Now Bonder wouldn't be able to pay all of next month's bill.

Myron Festig's mother, he day before, had called him and begged him, for the undredth time, to accept his aged father's offer to bec me his junior partner in his business. He should quit b ng a nogoodnik "artist" who couldn't support his wife a d child. Or, for that matter, himself.

Moreover, and this as muc as anything sent him skiing out of control on the slop of despair, his psychiatrist had gone on a two-weeks' va tion in Mexico.

And, that very morning, yron got word that one of the therapy group, a lovely ung woman whom Myron was becoming very fond of, had killed herself with a .45 automatic.

Tom Bonder flushed the toilet, and it filled up and ran all over the bathroom floor. Bonder suppressed his desire to yell out obscenities and denunciations of his landlord because he did not want to upset his granddaughter, and he called the plumber. This incident was the latest in a long series of blown fuses in the old and overloaded electrical circuits and the backing of dirty waters in the old and deteriorating plumbing.

Rachel Festig told Myron that he had to get another job and quickly. Or she was going to work, and he could stay home to take care of the child. Myron sat in the big worn easy chair and just looked at her, as if he were an oyster with five o'clock shadow and she were a strange fish he was trying to identify. Rachel became hysterical and raved for an hour (I could hear her across the street through my open window, I didn't need my tap-beam) about the psychic damage to Lisa if her mother left her to go to work. Myron was so silent and unresponsive that she became frightened.

The plumbers finally left. The baby, who had been awakened by their activities, finally went back to sleep. Tom Bonder sat down at his desk in the crowded bedroom to start writing a story for a mystery magazine. If he wrote it quickly enough and the editors did not dawdle reading it, and bought it, and then did not dawdle in sending his money, he might have enough to pay next month's bills. He wrote two paragraphs, using his pencil so that the typewriter wouldn't wake up the baby.

The thumping of Lisa's feet and her screaming as she ran back and forth from room to room disturbed him even more than usual. But he clamped his mental teeth and wrote on.

Then Rachel began to march along behind Lisa, and she sang loudly (she always said she could have been a great singer if she hadn't married Myron), and she clapped her hands over and over.

It was now nine p.m. The baby stirred in her crib. Then, after some especially heavy crashing of Lisa's feet, Pam cried out. Tom's daughter came into the back bedroom and tried to quiet her down.

Tom Bonder reared up from his desk, his flailing hand scattering papers onto the floor. He stalked into the kitchen and opened a bottom drawer. As usual, it stuck, and he had to get down on his knees and yank at it. This time, he did not mutter something about fixing it someday.

He took out the hand-axe and walked through the front room, hoping his wife would see it.

She curled her lip and said, "Don't be more of an ass than God made you, Tom. You're not scaring anybody with that."

And then, "Why aren't you writing? You said you couldn't talk to me because you had to write."

He glared at her and said nothing. The reasons for his anger were so obvious and justified that she must be deliberately baiting him because of her own turmoiled feelings.

Finally, he grunted, "That menagerie downstairs."

"Well, if you have to fantasize, you don't have to hold that axe. It makes me nervous. Put it away."

He went back into the kitchen. At that moment, I phoned.

His wife said, "Get the phone. If anybody wants me, I'm out to the store. I don't feel like talking to anyone tonight, except you, and you won't talk to me."

Violently, he picked up the phone and said, harshly, "Hello!"

I was watching the whole scene directly on the tap-beam, of course, and at the same time was displaying the Festig's front room on a viewer.

I mimicked Myron Festig's voice. "This is Myron. Would you please be more quiet up there? We can't think with all that noise."

Tom Bonder yelled an obscenity and slammed down the phone. He whirled, ran out into the hall, and charged down the steps with the axe still in his hand.

Rachel and Lisa had stopped their noisy parade, and Myron had risen from his chair at the thunder on the staircase.

I had started to dial the Festigs' number as soon as I'd finished with Tom Bonder. The phone rang when Bonder reached the bottom of the steps, Myron, who was closest to the phone, answered.

I mimicked the voice of Myron's mother. I said, "Myron! If you don't go into business with your father at once, I'll never ever have anything any more to do with you, my only son! God help me! What did I ever do to deserve a son like you? Don't you love your aged parents?" And I hung up.

Tom Bonder was standing outside the Festigs' door with the axe raised when I ran out of my apartment building. I was wearing a policeman's uniform, and I was ready for Mrs. Klugel if she should see me. I meant to tell her I was going to a costume ball. She did not, however, come out of her room since her favorite TV show was on.

I walked swiftly across the street, and not until I got on the sidewalk did Tom Bonder see me.

He could have been beating on the door with his axe in a maniac effort to get inside and kill the Festigs. But his abnormally powerful self-control had, as I'd hoped, reasserted itself. He had discharged much of his anger by the obscenity, the energy of aggression in charging down the stairs, and the mere act of raising the axe to strike the door. Now he stood like the Tin Woodman when the rain rusted his joints, motionless, his eyes on the door, his right arm in the air with his axe in his hand.

I coughed; he broke loose. He whirled and saw the uniform by the nearby street light. My face was in the shadows.

I said, "Good evening," and started back across the street as if I were going home after work. I heard the door slam and knew that Tom Bonder had run back into his apartment and doubtless was shaking with reaction from his anger and from relief at his narrow escape from being caught in the act by a policeman.

Once in my apartment, I used the tap-beams to observe the situation. Tom Bonder had opened the door and tossed the axe onto the floor in front of the Festigs' door.

It was his obscure way of communicating. Quit driving me crazy with your swinish uproar, or the next time. . . .

I'm sure that the dropping of the axe before the Festigs was, at the same time, an offer of peace. Here is the axe which I have brandished at you. I no longer want it; you may have it.

And there was a third facet to this seemingly simple but actually complicated gesture, as there is to almost every human gesture. He knew well, from what Rachel had told his daughter, and from what he had observed and heard, that Myron was on as high and thin a tight-rope as he. So, the flinging down of the axe meant also: Pick it up and use it.

Tom Bonder did not realize this consciously, of course. I had thought that Tom Bonder might do just what he had done. I knew him well enough to chance that he would. If he had acted otherwise, then I would have had to set up another situation.

Myron opened the door; he must have heard the thump of the hatchet and Bonder's steps as he went back up the stairs. He picked it up after staring at it for a full minute and returned to his easy chair. He sat down and put the axe on his lap. His fat fingers played with the wooden handle and a thumb felt along the edge of the head.

Rachel walked over to him and bent over so her face was only about three inches from his. She shouted at him; her mouth worked and worked.

I didn't know what she was saying because I had shut off the audio of their beam. I was forcing myself to watch, but I didn't want to hear.

This was the first time I had cut off the sound during a "stoking". At that moment, I didn't think about what I was doing or why. Later, I knew that this was the first overt reflection of something that had been troubling me for a long long time.

All the elements of the situation (I'm talking about the Festigs, now) had worked together to make Myron do what he did. But the final element, the fuse, was that Rachel looked remarkably like his mother and at that moment was acting and talking remarkably like her.

The black clouds which usually poured out of him had been slowly turning a bright red at their bases. Now the red crept up the clouds, like columns of mercury in a bank of thermometers seen through smoke. Suddenly, the red exploded, shot through the black, overwhelmed the black, dissolved it in scarlet, and filled the room with a glare.

Myron seemed to come up out of the chair like a missile from its launching pad. He pushed Rachel with one hand so hard that she staggered back halfway across the room, her mouth open, jelled in the middle of whatever she had been screaming.

He stepped forward and swung.

I forced myself to watch as he went towards the child. When Myron Festig was through with the two, and he took a long time, or so it seemed to me, he ran into the kitchen. A moment later, he came back out of the kitchen door with a huge butcher knife held before him with both hands, the point against the solar plexus. He charged the room, slammed into the wall and rammed its hilt into the wall. The autopsy report was to state that the point had driven into his backbone.

I turned the audio back on then, although I could hear well enough through my apartment window. A siren was whooping some blocks away. The porch light had been turned on, and the manager, his wife, and juvenile daughter were standing outside the Festigs' door. Presently, the door to the Bonders' apartment opened, and Mrs. Bonder came out. Tom Bonder and Thea followed a minute later.

The manager opened the door to the Festigs' apartment. Tom Bonder looked into the front room between the manager and the side of the doorway.

He swayed, then stepped back until he bumped into Mrs. Bonder. The blood was splashed over the walls, the floors, and the furniture. There were even spots of it on the ceiling.

The broken handle of the axe lay in a pool of blood.

I turned the beam away from the Festigs and watched Tom Bonder. He was on his knees, his arms dangling, hands spread open stiffly, his head thrown back, and his eyes rolled up. His mouth moved silently.

Then there was a cry. Pam, the baby, had gotten out of her crib and was standing at the top of the steps and looking down at the half-open door to the porch and crying for her mother. Thea ran up to her and held her in her arms and soothed her.

At the cry, Tom Bonder shook. No nimbus except the gray of sleep or trance or semi-consciousness had welled from him. But then a finger of white, a slim shaft of brightness, extended from his head. In a minute, he was enveloped in a starry blaze. He was on his feet and taking Mrs. Bonder by the hand and going up the steps. The police car stopped before the building. The siren died, but the red light on top of the car kept flashing.

I packed my stuff in my three bags and went out the back entrance. It was now highly probable that Tom Bonder would take the course I had planned. And, since he was a highly imaginative man, he would influence his granddaughter, who, being a Thrust Potential, would naturally incline toward the religious and the mystical. And toward love. And those in charge of her development would see that she came into prominence and then into greatness in later life. And, after the almost inevitable martyrdom, they would bring about the proper followup. Or try to.

They would. I wouldn't.

I was through. I had had enough of murder, suffering and bloodshed. A million, many millions, of Festigs haunted me. Somehow, and I know the crewmen and officers say it's impossible, I'd grown a heart. Or I'd had it given to me, in the same way the Tin Woodman got his heart.

I'd had enough. Too much. That is why I deserted and why I've been hiding for all these years. And why I've managed to get three others of the black gang to desert, too.

Now we're being hunted down. The hunters and the hunted are not known by you humans. You engines, so they call you.

But I fled here, and I met you, and I fell in love with you, not in a quite-human way, of course. Now you know who and what I am. But don't turn away. Don't make me leave you.

I love you, even if I can't make love to you.

Help me. I'm a mutineer, but unlike The Rooster Rowdy, I'm interested in mutinying because of you humans, not because I want to be first, to be The Captain.

We must take over. Somehow, there has to be a better way to run The Ship!

The Shadow of Space

I

The klaxon cleared its plastic throat and began to whoop. Alternate yellow and reds pulsed on the consoles wrapped like bracelets around the wrists of the captain and the navigator. The huge auxilliary screens spaced on the bulkheads of the bridge also flashed red and yellow.

Captain Grettir, catapulted from his reverie, and from his chair, stood up. The letters and numerals 20-G-DZ-R hung burning on a sector of each screen and spurted up from the wrist-console, spread out before his eyes, then disappeared, only to rise from the wrist-console again and magnify themselves and thin into nothing. Over and over again. 20-G-DZ-R. The code letters indicating that the alarm originated from the corridor leading to the engine room.

He turned his wrist and raised his arm to place the lower half of the console at the correct viewing and speaking distance.

"20-G-DZ-R, report!"

The flaming, expanding, levitating letters died out, and the long high-cheekboned face of MacCool, chief engineer, appeared as a tiny image on the sector of the console. It was duplicated on the bridge bulkhead screens. It rose and grew larger, shooting towards Grettir, then winking out to be followed by a second ballooning face.

Also on the wrist-console's screen, behind MacCool, were Comas, a petty officer, and Grinker, a machinist's mate. Their faces did not float up because they were not in the central part of the screen. Behind them was a group of marines and an 88-K cannon on a floating sled.

"It's the Wellington woman," MacCool said. "She used

28

the photer, lowpower setting, to knock out the two guards stationed at the engine-room port. Then she herded us— me, Comas, Grinker—out. She said she'd shoot us if we resisted. And she welded the grille to the bulkhead so it can't be opened unless it's burned off."

"I don't know why she's doing this. But she's reconnected the drive wires to a zander bridge so she can control the acceleration herself. We can't do a thing to stop her unless we go in after her."

He paused, swallowed and said, "I could send men outside and have them try to get through the engine room airlock or else cut through the hull to get her. While she was distracted by this, we could make frontal attack down the corridor. But she says she'll shoot anybody that gets too close. We could lose some men. She means w she says."

"If you cut a hole in the hull, she'd be out of air, dead in a minute," Grettir said.

"She's in a spacesuit," MacCool replied. "That's why I didn't have this area sealed off and gas flooded in."

Grettir hoped his face was not betraying his shock. Hearing an exclamation from Wang, seated near him, Grettir turned his head. He said, "How in the hell did she get out of sick bay?"

He realized at the same time that Wang could not answer that question. MacCool said, "I don't know, sir. Ask Doctor Wills."

"Never mind that now!"

Grettir stared at the sequence of values appearing on the navigator's auxiliary bulkhead-screen. The 0.5 of light speed had already climbed to 0.96. It changed every 4 seconds. The 0.96 became 0.97, then 0.98, 0.99 and then 1.0. And then 1.1 and 1.2.

Grettir forced himself to sit back down. If anything was going to happen, it would have done so by now; the TSN-X cruiser Sleipnir, 280 million tons, would have been converted to pure energy.

A nova, bright but very brief, would have gouted in the heavens. And the orbiting telescopes of Earth would see the flare in 20.8 light-years.

"What's the state of the emc clamp and acceleration-dissipaters?" Grettir said.

"No strain—yet," Wang said. "But the power drain . . . if it continues . . . 5 megakilowatts per 2 seconds, and we're just beginning."

"I think," Grettir said slowly, "that we're going to find out what we intended to find out. But it isn't going to be under the carefully controlled conditions we had planned."

The Terran Space Navy experimental cruiser *Sleipnir* had left its base on Asgard, eighth planet of Altair (alpha Aquilae), 28 shipdays ago. It was under orders to make the first attempt of a manned ship to exceed the velocity of light. If its mission was successful, men could travel between Earth and the colonial planets in weeks instead of years. The entire galaxy might be opened to Earth.

Within the past two weeks, the *Sleipnir* had made several tests at 0.8 times the velocity of light, the tests lasting up to two hours at a time.

The *Sleipnir* was equipped with enormous motors and massive clamps, dissipaters and space-time structure expanders ("l~~~~~ ~~~~~~~ners~~") required for near-lightspeeds an~~~ ~~~~~~ ~~~. No ship in Terrestrial history had ever had ~~~~~~~ power or the means to handle such power.

The drive itself—the cubed amplification of energy produced by the controlled mixture of matter, antimatter and half-matter—gave an energy that could eat its way through the iron core of a planet. But part of that energy had to be diverted to power the energy-mass conversion "clamp" that kept the ship from being transformed into energy itself. The "hole-opener" also required vast power. This device—officially the Space-Time Structure Expander, or Neutralizer—"unbent" the local curvature of the universe and so furnished a "hole" through which the *Sleipnir* traveled. This hole nullified 99.3 per cent of the resistance the *Sleipnir* would normally have encountered.

Thus the effects of speeds approaching and even exceeding lightspeed, would be modified, even if not entirely avoided. The *Sleipnir* should not contract along its length to zero nor attain infinite mass when it reached the speed of light. It contracted, and it swelled, yes, by only 1/777,777th what it should have. The ship would assume the shape of a disk—but much more slowly than it would without its openers, clamps and dissipaters.

Beyond the speed of light, who knew what would happen? It was the business of the *Sleipnir* to find out. But, Grettir thought, not under these conditions. Not willy-nilly.

"Sir!" MacCool said, "Wellington threatens to shoot anybody who comes near the engine room."

He hesitated, then said, "Except you. She wants to speak to you. But she doesn't want to do it over the intercom. She insists that you come down and talk to her face to face." Grettir bit his lower lip and made a sucking sound.

"Why me?" he said, but he knew why, and MacCool's expression showed that he also knew.

"I'll be down in a minute. Now, isn't there any way we can connect a bypass, route a circuit around her or beyond her and get control of the drive again?"

"No, sir!"

"Then she's cut through the engine-room deck and gotten to the redundant circuits also?"

MacCool said, "She's crazy but she's clear-headed enough to take all precautions. She hasn't overlooked a thing."

Grettir said, "Wang! What's the velocity now?"

"2.3 sl/pm, sir!"

Grettir looked at the huge star screen on the "forward" bulkhead of the bridge. Black except for a few glitters of white, blue, red, green, and the galaxy called XD-2 that lay dead ahead. The galaxy had been the size of an orange, and it still was. He stared at the screen for perhaps a minute, then said, "Wang, am I seeing right? The red light from XD-2 is shifting towards the blue, right?"

"Right, sir!"

"Then . . . why isn't XD-2 getting bigger? We're over-hauling it like a fox after a rabbit."

Wang said, "I think it's getting closer, sir. But we're getting bigger."

II

Grettir rose from the chair. "Take over while I'm gone. Turn off the alarm; tell the crew to continue their normal duties. If anything comes up while I'm in the engine area, notify me at once."

The exec saluted. "Yes, sir!" she said huskily.

Grettir strode off the bridge. He was aware that the officers and crewmen seated in the ring of chairs in the bridge were looking covertly at him. He stopped for a minute to light up a cigar. He was glad that his hands were not shaking, and he hoped that his expression was confident. Slowly, repressing the impulse to run, he continued across the bridge and into the jump-shaft. He stepped off backward into the shaft and nonchalantly blew out smoke while he sank out of sight of the men in the bridge. He braced himself against the quick drop and then the thrusting deceleration. He had set the controls for Dock 14; the doors slid open; he walked into a corridor where a g-car and operator waited for him. Grettir climbed in, sat down and told the crewman where to drive.

Two minutes later, he was with MacCool. The chief engineer pointed down the corridor. Near its end on the floor were two still unconscious Marines. The door to the engine room was open. The secondary door, the grille, was shut. The lights within the engine room had been turned off. Something white on the other side of the grille moved. It was Donna Wellington's face, visible through the helmet.

"We can't keep this acceleration up," Grettir said. "We're already going faster than even unmanned experimental ships have been allowed to go. There are all sorts of theories about what might happen to a ship at these speeds, all bad

"We've disproved several by now," MacCool said. He spoke evenly, but his forehead was sweaty and shadows hung under his eyes.

MacCool continued, "I'm glad you got here, sir. She just threatened to cut the *emc* clamp wires if you didn't show within the next two minutes."

He gestured with both hands to indicate a huge expanding ball of light.

"I'll talk to her," Grettir said. "Although I can't imagine what she wants."

MacCool looked dubious. Grettir wanted to ask him what the hell he was thinking but thought better of it. He said, "Keep your men at this post. Don't even look as if you're coming after me."

"And what do we do, sir, if she shoots you?"

Grettir winced. "Use the cannon. And never mind hesitating if I happen to be in the way. Blast her! But make sure you use a beam short enough to get her but not long enough to touch the engines."

"May I ask why we don't do that before you put your life in danger?" MacCool said.

Grettir hesitated, then said, "My main responsibility is to the ship and its crew. But this woman is very sick;

she doesn't realize the implications of her actions. Not fully anyway. I want to talk her out of this, if I can."

He unhooked the communicator from his belt and walked down the corridor toward the grille and the darkness behind it and the whiteness that moved. His back prickled. The men were watching him intently. God knew what they were saying, or at least thinking, about him. The whole crew had been amused for some time by Donna Wellington's passion for him and his inability to cope with her. They had said she was mad about him, not realizing that she really was mad. They had laughed. But they were not laughing now.

Even so, knowing that she was truly insane, some of them must be blaming him for this danger. Undoubtedly, they were thinking that if he had handled her differently, they would not now be so close to death.

He stopped just one step short of the grille. Now he could see Wellington's face, a checkerboard of blacks and whites. He waited for her to speak first. A full minute passed, then she said, "Robert!"

The voice, normally low-pitched and pleasant, was now thin and strained.

"Not Robert. Eric," he said into the communicator. "Captain Eric Grettir, Mrs. Wellington."

There was a silence. She moved closer to the grille. Light struck one eye, which gleamed bluely.

"Why do you hate me so, Robert?" she said plaintively. "You used to love me. What did I do to make you turn against me?"

"I am *not* your husband," Grettir said. "Look at me. Can't you see that I am not Robert Wellington? I am Captain Grettir of the *Sleipnir*. You *must* see who I *really* am, Mrs. Wellington. It is very important."

"You don't love me!" she screamed. "You are trying to get rid of me by pretending you're another man! But it won't work! I'd know you anywhere, you beast! You beast! I hate you, Robert!"

Involuntarily, Grettir stepped back under the intensity of her anger. He saw her hand come up from the shadows and the flash of light on a handgun. It was too late then; she fired; a beam of whiteness dazzled him.

Light was followed by darkness.

Ahead, or above, there was a disk of grayness in the black. Grettir traveled slowly and spasmodically towards it, as if he had been swallowed by a whale but was being

ejected towards the open mouth, the muscles of the
Leviathan's throat working him outwards.

Far behind him, deep in the bowels of the whale, Donna
Wellington spoke.

"Robert?"

"Eric!" he shouted. "I'm *Eric!*"

The *Sleipnir*, barely on its way out from Asgard, dawd-
ling at 6200 kilometers per second, had picked up the
Mayday call. It came from a spaceship midway between
the 12th and 13th planet of Altair. Although Grettir could
have ignored the call without reprimand from his superiors,
he altered course, and he found a ship wrecked by a
meteorite. Inside the hull was half the body of a man.
And a woman in deep shock.

Robert and Donna Wellington were second-generatio
Asgardians, Ph.D.'s in biotatology, holding master's papei
in astrogation. They had been searching for specimens o:
"space plankton" and "space hydras," forms of life born
in the regions between Altair's outer planets.

The crash, the death of her husband and the shattering
sense of isolation, dissociation and hopelessness during the
eighty-four hours before rescue had twisted Mrs. Wellington. Perhaps twisted was the wrong word. Fragmented was
a better description.

From the beginning of what at first seemed recovery,
she had taken a superficial resemblance of Grettir to her
husband for an identity. Grettir had been gentle and kind
with her at the beginning and had made frequent visits
to sick bay. Later, advised by Doctor Wills, he had been
severe with her.

And so the unforseen result.

Donna Wellington screamed behind him and, suddenly,
the twilight circle ahead became bright, and he was free.
He opened his eyes to see faces over him. Doctor Wills
and MacCool. He was in sick bay.

MacCool smiled and said, "For a moment, we
thought . . ."

"What happened?" Grettir said. Then "I know what she
did. I mean—"

"She fired full power at you," MacCool said. "But the
bars of the grille absorbed most of the energy. You got
just enough to crisp the skin off your face and to knock
you out. Good thing you closed your eyes in time."

Grettir sat up. He felt his face; it was covered with a
greasy ointment, pain-deadening and skin-growing *resec.*

"I got a hell of a headache."

Doctor Wills said, "It'll be gone in a minute."

"What's the situation?" Grettir said. "How'd you get me away from her?"

MacCool said, "I had to do it, Captain. Otherwise, she'd have taken another shot at you. The cannon blasted what was left of the grille. Mrs. Wellington—"

"She's dead?"

"Yes. But the cannon didn't get her. Strange. She took her suit off, stripped to the skin. Then she went out through the airlock in the engine room. Naked, as if she meant to be the bride of Death. We almost got caught in the outrush of air, since she fixed the controls so that the inner port remained open. It was close, but we got the port shut in time."

Grettir said, "I . . . never mind. Any damage t the engine room?"

"No. And the wires are reconnected for normal eration. Only—"

"Only what?"

MacCool's face was so long he looked like a frightened bloodhound.

"Just before I reconnected the wires, a funny . . . peculiar . . . thing happened. The whole ship, and everything inside the ship, went through a sort of distortion. Wavy, as if we'd all become wax and were dripping. Or flags flapping in a wind. The bridge reports that the fore of the ship seemed to expand like a balloon, then became ripply, and the entire effect passed through the ship. We all got nauseated while the waviness lasted."

There was silence, but their expressions indicated that there was more to be said.

"Well?"

MacCool and Wills looked at each other. MacCool swallowed and said, "Captain, we don't know where in hell we are!"

III

On the bridge, Grettir examined the forward EXT. screen. There were no stars. Space everywhere was filled with a light as gray and as dull as that of a false dawn on Earth. In the gray glow, at a distance as yet undetermined, were a number of spheres. They looked small, but if they were as large as the one immediately aft of the *Sleipnir*, they were huge.

The sphere behind them, estimated to be at a distance of fifty kilometers, was about the size of Earth's moon, relative to the ship. Its surface was as smooth and as gray as a ball of lead.

Darl spoke a binary code into her wrist-console, and the sphere on the starscreen seemed to shoot towards them. It filled the screen until Darl changed the line-of-sight. They were looking at about 20 degrees of arc of the limb of the sphere.

"There it is!" Darl said. A small object floated around the edge of the sphere and seemed to shoot towards them. She magnified it, and it became a small gray sphere.

"It orbits round the big one," she said.

Darl paused, then said, "We—the ship—came *out* of that small sphere. *Out* of it. *Through* its skin."

"You mean we had been inside it?" Grettir said. "And now we're outside it?"

"Yes, sir! Exactly!"

She gasped and said, "Oh, oh—sir!"

Around the large sphere, slightly above the plane of the orbit of the small sphere but within its sweep in an inner orbit, sped another object. At least fifty times as large as the small globe, it caught up with the globe, and the two disappeared together around the curve of the primary.

"Wellington's body!" Grettir said.

He turned away from the screen, took one step, and turned around again. "It's not right! She should be trailing along behind us or at least parallel with us, maybe shooting off at an angle but still moving in our direction.

"But she's been grabbed by the big sphere! She's in orbit! And her size; Gargantuan! It doesn't make sense! It shouldn't be!"

"Nothing should," Wang said.

"Take us back," Grettir said. "Establish an orbit around the primary, on the same plane as the secondary but further out, approximately a kilometer and a half from it."

Darl's expression said, "Then what?"

Grettir wondered if she had the same thought as he. The faces of the others on the bridge were doubtful. The fear was covered but leaking out. He could smell the rotten bubbles. Had they guessed, too?

"What attraction does the primary have on the ship?" he said to Wang.

"No detectable influence whatsoever, sir. The *Sleipnir* seems to have a neutral charge, neither positive nor negative in relation to any of the spheres. Or to Wellington's . . . body."

Grettir was slightly relieved. His thoughts had been so wild that he had not been able to consider them as anything but hysterical fantasies. But Wang's answer showed that Grettir's idea was also his. Instead of replying in terms of gravitational force, he had talked as if the ship were a subatomic particle.

But if the ship was not affected by the primary, why had Wellington's corpse been attracted by the primary?

"Our velocity in relation to the primary?" Grettir said

"We cut off the acceleration as soon as the wires w reconnected." Wang said.

"This was immediately after we came out into this . . this space. We didn't apply any retrodrive. Our velocity as indicated by power consumption, is ten megaparsecs per minute. That is," he added after a pause, "what the instruments show. But our radar, which should be totally ineffective at this velocity, indicates 50 kilometers per minute, relative to the big sphere."

Wang leaned back in his chair as if he expected Grettir to explode into incredulity. Grettir lit up another cigar. This time, his hands shook. He blew out a big puff of smoke and said, "Obviously, we're operating under different quote laws unquote *out here.*"

Wang sighed softly. "So you think so, too, Captain? Yes, different *laws.* Which means that every time we make a move through this space, we can't know what the result will be. May I ask what you plan to do, sir?"

By this question, which Wang would never have dared to voice before, though he had doubtless often thought it, Grettir knew that the navigator shared his anxiety. The umbilical had been ripped out; Wang was hurting and bleeding inside. Was he, too, beginning to float away in a gray void? Bereft as no man had even been bereft?

It takes a special type of man or woman to lose himself from Earth or his native planet, to go out among the stars so far that the natal sun is not even a faint glimmer. It also takes special conditioning for the special type of man. He has to believe, in the deepest part of his unconscious, that his ship is a piece of Mother Earth. He has to believe; otherwise, he goes to pieces.

It can be done. Hundreds do it. But nothing had pre-

pared even these farfarers for absolute divorce from the
universe itself.

Grettir ached with the dread of the void. The void
was coiling up inside him, a gray serpent, a slither of
nothingness. Coiling. And what would happen when it
uncoiled?

And what would happen to the crew when they were
informed—as they must be—of the utter dissociation?

There was only one way to keep their minds from slipping their moorings. They must believe that they could get
back into the world. Just as he must believe it.

"I'll play it by ear," Grettir said.

"What? Sir?"

"Play it by ear!" Grettir said more harshly than he
had intended. "I was merely answering your question.
Have you forgotten you asked me what I meant to do?"

"Oh, no, sir," Wang said. "I was just thinking. . ."

"Keep your mind on the job," Grettir said. He told
Darl he would take over. He spoke the code to activate
the ALL-STATIONS; a low rising-falling sound went into
every room of the *Sleipnir,* and all screens flashed a
black-and-green checked pattern. Then the warnings, visual
and audible, died out, and the captain spoke.

He talked for two minutes. The bridgemen looked as
if the lights had been turned off in their brains. It was
almost impossible to grasp the concept of their being outside their universe. As difficult was thinking of their
unimaginably vast native cosmos as only an "electron"
orbiting around the nucleus of an "atom." If what the
captain said was true (how could it be?), the ship
was in the space between the superatoms of a super-
molecule of a superuniverse.

Even though they knew that the *Sleipnir* had ballooned
under the effect of nearly 300,000 times the speed of
light, they could not wrap the fingers of their minds
around the concept. It turned to smoke and drifted away.

It took ten minutes, ship's time, to turn and to complete
the maneuvers which placed the *Sleipnir* in an orbit
parallel to but outside the secondary, or, as Grettir
thought of it, "our universe." He gave his chair back to
Darl and paced back and forth across the bridge while he
watched the starscreen.

If they were experiencing the sundering, the cutting-off,
they were keeping it under control. They had been told by
their captain that they *were* going back in, not that they

would make a *try* at re-entry. They had been through much with him, and he had never failed them. With this trust, they could endure the agony of dissolution.

As the *Sleipnir* established itself parallel to the secondary, Wellington's body curved around the primary again and began to pass the small sphere and ship. The arms of the mountainous body were extended stiffly to both sides, and her legs spread out. In the gray light, her skin was bluish-black from the ruptured veins and arteries below the skin. Her red hair, coiled in a Psyche knot, looked black. Her eyes, each of which was larger than the bridge of the *Sleipnir*, were open, bulging clots of black blood. Her lips were pulled back in a grimace, the teeth like a soot-streaked portcullis.

Cartwheeling, she passed the sphere and the ship.

Wang reported that there were three "shadows" on the surface of the primary. Those were keeping pace with the secondary, the corpse and the ship. Magnified on the bridge-bulkhead screen, each "shadow" was the silhouette of one of the three orbiting bodies. The shadows were only about one shade darker than the surface and were caused by a shifting pucker in the primary skin. The surface protruded along the edges of the shadow and formed a shallow depression within the edges.

If the shadow of the *Sleipnir* was a true replication of the shape of the vessel, the *Sleipnir* had lost its needle shape and was a spindle, fat at both ends and narrow-waisted.

When Wellington's corpse passed by the small sphere and the ship, her shadow or "print" reversed itself in shape. Where the head of the shadow should have been, the feet now were and vice versa.

She disappeared around the curve of the primary and, on returning on the other side, her shadow had again become a "true" reflection. It remained so until she passed the secondary, after which the shadow once more reversed itself.

Grettir had been informed that there seemed to be absolutely no matter in the space outside the spheres. There was not one detectable atom or particle. Moreover, despite the lack of any radiation, the temperature of the hull, and ten meters beyond the hull, was a fluctuating 70° plus-or-minus 20° F.

IV

Three orbits later, Grettir knew that the ship had diminished greatly in size. Or else the small sphere had expanded. Or both changes occurred. Moreover, on the visual screen, the secondary had lost its spherical shape and become a fat disk during the first circling of the ship to establish its orbit.

Grettir was puzzling over this and thinking of calling Van Voorden, the physicist chief, when Wellington's corpse came around the primary again. The body caught up with the other satellites, and for a moment the primary, secondary, and the *Sleipnir* were in a line, strung on an invisible cord.

Suddenly, the secondary and the corpse jumped toward each other. They ceased their motion when within a quarter kilometer of each other. The secondary regained its globular form as soon as it had attained its new orbit. Wellington's arms and legs, during this change in position, moved in as if she had come to life. Her arms folded themselves across her breasts, and her legs drew up so that her thighs were against her stomach.

Grettir called Van Voorden. The physicist said, "Out here, the cabin boy—if we had one—knows as much as I do about what's going on or what to expect. The data, such as they are, are too inadequate, too confusing. I can only suggest that there was an interchange of energy between Wellington and the secondary."

"A quantum jump?" Grettir said. "If that's so, why didn't the ship experience a loss or gain?"

Darl said, "Pardon, sir. But it did. There was a loss of 50 megakilowatts in 0.8 second."

Van Voorden said, "The *Sleipnir* may have decreased in relative size because of decrease in velocity. Or maybe velocity had nothing to do with it or only partially, anyway. Maybe the change in spatial interrelationships among bodies causes other changes. In shape, size, energy transfer and so forth. I don't know. Tell me, how big is the woman —corpse—relative to the ship now?"

"The radar measurements say she's eighty-three times as large. She increased. Or we've decreased."

Van Voorden's eyes grew even larger. Grettir thanked him and cut him off. He ordered the *Sleipnir* to be put in exactly the same orbit as the secondary but ten dekameters ahead of it.

Van Voorden called back. "The jump happened when
we were in line with the other three bodies. Maybe the
Sleipnir is some sort of *geometrical catalyst* under certain
conditions. That's only an analogy, of course."

Wang verbally fed the order into the computer-interface,
part of his wrist-console. The *Sleipnir* was soon racing
ahead of the sphere. Radar reported that the ship and
secondary were now approximately equal in size. The
corpse, coming around the primary again, was still the
same relative size as before.

Grettir ordered the vessel turned around so that the nose
would be facing the sphere. This accomplished, he had the
velocity reduced. The retrodrive braked them while the
lateral thrusts readjusted forces to keep the ship in the
same orbit. Since the primary had no attraction for the
Sleipnir, the ship had to remain in orbit with a constant
rebalancing of thrusts. The sphere, now ballooning, inched
towards the ship.

"Radar indicates we're doing 26.6 dekameters per second
relative to the primary," Wang said. "Power drain indicates
we're making 25,000 times the speed of light. That, by
the way, is not proportionate to what we were making
when we left our world."

"More braking," Grettir said. "Cut it down to 15 dm."

The sphere swelled, filled the screen, and Grettir involuntarily braced himself for the impact, even though he
was so far from expecting one that he had not strapped
himself into a chair. There had been none when the ship
had broken through the "skin" of the universe.

Grettir had been told of the distorting in the ship when it
had left the universe and so was not entirely surprised.
Nevertheless, he could not help being both frightened and
bewildered when the front part of the bridge abruptly
swelled and then rippled. Screen, bulkheads, deck and
crew waved as if they were cloth in a strong wind. Grettir
felt as if he were being folded into a thousand different
angles at the same time.

Then Wang cried out, and the others repeated his cry.
Wang rose from his seat and put his hands out before him.
Grettir, standing behind and to one side of him, was
frozen as he saw dozens of little objects, firefly-size, burning brightly, slip *through* the starscreen and bulkhead and
drift towards him. He came out of his paralysis in time to
dodge one tiny whitely glowing ball. But another struck his
forehead, causing him to yelp.

A score of the bodies passed by him. Some were white; some blue; some green; one was topaz. They were at all levels, above his head, even with his waist, one almost touching the deck. He crouched down to let two pass over him, and as he did so, he saw Nagy, the communications officer, bent over and vomiting. The stuff sprayed out of his mouth and caught a little glow in it and snuffed it out in a burst of smoke.

Then the forepart of the bridge had reasserted its solidity and constancy of shape. There were no more burning objects coming through.

Grettir turned to see the aft bulkheads of the bridge quivering in the wake of the wave. And they, too, became normal. Grettir shouted the "override" code so that he could take control from Wang, who was screaming with pain. He directed the ship to change its course to an "upward vertical" direction. There was no "upward" sensation, because the artificial g-field within the ship readjusted. Suddenly, the forward part of the bridge became distorted again, and the waves reached through the fabric of the ship and the crew.

The starscreen, which had been showing nothing but the blackness of space, speckled by a few stars, now displayed the great ~ray sphere in one corner and the crepuscular light. Gre. fighting the pain in his forehead and the nausea, gave a. her command. There was a delay of possibly thirty second., and then the *Sleipnir* began the turn that would take it back into a parallel orbit with the secondary.

Grettir, realizing what was happening shortly after being burned, had taken the *Sleipnir* back out of the universe He put in a call for corpsmen and Doctor Wills and the helped Wang from his chair. There was an odor of burned flesh and hair in the bridge which the air-conditioning system had not as yet removed. Wang's face and hands were burned in five or six places, and part of the long coarse black hair on the right side of his head was burned.

Three corpsmen and Wills ran into the bridge. Wills started to apply a pseudoprotein jelly on Grettir's forehead, but Grettir told him to take care of Wang first. Wills worked swiftly and then, after spreading the jelly over Wang's burns and placing a false-skin bandage over the burns, treated the captain. As soon as the jelly was placed on his forehead, Grettir felt the pain dissolve.

"Third degree," Wills said. "It's lucky those things— whatever they are—weren't larger."

Grettir picked up his cigar, which he had dropped on the deck when he had first seen the objects racing towards him. The cigar was still burning. Near it lay a coal, swiftly blackening. He picked it up gingerly. It felt warm but could be held without too much discomfort.

Grettir extended his hand, palm up, so that the doctor could see the speck of black matter in it. It was even smaller than when it had floated into the bridge through the momentarily "opened" interstices of the molecules composing the hull and bulkheads.

"This is *a galaxy*," he whispered.

Doc Wills did not understand. "A galaxy of our universe," Grettir added.

Doc Wills paled, and he gulped loudly.

"You mean . . .?"

Grettir nodded.

Wills said, "I hope . . . not our . . . Earth's . . . Galaxy!"

"I doubt it," Grettir said. "We were on the edge of the star fields farthest out, that is, the closest to the—skin?—of our universe. But if we had kept on going . . ."

Wills shook his head. Billions of stars, possibly millions of inhabitable, hence inhabited, planets, were in that little ball of fire, now cool and collapsed. Trillions of sentient beings and an unimaginable number of animals had died when their world collided with Grettir's forehead.

Wang, informed of the true cause of his burns, became ill again. Grettir ordered him to sick bay and replaced him with Gomez. Van Voorden entered the bridge. He said, "I suppose our main objective has to be our reentry. But why couldn't we make an attempt to penetrate the primary, the nucleus? Do you realize what an astounding . . .?"

Grettir interrupted. "I realize. But our fuel supply is low, very low. If—I mean, *when* we get back through the 'skin,' we'll have a long way to go before we can return to Base. Maybe too long. I don't dare exceed a certain speed during reentry because of our size. It would be too dangerous. . . . I don't want to wipe out any more galaxies. God knows the psychological problems we are going to have when the guilt really hits. Right now, we're numbed. *No!* We're not going to do any exploring!"

"But there may be no future investigations permitted!" Van Voorden said. "There's too much danger to the universe itself to allow any more research by ships like ours!"

"Exactly," Grettir said. "I sympathize with your desire to do scientific research. But the safety of the ship and crew comes first. Besides, I think that if I were to order an exploration, I'd have mutiny on my hands. And I couldn't blame my men. Tell me, Van Voorden, don't you feel a sense of . . . dissociation?"

Van Voorden nodded and said, "But I'm willing to fight it. There is so much . . ."

"So much to find out," Grettir said. "Agreed. But the authorities will have to determine if that is to be done."

Grettir dismissed him. Van Voorden marched off. But he did not give the impression of a powerful anger. He was, Grettir thought, secretly relieved at the captain's decision. Van Voorden had made his protest for Science's sake. But as a human being, Van Voorden must want very much to get "home."

V

At the end of the ordered maneuver, the *Sleipnir* was in the same orbit as the universe but twenty kilometers ahead and again pointed toward it. Since there was no attraction between ship and primary, the *Sleipnir* had to use power to maintain the orbit; a delicate readjustment of lateral thrust was constantly required.

Grettir ordered braking applied. The sphere expanded on the starscreen, and then there was only a gray surface displayed. To the viewers the surface did not seem to spin, but radar had determined that the globe completed a revolution on its polar axis once every 33 seconds.

Grettir did not like to think of the implications of this. Van Voorden undoubtedly had received the report, but he had made no move to notify the captain. Perhaps, like Grettir, he believed that the fewer who thought about it, the better.

The mockup screen showed, in silhouette form; the relative sizes of the approaching spheres and the ship. The basketball was the universe; the toothpick, the *Sleipnir*. Grettir hoped that this reduction would be enough to avoid running into any more galaxies. Immediately after the vessel penetrated the "skin," the *Sleipnir* would be again braked, thus further diminishing it. There should be plenty of distance between the skin and the edge of the closest star fields.

"Here we go," Grettir said, watching the screen which indicated in meters the gap between ship and sphere. Again he involuntarily braced himself.

There was a rumble, a groan. The deck slanted upwards, then rolled to port. Grettir was hurled to the deck, spun over and over and brought up with stunning impact against a bulkhead. He was in a daze for a moment, and by the time he had recovered, the ship had reasserted its proper attitude. Gomez had placed the ship into "level" again. He had a habit of strapping himself into the navigator's chair although regulations did not require it unless the captain ordered it.

Grettir asked for a report on any damage and, while waiting for it, called Van Voorden. The physicist was bleeding from a cut on his forehead.

"Obviously," he said, "it requires a certain force to penetrate the outer covering or energy shield or whatever it is that encloses the universe. We didn't have it. So—"

"Presents quite a problem," Grettir said. "If we go fast enough to rip through, we're too large and may destroy entire galaxies. If we go too slow, we can't get through."

He paused, then said, "I can think of only one method. But I'm ignorant of the consequences, which might be disastrous. Not for us but for the universe. I'm not sure I should even take such a chance."

He was silent so long that Van Voorden could not restrain himself. "Well?"

"Do you think that if we could make a hole in the skin, the rupture might result in some sort of collapse or cosmic disturbance?"

"You want to beam a hole in the skin?" Van Voorden said slowly. His skin was pale, but it had been that color before Grettir asked him the question. Grettir wondered if Van Voorden was beginning to crumble under the "dissociation."

"Never mind," Grettir said. "I shouldn't have asked you. You can't know what the effects would be any more than anyone else. I apologize. I must have been trying to make you share some of the blame if anything went wrong. Forget it."

Van Voorden stared, and he was still looking blank when Grettir cut off his image. He paced back and forth, once stepping over a tiny black object on the deck and then grimacing when he realized that it was too late for care. Millions of stars, billions of planets, trillions of creatures.

All cold and dead. And if he experimented further in trying to get back into the native cosmos, then what? A collapsing universe?

Grettir stopped pacing and said aloud, "We came through the skin twice without harm to it. So we're going to try the beam!"

Nobody answered him, but the look on their faces was evidence of their relief. Fifteen minutes later, the *Sleipnir* was just ahead of the sphere and facing it. After an unvarying speed and distance from the sphere had been maintained for several minutes, laser beams measured the exact length between the tip of the cannon and the surface of the globe.

The chief gunnery officer, Abdul White Eagel, set one of the fore cannons. Grettir delayed only a few seconds in giving the next order. He clenched his teeth so hard he almost bit the cigar in two, groaned slightly then said, "Fire!"

Darl transmitted the command. The beam shot out, ᴛ ꞓhed the skin and vanished.

The starscreen showed a black hole in the gray surface at the equator of the sphere. The hole moved away and then was gone around the curve of the sphere. Exactly 33 seconds later, the hole was in its original position. It was shrinking. By the time four rotations were completed, the hole had closed in on itself.

Grettir sighed and wiped the sweat off his forehead. Darl reported that the hole would be big enough for the ship to get through by the second time it came around. After that, it would be too small.

"We'll go through during the second rotation," Grettir said. "Set up the compigator for an automatic entry; tie the cannon in with the compigator. There shouldn't be any problem. If the hole shrinks too fast, we'll enlarge it with the cannon."

He heard Darl say, "Operation begun, sir!" as Gomez spoke into his console. The white beam spurted out in a cone, flicked against the "shell" or "skin" and disappeared. A circle of blackness three times the diameter of the ship came into being and then moved to one side of the screen. Immediately, under the control of the compigator, the retrodrive of the *Sleipnir* went into action. The sphere loomed; a gray wall filled the starscreen. Then the edge of the hole came into view, and a blackness spread over the screen.

"We're going to make it," Grettir thought. "The compigator can't make a mistake."

He looked around him. The bridgemen were strapped to their chairs now. Most of the faces were set, they were well disciplined and brave. But if they left as he did—they must —they were shoving back a scream far down in them. They could not endure this "homesickness" much longer. And after they got through, were back in the womb, he would have to permit them a most unmilitary behavior. They would laugh, weep, shout. And so would he.

The nose of the *Sleipnir* passed through the hole. Now; if anything went wrong, the fore cannon could not be used. But it was impossible that . . .

The klaxon whooped. Darl screamed, "Oh, my God! Something's wrong! The hole's shrinking too fast!"

Grettir roared, "Double the speed! No! Halve it!"

Increasing the forward speed meant a swelling in size of the *Sleipnir* but a contraction of the longitudinal axis and a lengthening of the lateral. The *Sleipnir* would get through the hole faster, but it would also narrow the gap between its hull and the edges of the hole.

Halving the speed, on the other hand, though it would make the ship smaller in relation to the hole, would also make the distance to be traversed greater. This might mean that the edges would still hit the ship.

Actually, Grettir did not know what order should be given or if any order would have an effect upon their chance to escape. He could only do what seemed best.

The grayness spread out from the perimeter of the starscreen. There was a screech of severed plastic running through the ship, quivering the bulkheads and decks, a sudden push forward of the crew as they felt the inertia, then a release as the almost instantaneous readjustment of the internal g-field canceled the external effects.

Everybody in the bridge yelled. Grettir forced himself to cut off his shout. He watched the starscreen. They were out in the gray again. The huge sphere shot across the screen. In the corner was the secondary and then a glimpse of a giant blue-black foot. More grayness. A whirl of other great spheres in the distance. The primary again. The secondary. Wellington's hand, like a malformed squid of the void.

When Grettir saw the corpse again, he knew that the ship had been deflected away from the sphere and was heading towards the corpse. He did not, however, expect a collision. The orbital velocity of the dead woman was greater than that of the secondary or of the *Sleipnir*.

Gretter, calling for a damage report, heard what he had expected. The nose of the ship had been sheared off. Bearing 45 crewmen with it, it was now inside the "universe," heading toward a home it would never reach. The passageways leading to the cut-off part had been automatically sealed, of course, so that there was no danger of losing air.

But the retrodrives had also been sliced off. The *Sleipnir* could drive forward but could not brake itself unless it was first turned around to present its aft to the direction of motion.

VI

Grettir gave the command to stabilize the ship first, then to reverse it. MacCool replied from the engine room that neither maneuver was, at the moment, possible. The collision and the shearing had caused malfunctions in the control circuits. He did not know what the trouble was, but the electronic trouble-scanner was searching through the circuits. A moment later, he called back to say that the device was itself not operating properly and that the troubleshooting would have to be done by his men until the device had been repaired.

MacCool was disturbed. He could not account for the breakdown because, theoretically, there should have been none. Even the impact and loss of the fore part should not have resulted in loss of circuit operation.

Grettir told him to do what he could. Meanwhile, the ship was tumbling and was obviously catching up with the vast corpse. There had been another inexplainable interchange of energy, position and momentum, and the *Sleipnir* and Mrs. Wellington were going to collide.

Grettir unstrapped himself and began walking back and forth across the bridge. Even though the ship was cartwheeling, the internal g-field neutralized the effect for the crew. The vessel seemed level and stable unless the starscreen was looked at.

Grettir asked for a computation of when the collision would take place and of what part of the body the *Sleipnir* would strike. It might make a difference whether it struck a soft or hard part. The difference would not result in damage to the ship, but it would affect the angle and velocity of the rebound path. If the circuits were repaired before the convergence, or just after, Grettir would have to know what action to take.

Wang replied that he had already asked the compigator for an estimate of the area of collision if conditions remained as they were. Even as he spoke, a coded card issued from a slot in the bulkhead. Wang read it, handed it to Grettir.

Grettir said, "At any other time, I'd laugh. So we will return—literally—to the womb."

The card had also indicated that, the nearer the ship got to Wellington, the slower was its velocity. Moreover, the relative size of the ship, as reported by radar, was decreasing in direct proportion to its proximity to the body.

Gomez said, "I think we've come under the influence of that . . . woman, as if she's become a planet and had captured a satellite. Us. She doesn't have any gravitational attraction or any charge in relation to us. But—"

But there are other factors," Grettir said to her. "Maybe they are spatial relations, which, in this 'space,' may be the equivalent of gravity."

The *Sleipnir* was now so close that the body entirely filled the starscreen when the ship was pointed towards it. First, the enormous head came into view. The blood-clotted and bulging eyes stared at them. The nose slid by like a Brobdingnagian guillotine; the mouth grinned at them as if it were to enjoy gulping them down. Then the neck, a diorite column left exposed by the erosion of softer ⌐k; the cleavage of the blackened Himalayan breasts, the naval, the eye of a hurricane.

Then she went out of sight, and the secondary and primary and the gray-shrouded giants far off wheeled across the screen.

Grettir used the All-Stations to tell the nonbridge personnel what was happening. "As soon as MacCool locates the trouble, we will be on our way out. We have plenty of power left, enough to blast our way out of a hundred corpses. Sit tight. Don't worry. It's just a matter of time."

He spoke with a cheerfulness he did not feel, although he had not lied to them. Nor did he expect any reaction, positive or negative. They must be as numb as he. Their minds, their entire nervous systems, were boggling.

Another card shot out from the bulkhead-slot, a cor-

rected impact prediction. Because of the continuing decrease in size of the vessel, it would strike the corpse almost dead-center in the naval. A minute later, another card
predicted impact near the coccyx. A third card revised that
to collision with the top of the head. A fourth changed
that to a strike on the lower part on the front of the right
leg.

Grettir called Van Voorden again. The physicist's face
shot up from the surface of Grettir's wrist-console but was
stationary on the auxiliary bulkhead-screen. This gave a
larger view and showed Van Voorden looking over his
wrist-console at a screen on his cabin-bulkhead. It offered
the latest impact report in large burning letters.

"Like the handwriting on the wall in the days of King
Belshazzar," Van Voorden said. "And I am a Daniel come
to judgment. So we're going to hit her leg, heh, *Many,
many tickle up her shin.* Hee, hee!"

Grettir stared uncomprehendingly at him, then cut him
off. A few seconds later, he understood Van Voorden's
pun. He did not wonder at the man's levity at a moment
so grave. It was a means of relieving his deep anxiety and
bewilderment. It might also mean that he was already
cracking up, since it was out of character with him. But
Grettir could do nothing for him at that moment.

As the *Sleipnir* neared the corpse, it continued to shrink.
However, the dwindling was not at a steady rate nor could
the times of shrinkage be predicted. It operated in spurts of
from two to thirty seconds duration at irregular intervals.
And then, as the 300th card issued from the slot, it became evident that, unless some new factor entered, the
Sleipnir would spin into the gaping mouth. While the head
rotated "downward," the ship would pass through the great
space between the lips.

And so it was. On the starscreen, the lower lip, a massive
ridge, wrinkled with mountains and pitted with valleys,
appeared. Flecks of lipstick floated by like vast meteors.
A tooth like a jagged skyscraper dropped out of sight.

The *Sleipnir* settled slowly into the darkness. The walls
shot away and upwards. The blackness outside knotted. Only a part of the gray "sky" was visible during that point of
the cartwheel when the fore part of the starscreen was
directed upwards. Then the opening became a thread of
gray, a strand, and was gone.

Strangely—or was it so odd?—the officers and crew lost
their feeling of dissociation. Grettir's stomach expanded

with relief; the dreadful fragmenting was gone. He now felt as if something had been attached, or reattached, to his naval. Rubb, the psychology officer, reported that he had taken a survey of one out of fifty of the crew, and each described similar sensations.

Despite this, the personnel were free of only one anxiety and were far from being out of danger. The temperature had been slowly mounting ever since the ship had been spun off the secondary and had headed towards the corpse. The power system and air-conditioning had stabilized at 80°F for a while. But the temperature of the hull had gone upwards at a geometric progression, and the outer hull was now 2500 K. There was no danger of it melting as yet; it could resist up to 56,000 K. The air-conditioning demanded more and more power, and after thirty minutes ship's time, Grettir had had to let the internal temperature rise to 98.2°F to ease the load.

Grettir ordered everybody into spacesuits, which could keep the wearers at a comfortable temperature. Just as the order was carried out, MacCool reported that he had located the source of malfunction.

"The Wellington woman did it!" he shouted. "She surely took care of us! She inserted a monolith subparticle switch in the circuits; the switch had a timer which operated the switch after a certain time had elapsed. It was only coincidence that the circuits went blank right after we failed to get back into our world!"

VII

"So she wanted to be certain that we'd be wrecked if she was frustrated in her attempts in the engine room," Grettir said. "You'd better continue the search for other microswitches or sabotage devices."

MacCool's face was long.

"We're ready to operate now only . . . hell! We can't spare any power now because we need all we can get to keep the temperature down. I can spare enough to cancel the tumble. But that's all."

"Forget it for now," Grettir said. He had contacted Van Voorden, who seemed to have recovered. He confirmed the captain's theory about the rise in temperature. It was the rapid contraction of the ship that was causing the emission of heat.

"How is this contraction possible?" Grettir said. "Are the atoms of the ship, and of our bodies, coming closer together? If so, what happens when they come into contact with each other?"

"We've already passed that point of diminishment," Van Voorden said. "I'd say that our own atoms are shrinking also."

"But that's not possible," Grettir replied. Then, "Forget about that remark. What is possible? Whatever happens is possible."

Grettir cut him off and strode back and forth and wished that he could smoke a cigar. He had intended to talk about what the *Sleipnir* would find if it had managed to break back into its native universe. It seemed to Grettir that the universe would have changed so much that no one aboard the ship would recognize it. Every time the secondary— the universe—completed a revolution on its axis, trillions of Earth years, maybe quadrillions, may have passed. The Earth's sun may have become a lightless clot in space or even have disappeared altogether. Man, who might have survived on other planets, would no longer be homo sapiens.

Moreover, when the *Sleipnir* attained a supercosmic mass on its way out of the universe, it may have disastrously affected the other masses in the universe.

Yet none of these events may have occurred. It was possible that time inside that sphere was absolutely independent of time outside it. The notion was not so fantastic. God Almighty! Less than seventy minutes ago, Donna Wellington had been inside the ship. Now the ship was inside her.

And when the electrons and the nuclei of the atoms composing the ship and the crew came into contact, what then? Explosion?

Or were the elements made up of divisible subelements, and collapse would go on towards the inner infinity? He thought of the 20th-century stories of a man shrinking until the molecules became clusters of suns and the nuclei were the suns and the electrons were the planets. Eventually, the hero found himself on an electron-planet with atmosphere, seas, rivers, plains, mountains, trees, animals and aboriginal sentients.

These stories were only fantasies. Atomic matter was composed of wavicles, stuff describable in terms of both waves and particles. The parahomunculus hero would be in a cosmos as bewildering as that encountered by the crew of the *Sleipnir* on breaking into the extra-universe space.

That fantasy galloping across the sky of his mind, swift as the original *Sleipnir*, eight-legged horse of All-Father Odin of his ancestor's religion, would have to be dismissed. Donna Wellington was not a female Ymir, the primeval giant out of whose slain corpse was formed the world, the skull the sky, the blood the sea, the flesh the Earth, the bones the mountains.

No, the heat of contraction would increase until the men cooked in their suits. What happened after that would no longer be known to the crew and hence of no consequence.

"Captain!"

MacCool's face was on the auxiliary screen, kept open to the engine room. "We'll be ready to go in a minute."

Sweat mingled with tears to blur the image of the engineer's face. "We'll make it then," Grettir said.

Four minutes later, the tumble was stopped, the ship was pointed upwards and was on its way out. The temperature began dropping inside the ship at one degree F per 30 seconds. The blackness was relieved by a gray thread. The thread broadened into ribbon, and then the ribbon became the edges of two mountain ridges, one below and the one above hanging upside down.

"This time," Grettir said, "we'll make a hole more than large enough."

Van Voorden entered the bridge as the *Sleipnir* passed through the break. Grettir said, "The hole repairs itself even more quickly than it did the last time. That's why the nose was cut off. We didn't know that the bigger the hole, the swifter the rate of reclosure."

Van Voorden said, "Thirty-six hundred billion years old or even more! Why bother to go home when home no longer exists?"

"Maybe there won't be that much time gone," Grettir said. "Do you remember Minkowski's classical phrase? *From henceforth space in itself and time in itself sink to mere shadows, and only a kind of union of the two preserves an independent existence.*

"That phrase applied to the world inside the sphere, our world. Perhaps *out here* the union is somehow dissolved, the marriage of space and time is broken. Perhaps no time, or very little, has elapsed in our world."

"It's possible," Van Voorden said. "But you've overlooked one thing, Captain. If our world has not been marked by time while we've been gone, *we* have been marked. Scarred by unspace and untime. I'll never believe in cause and effect and order throughout the cosmos again. I'll always be suspicious and anxious. I'm a ruined man."

Grettir started to answer but could not make himself heard. The men and women on the bridge were weeping, sobbing, or laughing shrilly. Later, they would think of that *out there* as a nightmare and would try not to think of it at all. And if other nightmares faced them here, at least they would be nightmares they knew.

A Bowl Bigger Than Earth

I

No squeeze. No pain.

Death has a wide pelvis, he thought—much la   when
he had time to reflect.

Now he was screaming.

He had had an impression of awakening from   's
deathbed, of being shot outwards over the edge of a bo
bigger than Earth seen from a space capsule. Sprawling
outwards, he landed on his hands and knees on a gentle
slope. So gentle it was. He did not tear his hands and
knees but slid smoothly onward and downward on th reat
curve. The material on which he accelerated lo   much
like brass and felt frictionless. Though he di not think of
it then—he was too panic-stricken to do anything but
react—he knew later that the brassy stuff had even less
resistance than oil become a solid. And the brass, or
whatever it was, formed a solid seamless sheet.

The only break was in the center, where the sheet ended.
There, far ahead and far below, the bowl curved briefly
upward.

Gathering speed, he slipped along the gigantic chute. He
tried to stay on his hands and knees; but, when he
twisted his body to see behind him, he shifted his weight.
Over he went onto his side. Squawling, he thrashed around,
and he tried to dig his nails into the brass. No use. He met
no resistance, and he began spinning around, around. He
did see, during his whirlings, the rim from which he had
been shoved. But he could see only the rim itself and,
beyond, the blue cloudless sky.

Overhead was the sun, looking just like the Terrestrial
sun.

He rolled over on his back and succeeded during the maneuver in stopping the rotations. He also managed to see his own body. He began screaming again, the first terror driven out and replaced by—or added to as a higher harmonic—the terror of finding himself in a sexless body.

Smooth. Projectionless. Hairless. His legs hairless, too. No navel. His skin a dark brown—like an Apache's.

Morfiks screamed and screamed, and he gripped his face and the top of his head. Then he screamed higher and higher. The face was not the one he knew (the ridge of bone above the eyes and the broken nose were not there), and his head was smooth as an egg.

He fainted.

Later, although it could not have been much later, he came to his senses. Overhead was the bright sun and beneath him was the cool nonfriction.

He turned his face to one side, saw the same brass and had no sensation of sliding because he had no reference point. For a moment he thought he might be at the end of his descent. But on lifting his head he saw that the bottom of the bowl was closer, that it was rushing at him.

His heart was leaping in his chest as if trying to batter itself to a second death. But it did not fail. It just drove the blood through his ears until he could hear its roar even ab the air rushing by.

He lowered his head until its back was supported by the ass, and he closed his eyes against the sun. Never in all his life (lives?) had he felt so helpless. More helpless than a newborn babe, who does not know he is helpless and who cannot think and who will be taken care of if he cries.

He had screamed, but no one was running to take care of him.

Downward he slipped, brassy-yellow curving away on both sides of him, no sensation of heat against his back where the skin should have burned off a long time ago and his muscles should now be burning.

The incline began to be less downward, to straighten out. He shot across a flat space which he had no means of estimating because he was going too fast.

The flatness gave away to a curving upwards. He felt that he was slowing down; he hoped so. If he continued at the same rate of speed, he would shoot far out and over the center of the bowl.

Here it came! The rim!

He went up with just enough velocity to rise perhaps

seven feet above the edge. Then, falling, he glimpsed a city of brass beyond the people gathered on the shore of a river but lost sight of these in the green waters rushing up towards him directly below.

He bellowed in anguish, tried to straighten out, and flailed his arms and legs. In vain. The water struck him on his left side. Half-stunned, he plunged into the cool and dark waters.

By the time he had broken the surface again, he had regained his senses. There was only one thing to do. Behind him, the brassy wall reared at least thirty feet straight up. He had to swim to the shore, which was about four hundred yards away.

What if he had not been able to swim? What if he chose to drown now rather than face the unknown on the beach?

A boat was his answer. A flat-bottomed boat of brass rowed with brass oars by a brown-skinned man (man?). In the bow stood a similar creature (similar? exactly alike) extending a long pole of brass.

The manlike thing in the bow called out, "Grab hold, and I'll pull you in."

Morfiks replied with an obscenity and began swimming toward the beach. The fellow with the pole howled, "A trouble-maker, heh? We'll have no antisocial actions here, citizen!"

He brought the butt of the pole down with all his strength.

It was then that Morfiks found that he was relatively invulnerable. The pole, even if made of material as light as aluminum and hollow, should have stunned him and cut his scalp open. But it had bounced off with much less effect than the fall into the river.

"Come into the boat," said the poleman. *"Or nobody here will like you."*

II

It was this threat that cowed Morfiks. After climbing into the boat, he sat down on the bench in front of the rower and examined the two. No doubt of it. They were twins. Same height (both were sitting now) as himself. Hairless, except for long curling black eyelashes. Same features. High foreheads. Smooth hairless brows. Straight

noses. Full lips. Well developed chins. Regular, almost
classical features, delicate, looking both feminine and
masculine. Their eyes were the same shade of dark brown.
Their skins were heavily tanned. Their bodies were slimly
built and quite human except for the disconcerting lack of
sex, navel and nipples on the masculine chests.

"Where am I?" said Morfiks. "In the fourth dimension?"

He had read about that in the Sunday supplements and
some of the more easily digesteds.

"Or in Hell?" he added, which would have been his first
question if he had been in his Terrestrial body. Nothing
that had happened so far made him think he was in
Heaven.

The pole rapped him in the mouth, and he thought that
either the poleman was pulling his punches or else his new
flesh was less sensitive than his Terrestrial. The last must
be it. His lips felt almost as numb as when the dentist gave
him novocaine before pulling a tooth. And his meager
buttocks did not hurt from sitting on the hard brass.

Moreover, he had all his teeth. There were no fillings or
bridges in his mouth.

"You will not use *that* word," said the poleman. "It's not
nice, and it's not true. The protectors do not like that word
and will take one hundred percent effective measures to
punish anybody responsible for offending the public taste
with it."

"You mean the word beginning with H?" said Morfiks
cautiously.

"You're catching on fast, citizen."

"What do you call this . . . place?"

"Home. Just plain home. Allow me to introduce myself.
I'm one of the official greeters. I have no name; nobody
here does. Citizen is good enough for me and for you.
However, being a greeter doesn't make me one whit better
than you, citizen. It's just my job, that's all. We all have
jobs here, all equally important. We're all on the same
level, citizen. No cause for envy or strife."

"No name?" Morfiks said.

"Forget that nonsense. A name means you're trying to
set yourself apart. Now, you wouldn't think it was nice if
somebody thought he was better than you because he had
a name that was big in We-know-where, would you? Of
course not."

"I'm here for . . . how long?" Morfiks said.

"Who knows?"

"Forever?" Morfiks said dismally.

The end of the pole butted into his lips. His head rocked back, but he did not hurt much.

"Just think of the present, citizen. Because that is all that exists. The past doesn't exist; the future can't. Only the present exists."

"There's no future?"

Again, the butt of the pole.

"Forget that word. We use it on the river when we're breaking in immigrants. But once on the shore, we're through with it. Here, we're practical. We don't indulge in fantasy."

"I get your message," Morfiks said. He damped the impulse to leap at the poleman's throat. Better to wait until he found out what the set-up was, what a man could or could not get away with.

The rower said, "Coming ashore, citizens."

Morfiks noticed that the two had voices exactly alike, and he supposed his own was the same as theirs. But he had a secret triumph. His voice would sound different to himself; he had that much edge on the bastards.

The boat nudged onto the beach, and Morfiks followed the other two onto the sand. He looked quickly behind him and now saw that there were many boats up and down the river. Here and there a body shot up over the rim of the brassy cliff and tumbled down into the waters as he had a few minutes ago.

Beyond the lip of the cliff rose the swell of the brass slide down which he had hurtled. The slide extended so far that he could not see the human figures that undoubtedly must be standing on the edge where he had stood and must just now be in the act of being pushed from behind. Five miles away, at least, five miles he had slid.

A colossal building project, he thought.

Beyond the city of brass rose another incline. He understood now that he had been mistaken in believing the city was in the middle of a bowl. As far as he could see, there was the river and the city and the cliffs and slides on both sides. And he supposed that there was another river on the other side of the city.

The city reminded him of the suburban tract in which he had lived on Earth. Rows on rows of square brass houses, exactly alike, facing each other across twenty-foot wide streets. Each house was about twelve feet wide. Each had a flat roof and a door in front and back, a strip of windows which circled the house like a transparent belt. There were no yards. A space of two feet separated each house from its neighbor.

A person stepped out of the crowd standing on the beach. This one differed from the others only in having a band of some black metal around the biceps of its right arm.

"Officer of the Day," it said in a voice exactly like the two in the boat. "Your turn will come to act in this capacity. No favorites here."

It was then that Morfiks recognized the possibilities of individualism in voice, of recognizing others. Even if everybody had identical dimensions in larynxes and the resonating chambers of palate and nasal passages, they must retain their habits of intonation and choice of pitch and words. Also, despite identical bodies and legs, they must keep some of their peculiar gestures and methods of walking.

"Any complaints about treatment so far?" said the O.D.

"Yes," said Morfiks. "This jerk hit me three times with its pole."

"Only because we love it," said the poleman. "We struck it—oh, very lightly!—to correct its ways. As a father—pardon the word—punishes a child he loves. Or an older brother his little brother. We are all brothers . . ."

"We are guilty of antisocial behavior," said the O.D. sternly. "We're very very sorry, but we must report this incident to the Protectors. Believe us, it hurt us . . ."

"Worse than it hurts us," said the poleman wearily. "We know."

"We'll have to add cynicism to the charge," said the O.D. "K.P. for several months if we know the Protectors. Should anybody be guilty again—"

The O.D. told Morfiks to walk with it, and it briefed Morfiks as they went through the streets. These were made of a pale violet rubbery substance only slightly warm to the feet despite the sun beating down upon it. Morfiks would be given his own home. He was lord and master there and could do whatever he wished in it as long as he did not break any rules of public morality.

"You mean I can invite anybody I want to and can keep out anybody I want to?"

"Well, you can invite anybody you want. But don't throw anybody out who comes in uninvited. This is, unless the uninvited behaves antisocially. In which case, notify the O.D., and we'll notify a Protector."

"How can I be master of my house if I can't choose my guests?" Morfiks said.

"The citizen doesn't understand," said the O.D. "A citizen should not want to keep another citizen out of his house. Doing so is saying that a citizen doesn't love all citizens as brothers and sisters. It's not nice. We want to be nice, don't we?"

Morfiks replied that had always been known as a nice guy, and he continued to listen to the O.D. But, on passing an area where a large field coated with the violet rubber broke the monotonous rows of houses, he said, "Looks like a children's playground with all those swings, seesaws, games, trampolines. Where are the kids? And how—"

"Only the Protectors know what happens to the children who come from We-Know-Where," said the O.D. "It's better, much, much better, not to ask them ab   In fact, it's very good not to see or talk to a Protector.

"No, the playgrounds are for the amusement of us citizens. However, the Protectors have been thinking about taking them down. Too many citizens quarrel about who gets to use them, instead of amicably arranging predecedence and turns. They actually dare to fight each other even if fighting's forbidden. And they manage, somehow, to hurt each other. We don't want anybody to get hurt, do we?"

"I guess not. What do you do for entertainment, otherwise?"

"First things first, citizen. We don't like to use any of the personal pronouns except *we*, of course, and *us* and *our* and *ours*. *I, me, they, you* all differentiate. Better to forget personal differences here, heh? After all, we're just one big happy family, heh?"

"Sure," Morfiks said. "But there must be times when a citizen has to point out somebody. How do I—we—identify someone guilty of, say, antisocial behavior?"

"It doesn't matter," said the O.D. "Point out anyone. Yourself—if you'll pardon the word—for instance. We all share in the punishment, so it makes no difference."

"You mean *I* have to be punished for someone else's crime? That isn't *fair!*"

"It may not seem so to us at first," said the O.D. "But consider. We're brothers, not only under the skin but on the skin. If a crime is committed, the guilt is shared by all because, actually, all are responsible. And if punishment is given to all, then all will try to prevent crime. Simple, isn't it? And fair, too."

"But you—we—said that the poleman would be given K.P. Does that mean we all go on K.P.?"

"We did not commit a felony, only a misdemeanor. If we do it again, we are a felon. And we suffer. It's the only nice thing to do, to share, right?"

Morfiks did not like it. He was the one hit in the teeth, so why should he, the victim, have to take the punishment of the aggressor?

But he said nothing. He had gotten far on We-Know-Where by keeping his mouth shut. It paid off; everybody had thought he was a nice guy. And he *was* a nice guy.

There did seem to be one fallacy in the set-up. If being a stool pigeon meant you, too, suffered, why turn anybody in? Wouldn't it be smarter to keep quiet and inflict the punishment yourself on the aggressor?

"Don't do it, citizen," said the O.D.

Morfiks gasped.

The O.D. smiled and said, "No, we can't read minds. But every immigrant thinks the same thing when told about the system. Keeping quiet only results in double punishment. The Protectors—whom this citizen has never seen face to face and doesn't want to—have some means of monitoring our behavior. They know when we've been antisocial. The offender is, of course, given a certain amount of time in which to confess the injury. After that . . ."

To keep himself from bursting into outraged denunciation of the system, Morfiks asked more questions.

Yes, he would be confined to this neighborhood. If he traveled outside it, he might find himself in an area where his language was not spoken. That would result in his feeling inferior and different because he was a foreigner. Or, worse, superior. Anyway, why travel? Any place looked like every place.

Yes, he was free to discuss any subject as long as it did not concern We-Know-Where. Talking of that place led to discussions of—forgive the term—*one's* former identity and prestige. Besides, controversial subjects might arise and so lead to antisocial behavior.

Yes, this place was not constructed, physically, like We-Know-Where. The sun might be a small body; some eggheads had estimated it to be only a mile wide. The run orbited around the strip, which was composed of the slides, two rivers and the city between the rivers, all of which hung in space. There was some speculation that his place was in a pocket universe the dimensions of which were

stature different than the one you had on Earth. Or pumping something inside our skulls to take care of brains being too small for the skulls They gave us."

"Yeah, yeah," Morfiks said. He knew what Billie was going to propose, or he thought he did. He was breathing hard; a tingle was running over his skin; a warmth was spreading out from the pit of his stomach.

"Well," said Billie, "I always heard that it was all in your head. And that's true. Of course, there's only so much you can do, and maybe it isn't as good as it was on You-Know-Where. But it's better than nothing. Besides, like they say, none of it's bad. It's all good, some is just better than others."

"You mean?"

"Just close your eyes," Billie crooned, "and imagine I'm a woman. I'll tell you how I looked, how I was stacked. And you think about it. Then you tell me how you looked, don't hold anything back, no need to be bashful here, described everything down to the last detail. And I'll imagine how you were."

"Think it'll work?" Morfiks said.

Billie, her eyes closed, softly sang, "I know it will, baby. I've been around some since I came here."

"Yeah, but what about the punishment?"

Billie half-opened her eyes and said, scornfully, "Don't believe all that jazz, Johnny boy. Besides, even if They do catch you, it's worth it. Believe me, it's worth it."

"If only I thought I could put one over on Them," Morfiks said. "It'd be worth taking any risk."

Billie's answer was to kiss him. Morfiks, though he had to repress revulsion, responded. After all, it was only the bald head that made Billie look like a half-man.

They struggled fiercely and desperately; their kisses were as deep as possible.

Suddenly Morfiks pushed Billie away from him.

"It's worse than nothing," he panted. "I think something's going to happen, but it never quite does. It's no use. Now I feel awful."

Billie came towards him again, saying, "Don't give up so easy, honey. Rome wasn't erected in a day. Believe me, you can do it. But you got to have faith."

"No, I'm licked," Morfiks said. "Maybe if you did look like a woman, instead of just a carbon copy of me. Then . . . no, that wouldn't be any good. I'm just not designed for the job; neither are you. They got us where it hurts."

Billie lost her half-smile; her face twisted.

"Where it hurts!" she shrilled. "Let me tell you, Buster, if you can't get your kicks being a man here, you can by hurting somebody! That's about all that's left!"

"What do you mean?" Morfiks said.

Billie laughed loudly and long. When she mastered herself, she said, "I'll tell you one good thing about looking like everybody else. Nobody knows what you really are inside. Or what you were on Earth. Well, I'll tell you about myself.

"I was a man!"

Morfiks sputtered. His fists clenched. He walked towards Billie.

But he did not strike her . . . him . . . it.

Instead, he smiled, and he said, "Well, let me tell you something. My real name was Juanita."

Billie became pale, then red.

"You . . . you!"

The next few days, Morfiks spent four hours each morning on the building of new houses. It was easy work. The walls and sections of the roof were brought in on wagons of brass pulled by citizens. Supervised by foremen, the laborers raised the walls, secured the bottoms to the brass foundation of the city with a quick-drying glue and then fastened the walls together by gluing down strips of the violet stuff at the corners of the walls.

Morfiks took his turn being a foreman for one day after he had gotten enough experience. He asked a citizen where the material for the houses and the rubber and the glue came from.

"And where's the food grown?"

The citizen looked around to make sure no one could hear them.

"The original brass sheets and rubber are supposed to have originated from the blind end of this universe," he said. "It's spontaneously created, flows like lava from a volcano."

"How can that be?" Morfiks said.

The citizen shrugged. "How should I know? But if you remember one of the theories of creation back on You-Know-Where, matter was supposed to be continuously created out of nothing. So if hydrogen atoms can be formed from nothing, why not brass and rubber lava?"

"But brass and rubber are organized configurations of elements and compounds!"

"So what? The structure of this universe orders it."

"And the food?"

"It's brought up on dumbwaiters through shafts which lead down to the underside. The peasants live there, citizen, and grow food and raise some kind of cattle and poultry."

"Gee, I'd like that," Morfiks said. "Couldn't I get a transfer down there? I'd like to work with the soil. It'd be much more interesting than this."

"If you were supposed to be a peasant, you'd have been transformed down there to begin with," the citizen said. "No, you're a city-dweller, brother, and you'll stay one. You predetermined that, you know, in You-Know-Where."

"I had obligations," Morfiks said. "What'd you expect me to do, shirk them?"

"I don't expect nothing except to get out of here some day."

"You mean we can get out? How? How?"

"Not so loud with that *you*," the citizen growled. "Yeah, or so we heard, anyway. We never saw a corpse but we heard about some of us dying. It isn't easy, though."

"Tell me how I can do it," Morfiks said. He grabbed the citizen's arm but the citizen tore himself loose and walked away swiftly.

Morfiks started to follow him, then could not identify him because he had mingled with a dozen others.

In the afternoons, Morfiks spent his time playing shuffleboard, badminton, swimming or sometimes playing bridge. The brass plastic cards consisted of two thicknesses glued together. The backs were blank, and the fronts were punched with codes indicating the suits and values. Then, after the evening meals in the communal halls, there were always neighborhood committee meetings. These were to settle any disputes among the local citizens. Morfiks could see no sense in them other than devices to keep the attendants busy and tire them out so that they would be ready to go to bed. After hours of wrangling and speech-making, the disputants were always told that the fault lay equally on both sides. They were to forgive each other, shake hands and make up. Nothing was really settled, and Morfiks was sure that the disputants still burned with resentments despite their protestations that all was now well with them.

What Morfiks found particularly interesting was the public prayer—if it could be called that—said by an O.D. before each meeting. It contained hints about the origins and reasons for this place and this life but was not specific enough to satisfy his curiosity.

"Glory be to the Protectors, who give us this life. Blessed be liberty, equality and fraternity. Praise be to security, conformity and certainty. None of these did we have on We-Know-Where, O Protectors, though we desired them mightily and strove always without success to attain them. Now we have them because we strove; inevitably we came here, glory be! For this cosmos was prepared for us and when we left that vale of slippery, slidery chaos, we squeezed through the walls and were formed in the template of passage, given these bodies, sexless, sinless, suitable. O Mighty Protectors, invisible but everywhere, we know that We-Know-Where is the pristine cosmos, the basic world, dirty, many-aspected, chaos under the form of seeming order, evil but necessary. The egg of creation, rotten but generative. Now, O Protectors, we are shaped forever in that which we cried for on that other unhappy universe. . . ."

There was more but most of it was a repetition in different words. Morfiks, sitting in the brass pews, his head bowed, looked up at the smooth hemisphere of the ceiling and walls and the platform on which the O.D. stood. If he understood the O.D., he was bound here forever, immortal, each day like the next, each month an almost unvarying image of the preceding, year after year, century after century, millennia after millennia.

"Stability, Unseen but Everfelt Protectors. Stability! A place for everyone and everyone in a place!"

The O.D. was saying that there were such things as souls, a configuration of energy which exactly duplicated the body of the person when he had existed on We-Know-Where. It was undetectible by instruments there and so had been denied by many. But when one died there, the configuration was released from the attraction of the body, was somehow pushed from one universe into the next.

There were billions of these, all existing within the same space as the original universe but polarized and at angles to it. A "soul" went to that universe for which it had the most attraction.

Indeed, the universe to which it traveled had actually been created by men and women. The total cumulative effect of desire for just such a place had generated this place.

If Morfiks interpreted the vague statements of the O.D. correctly, the structure of this universe was such that when a "soul" or cohesive energy configuration came through the "walls," it naturally took the shape in which all citizens found themselves. It was like hot plastic being poured into a mold.

Morfiks dared question a citizen who claimed to have been here for a hundred years. "The O.D. said all questions have been settled, everything is explained. What's explained? I don't understand any more about the origins or reasons for things here than I did on We-Know-Where."

"So what's new?" the citizen said. "How can you understand the ununderstandable? The main difference here is that you don't ask questions. There are many answers, all true, to one question, and this place is one answer. So quit bugging me. You trying to get me—uh, us— into trouble? Hey, O.D.!"

Morfiks hurried off and lost himself in a crowd before he could be identified. He burned with resentment at the implications of this world. Why should he be here? Sure, on We-Know-Where he had stayed with one company for 20 years, he had been a good family man, a pal to his kids, a faithful husband, a pillar of the best church in the neighborhood, had paid off his mortgages, joined the Lions, Elk, and Moose and the Masonic Lodge, the PTA, the Kiwanis, the Junior Chamber of Commerce and been a hard worker for the Democrats. His father before him had been a Democrat, and though he had had many misgivings about some of the policies, he had always followed the party line. Anyway, he was a right-wing Democrat, which made him practically the same thing as a left-wing Republican. He read the *Reader's Digest, Look, Life, Time, Wall Street Journal, Saturday Evening Post,* and had always tried to keep up with the bestsellers as recommended by the local newspaper reviewer. All this, not because he really wanted it but because he felt that he owed it to his wife and kids and for the good of society. He had hoped that when he went "over yonder" he would be rewarded with a life with more freedom, with a number of unlimited avenues for the things he really wanted to do.

What were those things? He didn't remember now, but he was sure that they were not what was available here.

"There's been a mistake," he thought. "I don't belong here. Everything's all screwed up. I shouldn't be here. This is an error on somebody's part. I got to get out. But how can I get out of here any more than I could get out of We-Know-Where? There the only way out was suicide and I couldn't take that, my family would have been disgraced. Besides, I didn't feel like it.

"And here I can't kill myself. My body's too tough and there's nothing, no way for me to commit suicide. Drowning? That won't work. The river's too well guarded, and if you did slip by the guards long enough to drown, you'd be dragged out in no time at all and resuscitated. And then punished."

IV

On the fourth night, what he had been dreading happened. His punishment. He woke up in the middle of the night with a dull toothache. As the night went on, the ache became sharper. By dawn, he wanted to scream.

Suddenly, the batwings on his doorway flew open, and one of his neighbors (he presumed) stood in the room. He/she was breathing hard and holding his/her hand to his/her jaw.

"Did you do it?" said the neighbor in a shrill voice.

"Do what?" Morfiks said, rising from the couch-bed.

"Antisocial act," the intruder said. "If the culprit confesses, the pain will cease. After a while, that is."

"Did you do it?" Morfiks said. For all he knew, he might be talking to Billie again.

"Not me. Listen, newcomers often—always—commit crimes because of a mistaken notion a crime can't be detected. But the crime is always found out."

"There are newcomers who aren't born criminals," Morfiks said. Despite his pain, he intended to keep control too.

"Then you, and I mean *you*, won't confess?"

"The pain must be breaking some people apart," said Morfiks. "Otherwise, some wouldn't be using the second person singular."

"Singular, hell!" the citizen said, breaking two tabus with two words. "Okay, so it doesn't make much difference if you or me or the poor devil down the street did it. But I got a way of beating the game."

"And so bringing down more punishment on us?"

"No! Listen, I was a dental assistant on We-Know-Where. I know for a fact that you can forget one pain if you have a greater."

Morfiks laughed as much as his tooth would permit him, and he said, "So, what's the advantage there?"

The citizen smiled as much as his toothache would permit. "What I'm going to propose will hurt you. But it'll end up in a real kick. You'll enjoy your pain, get a big thrill out of it."

"How's that?" Morfiks said, thinking that the citizen talked too much like Billie.

"Our flesh is tough so we can't hurt each other too easily. But we can be hurt if we try hard enough. It takes perseverence, but then what doesn't that's worthwhile?"

The citizen shoved Morfiks onto the couch, and, before Morfiks could protest, he was chewing on his leg.

"You do the same to me," the citizen mumbled between bites. "I'm telling you, it's great! You've never had anything like it before."

Morfiks stared down at the bald head and the vigorously working jaws. He could feel a little pain, and his toothache did seem to have eased.

He said, "Never had anything like what?"

"Like blood," the citizen said. "After you've been doing this long enough, you'll get drunk on it."

"I don't know. There, uh, seems something wrong about this."

The citizen stopped gnawing.

"You're a greenhorn! Look at it this way. The protectors tell us to love one another. So you should love me. And you can show your love by helping me get rid of this toothache. And I can do the same for you. After a while, you'll be like all of us. You won't give a damn; you'll do anything to stop the pain."

Morifks got into position and bit down hard. The flesh felt rubbery. Then he stopped and said, "Won't we get another toothache tomorrow because of what we're doing now?"

"We'll get an ache somewhere. But forget about tomorrow."

"Yeah," Morfiks said. He was beginning to feel more pain in his leg. "Yeah. Anyway, we can always plead we were just being social."

The citizen laughed and said, "How social can you get, huh?"

Morfiks moaned as his crushed nerves and muscles began to bleed. After a while, he was screaming between his teeth, but he kept biting. If he was being hurt, he was going to hurt the citizen even worse.

And what the hell, he was beginning to feel a reasonable facsimile to that which he had known up there on We-Know-Where.

Riverworld

I

Tom Mix's boat sailed around the bend of the river first. The pursuing boat sped around a few seconds less than a minute later. Both craft, the large chaser and the small chased, were bamboo catamarans: double-hulled, single-masted, fore-and-aft rigged with spinnakers. The sails were fashioned from the paperthin but tough intestinal lining of the river-serpent fish.

It was an hour before dusk. The shadows of the western mountains of the valley fell across the hills at their feet and stained half of the plain bordering the river. People were gathered in groups by the great mushroom-shaped stones that lined the riverbank, each a mile apart. About the time that the sinking sun touched the peaks, the stones would roar and spout flame and the hundreds of cylindrical gray containers on top of each stone would be filled with the evening meal, the liquor, the tobacco, the dreamgum.

Pushed by the wind and the strong current in the middle of the river, the vessels scudded along. At the turn, the stream broadened from its normal width of a mile to three miles, forming a "lake." Many fishing boats were out on the river; thus, the two newcomers found themselves in the midst of a fleet.

The fleeing catamaran tacked to run between two fishing craft that were separated by only thirty feet. So close was the pursuing boat to its quarry by then, it had a quick decision to make. It could either follow the path of the first through the narrowing lane, or it could swing away to avoid a collision. The steersman took the course that would not permit the smaller vessel to gain distance—

if he were lucky or skillful enough. The big boat leaned over and cut towards the opening. But by then the fishing craft had drifted too closely together.

All three crews shouted. The catamaran crashed bow first into the side of the nearest fisher near its bow. Only half the size of the catamaran, the single-hulled bamboo boat swung around, its stern traveling towards the left hull of the catamaran. Those in the smaller craft were hurled to the deck. All ten men aboard the catamaran were also knocked down by the impact; three went over the side and into the water.

The pursued now became the attacker. It turned and beat up the wind towards the two caught in the collision. Although both were sinking from the water pouring into the stoved-in bows, they were settling very slowly. The captain of the catamaran shouted some orders; his men picked up their weapons and gathered near the port. Obviously, they intended to board the other boat; though for what purpose the others did not know.

Now the smaller catamaran neared the two cripples. There were only three on its deck, a woman at the helm, a man handling the sailropes, and Tom Mix in the bow. The woman wore the usual garb of the female river-dweller in this area, a brilliantly colored towel as a kilt around her waist and a thinner piece of cloth around her breasts. The sailhandler wore only a towel-kilt. But the man in the bow had a ten-gallon hat of woven straw on his head, a long black cloak made of towels fastened together with magnetic tabs and cowboy boots of river-serpent leather. Now, as his boat neared the others, he slipped off the boots and stood barefooted; his cloak and hat followed to the deck.

Mix picked up a heavy war-boomerang from the deck. It was two feet long, fashioned by sharp flint from a piece of hard white oak. One of its ends turned at the angle of 30 degrees. A formidable weapon in the hand of a skilled thrower, it could break a man's arm at a distance of 500 feet.

At his feet lay a chert-headed axe, four more boomerangs, several oak spears with flint tips and a leather sling and leather bag of sling-stones. As soon as Mix's craft came close enough to the other, he braced himself and threw the boomerang. It flew towards its target, the sun flashing off its pale surface, and struck a man in the neck. The man fell sidewise on the deck.

The others yelled and spread out along the deck, any intention of boarding the fisher boat forgotten. They threw clubs and spears, but all three on Mix's boat hugged the deck, and the missiles hit no one. Immediately afterward, Mix jumped up and hurled a spear. It fell short of its mark, the torso of the nearest man, but it pierced his foot. He screamed and hopped around the deck until two men got him down and pulled the spear out.

During this encounter, the second fisher had come alongside and was starting to take those on the sinking fisher aboard. Seeing this, the catamaran captain ordered his crew to take the riverworthy boat. He led the attack; his men followed him onto the fisher alongside. This contained two men and a woman who had not yet gotten off; the other fisher now held four women and two men.

All of these turned to defend themselves. They thrust spears tipped with sharp bamboo blades. One woman whirled a stone in a sling over her head. The rock caught a man in his solar plexus. He doubled over, staggered back and started to fall just as a thrown spear plunged into his arm. One of his crew stumbled over him and received the point of a blade with the full weight of a defender on it.

Shrieking, one of the women fell into the water between the boats, a spear in her breast. Then the defenders and attackers closed in a melee.

A moment later the other catamaran slid by. Mix worked smoothly with all the speed and finesse of a man who had practiced for hundreds of hours. His sling whirled three times and struck his target each time. Fortunately, he knew his pursuers and so did not have to worry about identity. One stone caught a man in the side of the neck. Another hit at the base of the spine. The third almost missed, but the captain of the boarders was sent writhing to the deck with a smashed kneecap. A knife slashed his jugular.

Again the little catamaran turned back toward the three boats, side by side, this time so swiftly that one of the hulls lifted completely from the water, and the sail swung violently around. It capsized almost, but it settled back; and with the wind behind it, it raced back up to its destination. Mix crouched by the bow, threw a spear that hit a man in the side and followed with a leap that brought him on the deck among the battlers.

His heavy axe rose and fell twice.

Suddenly outnumbered, the attackers tried to run back

to their boat. Only one made it, and he was forced to dive into the river. Mix picked up a boomerang from the deck, lifted his arm to throw it at the bobbing head, then lowered it. Boomerangs were too hard to come by to waste on somebody who could no longer be a threat.

By then, the catamaran had been secured to the undamaged fisher with ropes of plaited bamboo fibers. Mix crossed the two sinking boats to the fisher. Except for the groaning of the wounded and the weeping of a woman, all were silent. They looked pale and spent; the fire of battle was gone from their faces.

Mix put his ten-gallon hat back on, secured the long black cloak around his neck, and slipped on his dark-red and sable riverserpent boots. He came back to the fisher deck, removed his hat with a flourish, grinned, and said, "Tom Mix at your service, ladies and gentlemen. And many thanks for your help in saving us."

A man said, "Bare bones o' God, stranger, I scarcely comprehend your speech. Yet it seems to be somewhat English."

Mix put his hat back on and rolled his ~~~ as if beseeching help from above. "Still in the 17th ~~~ ury! Well, at least I can understand your lingo a little bit. What's your handle, amigo?"

"Handle? Amigo?"

"Your name, friend. And who's your boss? I'd like to offer my services. I need him, and I think he's going to need me."

"Stafford's the lord hereabouts," a woman said. She was looking at him strangely. The others were, too. But it was not only he they regarded so peculiarly. The man who had handled the sail on the catamaran and was now standing by Mix's side was receiving as much attention.

Mix grinned and said, "No, he's not my twin brother or any sort of brother to me, aside from that kinship that comes from being human. He was born on Earth some thousand years before me and in a place far off from my native Pennsylvania. It's only a trick of fate he resembles me so. A lucky one for him, otherwise he might not have gotten loose from Kramer."

He did not explain his remark. "My friends and I have had a tough time for the last couple of days. We're tired and hungry. I'd like permission to stay at your place for a few days before we go on down the river. Do you think your boss . . . lord . . . would object?"

"Far from it, sir," the woman said. "He welcomes good fighting men in the hopes they'll stay. And he rewards them well. But tell me, these men—they must be Kramer's—why were they so intent on killing you they chased you into a place where they are forbidden to enter under pain of death?"

"That's a long story," said Mix. He smiled. His smile was very attractive, and he knew it. "You evidently know of Kramer the Burner. These two—Bithniah and Yeshua—were prisoners of his. I got them loose, along with a bunch of others. We three were the only ones to make it to a boat. The rest you know."

Abruptly, he turned away to give orders to his two boat-mates. All boarded the catamaran, untied the ropes binding the two boats, hoisted sail, and slipped away. The woman steered toward the western shore; he stood in the prow with his long black cloak whipping to one side of him while he stared at the scene ahead.

II

As almost everywhere in the never-ending valley, there was the plain, a mile wide and flat as the floor of a house. This was covered with the short-bladed grass that no amount of trampling could kill. Beyond the plain, the hills began. These started out as mounds about 20 feet high but became broader and higher as they progressed toward the mountains. Unlike the plain, which had only a few trees here and there, the hills were thick with forest. Eighty out of every hundred were the indestructible "irontrees," the deep-rooted monsters with bark that resisted fire and would shrug off the swing of the sharpest steel axe—if any had existed on this world. Among them grew the five hundred to thousand-feet high pines, oak, ash, elm, alder and other varieties. Beneath the trees grew long-bladed grass and the bamboo groves.

Beyond the hills, the mountains soared. The lower parts were rugged with canyons and fissures and little plateaus. But, at the five thousand foot height, the mountains became an unbroken cliff. Smooth as glass, they soared straight up for another five thousand feet or even leaned outwards near the top. They were unclimbable, as every man who had tried them could testify.

Both sides of the valley were alike. However, one area of the river did differ from another in a few respects. A man could sail for ten thousand miles and see only green in the vegetation. Then, suddenly, as if a thin wall divided one area from another, the valley bloomed. Huge vines wreathed themselves around every tree and even the larger bamboo. From the vines grew flowers of many sizes, shapes, and every shade of the spectrum.

For ten thousand miles both sides of the river valley would explode with color. Then, just as abruptly as it had ceased, the trees would resume their ascetic green.

But this area trumpeted with the flourish of hue.

Mix gave the order, and Yeshua lowered the sail. Bithniah steered the catamaran straight onto the bank, which rose gently from the river, up onto the grass. Many hands among the crowd on the bank seized the boat and drew its hulls entirely onto the land. Yeshua finished furling the sail, and he and the woman came down onto the grass.

The three newcomers were surrounded by men and women eager to get answers to their questions. Yeshua and Bithniah spoke English, but with a heavy accent that made them unintelligible to anybody unused to them. Mix barely started a sentence before he was interrupted by other interrogators. In a few minutes, he was rescued. Some men dressed in leather cuirasses and helmets, 17th-century style, arrived. They were soldiers sent by Stafford to bring Mix and his friends to the Council Hall. Mix glanced at the sun, which was about to touch the tip of the mountains.

"I'm hungry. Couldn't we wait until we charged our buckets?"

He gestured at the mushroom-shaped stone structure, six feet high and several hundred broad, that stood a few feet from the river's edge. The gray cylinders of the others were inserted in the depressions on the surface.

"Buckets?" said the sergeant. "We call them copias, stranger. Short for cornucopia. Give me your copias. We will charge them for you, and you can fill your bellies after Stafford's seen you."

Mix shrugged, for he was in no position to argue. The three walked with the soldiers at an angle across the plain towards a hill. On top of it was a blockhouse built of giant bamboo logs. The gate fronting on the river was open, and through this the party went into a yard. The

Council House itself was a long hall in the middle of the yard.

Stafford and his council were sitting at a round table of pine on a platform at the far end of the hall. Pine torches impregnated with fish oil had been lit and set in brackets on the walls. The smoke rose towards the blackened rafters, but the stench of fish spread through the hall. Underlying it was another stink, that of unwashed human bodies.

The sergeant halted them and reported to Stafford, who rose from the table to greet the strangers courteously. He was a tall, slimly built man with an aristocratic, aquiline face. In a pleasant voice thick with a Northern burr, he asked them to sit down. He offered them their choice of wine, whiskey or liqueur. Mix, knowing that liquor came only from the miracle buckets—or copias—and the supply was therefore limited, took the offer as a good sign. Stafford would not be so generous with expensive commodities to people he intended to treat as hostiles. Mix sniffed, smiled at the scent of excellent bourbon, and tossed it down.

"I know what happened on the river," Stafford said. "But I don't know why Kramer's men were so desperate to kill you that they dared to trespass in my waters."

Tom Mix began his story. Now and then, Stafford nodded to an officer to give Mix another drink. Occasionally, he stopped Mix because he did not understand a 20th-century word or phrase.

It was evident his hospitality was not all based on good-heartedness. A drunken and tired man, if he were a spy, might slip. But Mix was a long way from having enough to make him loose-tongued, even on a growling belly. Moreover, he had nothing to hide. Well, not much, anyway.

"How far do you want me to go back in my story?" he said.

Stafford laughed. "For the present, leave your Earthly life out."

"Well, ever since All Souls' Day"—a term for the general resurrection of at least half of humanity on the planet—"I have been wandering down the river. I was born in 1871 A.D. and died in 1940 A.D. But it was my fate to be raised from the dead in an area occupied by 15th-century Poles. I didn't hang around them long; I shook the dust off my feet and took off like a stripe-tailed ape. It didn't take me long to find out there weren't any horses on this world, or any animals except man, earthworms and fish. So I built me a boat. I wanted to get back to folks of my own times, those I could talk to and who'd heard of me. I had some fame in my time, but I won't go into that here.

"I figured out that, if people were strung along this valley according to time sequence on Earth—although there were many exceptions—the 20th-centurians ought to be near the river's mouth. I had about ten men and women with me, and we sailed with the wind and the current for, let's see close to five years now. Now and then we'd stop to rest or to work."

"Work?"

"As mercenaries. We picked up extra cigarettes, liquor, good food. In return, we helped out some people that needed helping real bad and had a good cause. Most of my crew were veterans of wars on Earth. One of them had been a general in the American Civil War. I'm graduate of Virginia Military Institute, and I fough several wars in my younger days on Earth. The Spanis. American War, the Boxer Rebellion, the Boer War. You probably don't know about those.

"A couple of times we were captured by slavers when we landed at some seemingly friendly place to fill our buckets. We always escaped, but the time came when I was the only one left of the original group—the others were all killed, even my lovely little Egyptian. Maybe I'll run into them again some day. They could just as well be re-resurrected downriver as upriver."

He paused, then said, "It's funny. Among all the millions, maybe billions of faces I've seen while coming down the river, I've not seen one I knew on Earth."

Stafford said, "I met a 20th-centurian who calculated that there could be at least 25 billion human beings on this world."

Tom Mix nodded and said, "Yeah. I know. But you'd think that in five years, just one . . . well, it's bound to happen some day. So, I built this last boat of mine about 5,000 miles back, a year ago. My new crew and I did pretty well until we put in at one of Kramer's rocks for a meal. We'd been eating fish and bamboo shoots and acorn-nut bread for some time, and the others were aching for a smoke and a shot of booze. I took a chance and lost. We were brought before Kramer himself, an ugly fat guy from 15th-century Germany.

"Like a lot of nuts, he hasn't accepted the fact that

this world isn't exactly what he thought the afterlife was going to be. He was a bigshot on Earth. An inquisitor. He had burned a hell of a lot of men, women and children, after torturing them for the greater glory of God."

Yeshua, sitting near Mix, muttered something. Mix fell silent for a moment. He was not sure that he had not gone too far.

Although he had seen no signs of such, it was possible that Stafford and his people might just be as lunatic in their way as Kramer was in his. During their Terrestrial existence, most of the 17th-centurians had had a rockfast conviction in their religious beliefs. Finding themselves here in the strange place neither heaven nor hell, they had suffered a great shock. Some of them had not recovered.

There were those adaptable enough to cast aside their former religion and seek the truth. But too many, like Kramer, had rationalized their environment. Kramer, for instance, maintained that this world was a purgatory. He had been shaken to find that not only Christians but all heathens we. here. But he had insisted that the teachings of the Church had been misunderstood on Earth. They had been deliberately perverted in their presentation by Satan-inspired priests. But he clearly saw The Truth now.

However, those who did not see as he did must be shown. Kramer's method of revelation, as on Earth, was the wheel and the fire.

When Mix had been told this, he had not argued with Kramer's theory. On the contrary, he was enthusiastic—outwardly—in offering his services. He did not fear death, because he knew that he would be resurrected twenty-four hours later elsewhere along the river. But he did not want to be stretched on the wheel and then burned.

He waited for his chance to escape.

One evening a group had been seized by Kramer as they stepped off a boat. Mix pitied the captives, for he had witnessed Kramer's means of changing a man's mind. Yet there was nothing he could do for them. If they were stupid enough to refuse to pretend that they agreed with Kramer, they must suffer.

"But this man Yeshua bothered me," Mix said. "In the first place, he looked too much like me. Having to see him burn would be like seeing myself in the flames. Moreover, he didn't get a chance to say yes or no. Kramer asked him if he was Jewish. Yeshua said he had been on Earth, but he now had no religion.

"Kramer said he would have given Yeshua a chance to become a convert, that is, believe as Kramer did. This was a lie, but Kramer is a mealymouthed slob who has to find justification for every rotten thing he does. He said that he gave Christians and all heathens a chance to escape the fire—except Jews. They were the ones who'd crucified Jesus, and they should all pay. Besides, a Jew couldn't be trusted. He'd lie to save his own skin.

"The whole boatload was condemned because they were all Jews. Kramer asked where they were going, and Yeshua said they were looking for a place where nobody had ever heard of a Jew. Kramer said there wasn't any such place; God would find them out no matter where they went. Yeshua lost his temper and called Kramer a hypocrite and an anti-Christ. Kramer got madder than hell and told Yeshua he wasn't going to die as quickly as the others.

"About then, I almost got thrown into prison with them. Kramer had noticed how much we looked alike. He asked me if I'd lied to him when I told him I wasn't a Jew. How come I looked like a Jew if I wasn't? Of course, this was the first time he thought of me looking like a Jew, which I don't. If I was darker, I could pass for one of my Cherokee ancestors.

"So I grinned at him, although the sweat was pouring out of my armpits so fast it was trickling down my legs, and I said that he had it backwards. Yeshua looked like a Gentile, that's why he resembled me. I used one of his own remarks to help me; I reminded him he's said Jewish women were notoriously adulterous. So maybe Yeshua was half-Gentile and didn't know it.

"Kramer gave one of those sickening belly laughs of his; he drools until the spit runs down his chin when he's laughing. And he said I was right. But I knew my days were numbered. He'd get to thinking about my looks later, and he'd decide that I was lying. To hell with that, I thought, I'm getting out tonight.

"But I couldn't get Yeshua off my mind. I decided that I wasn't just going to run like a cur with its tail between its legs. I was going to make Kramer so sick with my memory his pig's belly would ache like a boil every time he thought of me. That night, just as it began to rain, I killed the two guards with my axe and opened the stockade gates. But somebody was awake and gave the alarm. We ran for my boat, had to fight our way to it, and only Yeshua, the woman Bithniah and I got away. Kramer must have given orders that the men who went after us had better not return without our heads. They weren't about to give up."

Stafford said, "God was good enough to give us eternal youth in this beautiful world. We are free from want, hunger, hard labor and disease. Yet men like Kramer want to turn this Garden of Eden into hell. Why? I do not know. He is a madman. One of these days, he'll be marching on us, as he has on the people to the north of his original area. If you would like to help us fight him, welcome!"

"I hate the murdering devil!" Mix said. "I could tell you things . . . never mind, you must know them."

"To my everlasting shame," Stafford replied, "I must confess that I witnessed many cruelties and injustices on Earth, and I not only did not protest, I encouraged them. I thought that law and order and religion, to be maintained, needed torture and persecution. Yet I was often sickened. So when I found myself in a new world, I determined to start anew. What had been right and necessary on Earth did not have to be so here."

"You're an extraordinary man," Mix said. "Most people have continued to think exactly what they thought on Earth."

III

By then, he was beginning to feel heady. Fortunately, the copias were brought in, and they were allowed to eat. Mix opened the tall gray cylinder and removed the containers from their snap-up racks. These held a thick cubical boneless steak, two slices of bread with butter, a lettuce salad, a baked potato with butter and sour cream, a chocolate bar, a 3-ounce shot of whiskey, a pack of cigarettes, two cigars and a stick of dreamgum.

Normally, Mix used tobacco for barter, since he did not smoke, but he thought it politic to pass it around to Stafford and his councilmen.

Yeshua, on opening his cylinder, looked disgusted. Instead of satisfying his hunger, which must have been as ravenous as Mix's, he stared gloomily at the ceiling. Mix asked him what was wrong. Bithniah, who was eating greedily, laughed and said, "Even though he has renounced his religion with his mind, his stomach can't forget the laws of Moses. There is a big tender piece of ham in his copia, and it has sickened him."

"Aren't you a Hebrew, too?" Mix asked.

"Yes, but I don't let it bother me. When I am hungry, I will eat anything. I learned that on Earth when I was a young girl and we were roaming in the desert. I never allowed the others to see me eating unclean food, of course, else I'd have been killed. But then I did many things that Yahweh was supposed to frown upon."

Mix said, "Yeshua, I'll trade my steak for your ham."

"I'm not sure that the animal was slaughtered correctly," Yeshua said.

"I don't think there's any slaughter involved," Mix replied, "I've been told that the buckets must convert energy into matter. Somehow the power that the stones give off three times a day is transformed by a mechanism in the false bottom of the bucket. There must also be a kind of program in the mechanism, because the buckets have different food every day. I've kept watch on it and noticed that I always get steak on certain days, a cake of soap every third day and so on.

"The scientist that explained it to me said—though he admitted he was only guessing—that there are matrices in the bucket that contain models for certain kinds of matter. They put together the atoms and molecules of the energy to form steak, cigars, or what have you. So, there's no slaughter."

"I'll take the steak and with thanks," Yeshua said.

Stafford, who had been listening with interest, spoke. "The first general resurrection, and the resurrection of those killed here since that day, must operate on the same principles. But who is doing all this for us and why?"

Mix shrugged and said, "Who knows? I've heard a lot of wild theories. But I did run into a man who knew a 19th-century Englishman named Burton. He said Burton had told him that he had accidentally awakened before Resurrection Day. He was in a very strange place, a titanic room where there were millions of bodies. Some were in the process of being restored to wholeness and youth. He tried to escape, but two men caught him and made him unconscious again, and he woke up with the rest of us on That Day, naked as a jaybird and with his bucket in his hand.

"Burton thought that some beings, maybe Earthmen of the post-20th-century, had found a way to record events in time. They'd taken records of every human being that existed, formed matter that re-created the original beings, restored the being to health and youth, made new recordings and transformed them in this rivervalley.

"This valley, by the way, must also be their work. A river that's at least ten million miles long and flows uphill at places, has to have been built by sentient beings, not by Nature."

"What you say seems reasonable," Stafford replied. "However, what appears to be reasonable may not conform to the facts. I am inclined to agree with you. But I still do not know what purpose there is in our being here."

Mix yawned and stretched. "I don't either, but I intend to make the best of what I do have while I have it. I know we'll have to pay for this one way or the other. You get nothing free. If it's okay with you, I'd like to hit the hay. First, though, I'd like to take a bath."

Stafford smiled. "You 20th-centurians are as enamored of bathing as the ancient Romans were reputed to be. I say reputed, because the few I've met were, to put it charitably, unwashed. Yet the river is only a few steps away. Perhaps it was the decadent ruling class of the Romans that was so clean?"

Mix grinned, but he felt angry. Something in Stafford's tone indicated he felt that Mix and his kind had a ridiculous obsession, maybe a somewhat immoral attitude. Mix swallowed the comment he wanted to make, that the council hall stank like a congress of baboons. But he was in no position to insult his host, nor should he. The man was only expressing the attitude of his time.

Stafford told Mix that there were several unoccupied cottages nearby. Those who had been killed by Kramer's men on the river had lived in them. The cottage automatically reverted to the state, which usually sold them to newcomers or rented them for tobacco, liquor or services rendered.

Mix, Yeshua and Bithniah followed a Sergeant Channing, who held a torch, although it was not needed. The night sky, ablaze with giant stars and luminous sheets of gasclouds, cast a brighter light than the Earth's full moon. The river sparkled beneath it. The four went to its bank, and the three newcomers walked into the water up to their hips. Yeshua and Bithniah kept their kilts on, so Mix did the same. When with a group that bathed in the nude, a common practice along the river, he undressed. When Mix was with those who retained their modesty, he observed their custom.

With soap from their copias, they washed the grime and sweat off and returned to the land to dry themselves with other towels. Mix watched Bithniah. She was a short dark woman with a full bosom, a narrow waist and shapely legs, but with too broad hips. She had long thick glossy blueblack hair and a pretty face, if you liked long noses. Her eyes were huge and dark, and even during the flight they had given Mix some curious glances. He told himself that Yeshua had better watch her; she looked to him like an alleycat in mating season.

Yeshua now, he was something different. The only resemblance he had to Mix was physical. He was quiet and withdrawn, except for that one outburst against Kramer, and he seemed to be always thinking of something far away. Despite his silence, he gave an impression of great authority—rather, of a man who had once had it but was now deliberately suppressing it. Or, perhaps, of a man who rejected all claim to authority.

"You know," Mix said to Yeshua, "shortly before I came to Kramer's territory, something puzzling happened to me. A little dark man rushed at me crying out in a foreign tongue. He tried to embrace me; he was weeping and moaning, and he kept repeating a name over and over. I had a hell of a time convincing him he'd made a mistake. Maybe I didn't. He tried to get me to take him along, but I didn't want anything to do with him. He made me nervous, the way he kept on staring at me.

"I forgot about him until just now. I'll bet he thought I was you. Come to think of it, he did say your name quite a few times."

Yeshua came out of his absorption. "Did he say what his name was?"

"I don't know. He tried four or five different languages on me, including English, and I couldn't understand him in any of them. But he did repeat a word more than once. Mattithayah. Mean anything to you?"

Yeshua did not reply. He shivered and draped a long towel over his shoulders. Mix knew that something inside Yeshua was chilling him. The heat of the daytime, which reached about 80 degrees at high noon (there were no thermometers), faded away slowly. The high humidity of the valley retained it until the invariable rains fell a few hours after midnight. Then the temperature dropped swiftly to an estimated 65°, and stayed there until dawn.

Sergeant Channing led them to their residences. These were small one-room bamboo huts with roofs thatched with the giant leaves of the irontree. Inside each was a table, several chairs, and beds, all of bamboo. Channing bade them good night and walked off, but Mix knew that he would probably give orders to sentinels stationed out of sight nearby.

IV

Mix fell asleep at once but wakened as soon as the rays of the sun fell on his face through the open window. He rose, put on his kilt, and splashed water from a broad shallow fired-clay basin on the table. He did not have to bother about shaving, for all men had been resurrected permanently beardless.

He took a roll of paper (the copias provided this, too), and found his desired destination by following his nose. This was a long bamboo hut built over a deep ditch.

He found that, if daily bathing was not widespread, other sanitary customs were observed. The deposits were hauled up at regular intervals to be dropped in a deep canyon (aptly and directly named) in the mountains. Mix asked if there was any sulfur in the area. He was told that there was none. That explained to him why these people did not extract nitrate crystals from processed excrement and mix it with charcoal and sulfur to make gunpowder. In other areas of the valley, bombs and rockets in bamboo cases were common.

On returning to his cottage, he intended to invite Yeshua and his woman to go with him to the nearest charging stone. A few paces from their door, he halted. They were arguing loudly in their heavily accented English. Later, he wondered why they did not use Hebrew or Aramaic, which would have been ununderstandable to any overhearer. Discreet inquiry would reveal that Bithniah did not know Aramaic. Also, her Hebrew was too archaic and had too many Egyptian and colloquial words, which later had dropped out of the language. Moreover, Yeshua knew Hebrew only as a liturgical and scholarly tongue and could converse in it only with hesitation. The only common speech to both was 17-century English, and their use of it was, to Tom Mix, a half-garble.

"I will not go up with you to live in the mountains!" Bithniah said. "I don't want to be alone, to sit on top of a rock with no one but a walking tomb to talk to. I love people, and I love to talk. No, I will not go!"

"I won't stop you from going down into the plains to talk," Yeshua said. "Now do I plan to live entirely as a hermit. I'll have to work, probably as a carpenter, but I don't . . ."

Here Mix couldn't understand the next few sentences. He had no trouble comprehending most of Bithniah's retort, however.

"I don't know why I stick to you! But I know why you want me around! It's just because I knew Mosheh and Aaron and I was on the march from Egypt! Your only interest in me is to drain me of all I know about your great hero Mosheh! Well, let me tell you, Yeshua, he was a louse! He was always preaching against adultery and strange women, but I happen to know what he practiced! Believe me, I was one of the women!"

Yeshua said, "I am interested in what you have to say about your life, although there are times when I wish I'd never heard a word of it. But great is the truth."

Here he continued in Hebrew or Aramaic, evidently quoting something.

"Stick to English!" Bithniah screamed. "I got so fed up with the so-called holy men always quoting proverbs and the holy writings, and all the time their own sins stank like a camel! Furthermore, you know all about me, you told me nothing about yourself. All I know is that you were a holy man, or you claimed to be. Maybe you're telling me the truth. I think that your religion ruined you. Certainly you're no good except when you take that dreamgum and you're out of your mind. What kind of a man is that, I ask you? Personally, I think . . ."

Yeshua's voice, suddenly so low that Mix could not make out the words, interrupted Bithniah. Mix strained to hear, then shrugged. He glanced at the sun. A few minutes more, and the stones would give up their energy. If they did not hurry, they'd have to go breakfastless, unless they wanted to eat fish, of which he was very tired.

He knocked loudly on the door. The two within fell silent. Bithniah swung the door open violently, but she managed to smile at him as if nothing had occurred. "Yes, I know. We'll be with you at once."

"Not I," said Yeshua. "I don't feel hungry now."

"That's right!" Bithniah said loudly. "Try to make me feel guilty, blame your upset stomach on me. Well, I'm hungry, and I'm going to eat, and you can sit here and sulk for all I care!"

"No matter what you say, I am going to live in the mountains."

"Go ahead! You must have something to hide! Who's after you? Who are you that you're so afraid of meeting people? Well, I have nothing to hide!"

Bithniah picked up her copia by the handle and stormed out. Mix walked along with her and tried to make pleasant conversation. But she was too angry to cooperate. As it was, they had just come into sight of the nearest mushroom-shaped rock, located between two hills, when blue flames soared up from the top and a roar like a lion's came to them. Bithniah stopped and burst into her native language. Obviously she was cursing. Mix contented himself with one short word.

"Got a smoke?" she said.

"In my hut. But you'll have to pay me back later. I usually trade my cigarettes for liquor."

"Cigarettes? That's your word for pipekins?"

He nodded and they returned to his hut. Yeshua was not in sight. Mix purposely left his door open. He trusted neither Bithniah nor himself.

Bithniah glanced at the door. "You must think me a fool. Right next door to Yeshua!"

Mix grinned. "You never lived in Hollywood."

He gave her a cigarette. She used the lighter that the copia had furnished: a thin metallic box which extended a whitely glowing wire when pressed on the side.

"You must have overheard us," she said. "Both of us were shouting our fool heads off. He's a very difficult man. Sometimes he frightens me, and I don't scare easily. There's something very deep—and very different, almost alien, maybe unhuman, about him. Not that he isn't very kind or that he doesn't understand people. He does, too much so.

"But he seems so aloof most of the time. Sometimes, he laughs very much, and he makes me laugh, for he has a

wonderful sense of humor. Other times, though, he de-
livers harsh judgments, so harsh they hurt me because I
know that I'm included in the indictment. Now, I don't
have any illusions about men or women. I know what they
are and what to expect. But I accept this. People are
people, although they often pretend to be better than
they are. But expect the worst, I say, and you now and
then get a pleasant surprise because you don't get the
worst."

"That's pretty much my attitude," Mix said. "Even
horses aren't predictable, and men are much more complicated. So you can't always tell what a horse or a
man's going to do or what's driving him. One thing you can
bet on. You're Number One to yourself, but to the other
guy, Number One is himself or herself. If somebody acts
like you're Number One, and she's sacrificing herself for
you, she's just fooling herself."

"You sound as if you'd had some trouble with your
wife."

"Wives. That, by the way, is one of the things I like
about this world. You don't have to go through any courts
or pay any alimony when you split up. You just pick up
your bucket, towels and weapons, and take off. No property settlements, no in-laws, no kids to worry about."

"I bore twelve children," she said. "All but three died
before they were two years old. Thank God, I don't have
to go through that here."

"Whoever sterilized us knew what he was doing," Mix
said. "If we could have kids, this valley'd be jammed tight
as a pig trough at feeding time.

He moved close to her and grinned. "Anyway, we men
still have our guns, even if they're loaded with blanks."

"You can stop where you are," she said, although she
was still smiling. "Even if I leave Yeshua, I may not
want you. You're too much like him."

"I might show you the difference," he said, but he
moved away from her and picked up a piece of dried
fish from his leather bag. Between bites, he asked her
about the Mosheh she had mentioned in her quarrel.

"Would you get angry or beat me if I told you the
truth?" she said.

"No, why should I?" he asked.

"Because I've learned to keep my mouth shut about my
Earthly life. The first time I told about it, I was beaten
badly and thrown into the river. The Englishmen I was
talking to were, what were they called? Oh, yes, Puritans!

They were outraged; I was lucky not to have been tortured and burned."

"I'd like to hear the real story," he said. "I could care less if it's not what I learned in Sunday school."

"You won't tell anybody else around here?"

"Cross my heart and promise to fall off Tony."

V

She looked blankly at him, then decided that he was giving a twentieth-century oath. She was, she said, born in the province of Goshen of the land of Egypt. Her tribe was that of Judah and they were not, technically, slaves. The Hebrews had originally come in to work for the state under contract. Conditions were not as bad as those depicted in the Book of Exodus.

She had never, of course, read this book or any of the Judaic scriptures. The first she had heard of them was from the inhabitants of the area of the rivervalley in which she had been resurrected.

There was a mixture of religions in the several tribes of Goshen. Her mother worshipped El, the original god of the Hebrews, among others. Her father favored the gods of Egypt, but he occasionally participated in the rites of El. She knew Mosheh (or Moses, as the English called him). She grew up with him. He was a wild kid (her own words), half-Hebrew, half-Egyptian. When Mosheh was about ten he had been adopted by an Egyptian priest who had lost his two sons. Five years later, Mosheh was back with the Hebrews. His fosterfather had been arrested and charged with practicing the forbidden religion of Aton, founded by the accursed Pharaoh Akhnaton. The fosterfather was executed.

Years later, Mosheh announced that the Hebrews had been taken under custody by an unknown god, Yahweh of the Midianites. This came as a surprise to the Hebrews, most of whom had never heard of Yahweh. But Mosheh was a man who had seen a vision; he seemed truly to burn as brightly with the light of Yahweh as the burning bush of which he told. And he offered them release from their bondage.

"What about the plagues, the river of blood, the slaying of the firstborn of the Egyptians?"

Bithniah laughed. "I saw nothing like that. There was a plague raging through the land, but it was killing as many Hebrews as Egyptians."

"What about the tablets of stone?"

"Mosheh did write the commandments on two tablets, but I couldn't read them. Three-fourths of the tribe couldn't. I never learned to read or write anything except a few simple Egyptian signs."

Mix wanted to question her further, but he was interrupted by a soldier. Stafford wanted to see the three of them. Yeshua came out of his hut at the summons and followed them without saying a word.

They entered the Council Hall and were greeted by Stafford. He asked them pointblank if they intended to stay.

All three answered that they would. Stafford said, "Very well. We believe that the citizen owes the state certain debts in return for its protection. Now, what would you wish to do?"

They talked a while. The result was that Mix entered the army as a private. Stafford apologized for the lowly position. He realized that a man of his training and experience should have a commisison. But it was the policy to start all newcomers off at the bottom. This avoided unhappiness and jealousy among those who had established their status.

However, since Mix had stone weapons of his own, and there were few of these in this area, Mix would be assigned to the elite squad of axemen. After a few months, he could be promoted to a sergeancy. That was the lowest permanent rank in the axemen.

Yeshua asked for a job as a carpenter. He did not want anything to do with the military, for he objected to shedding human blood. Stafford frowned at this. It was the state's policy to call on all able bodies, men or women, to fight for Albion. However, in view of Yeshua's ownership of flint tools and his undoubted usefulness, he could be admitted as a second-class citizen. This meant that he would not get any of the bonuses given out by the state every three months: the extra cigarettes, liquor, etc. At the same time, he would have to contribute a certain amount from his own copia to the state treasury. And, in case of war, he would have to submit to being kept in a stockade until the fighting was over. The state did this to make sure that the second-class citizens, of whom there were not many, would not get in the way of the military.

Yeshua agreed to this.

Bithniah was assigned to a woman's labor division. At present, this was busy adding to the southern wall dividing Albion from its neighboring state, Anglia.

Mix reported to Captain Hawkins. He spent the morning drilling and practicing throwing his axe and spears. That afternoon, he instructed craftsmen how to make boomerangs, unknown to this area.

Several hours before dusk, he was dismissed. After bathing in the river, he returned to his hut. Bithniah was home but Yeshua was gone.

"He went up into the mountains," she said. "He wanted to become pure again!"

She raved on until Mix quit listening. He waited until she had run out of breath and tears, then he asked her if she wanted to move into his cottage. She replied that he reminded her too much of Yeshua, and would he please leave? Mix shrugged and went to the nearest stone to charge his co ia.

While the , he met a pretty blonde who had recently parted with er hutmate because of their quarrels over his unreasonable jealousy. Delores and he had more in common than a desire to find a mate. Their lives on Earth had not had a chronological overlap, for she was born five years after he had rammed his car into the barricade on the road between Phoenix and Tucson, Arizona. She had never seen any of his movies, but she did know who he was. Since one of her father's childhood heroes was Tom Mix, she had heard her father discuss him more than once. And, when the family had moved to Arizona for a while, her father had insisted they go see the monument that marked the site of the accident.

For the first time, Mix heard details of what happened after his death. He felt hurt that the onlookers had been more interested in catching the many dollar bills that had flown like green snow around the barricade than in determining whether he was alive or not. But in a few minutes, he smiled to himself.

That the money meant more than a human life to those workers was only natural. If he had been in their skins, and their situation, he might have done the same. The sight of a thousand-dollar bill blown along by the wind was very tempting—to those who did not earn in two years what he made in a week. He could not really blame the slobs.

Mix and Delores Rambaut went to her hut to live, since her former mate had walked out and, therefore, lost his right to the property. Mix would have to make a formal application and pay a slight tax, cigarettes or labor, for the use of the house, but the whole procedure was routine.

He was looking forward to night when he was summoned by Stafford. The lord was grave and perturbed.

"My spies in Kramer's land tell me he is getting ready for a big attack. But they don't know on whom, for Kramer has not told even his highest officers. He knows that we have spies there, just as he undoubtedly has here."

"I hope you still don't think that I'm a spy," Mix said.

Stafford smiled slightly. "No. I've checked out your story. You're not a spy unless you're part of a diabolically clever plot by Kramer to sacrifice a good boat and fighting men to convince me you're what you claim to be. I doubt it, for Kramer is not the sort of man to release Jewish prisoners. On one hand, I can't believe Kramer could find among his followers the caliber of man to deliberately allow himself to be killed to further Kramer's ambitions. On the other hand, he does have a number of religious fanatics who might do just that."

It soon became apparent why Stafford was consulting him, a stranger, a lowly private, and an American colonist. For Stafford, despite his outward politeness, could not conceal his feelings of his own superiority, both as a blue-blooded lord and an Englishman. Mix was a "provincial," one of the inferior and wild breeds. Mix, aware of this, felt only slight resentment and more than a slight amusement. What would Stafford say if he were told that England had become the American "province" in Mix's time?

Stafford, however, was impressed by the showing of Mix in the river battle and his Earthly military background. Moreover, Mix knew Kramer's land, and he had made the statement the night before that the only way to defeat Kramer was to beat him to the punch.

Just what did he mean by that?

"As I understand it," Mix said, "Kramer's method of expansion is to leapfrog one state and conquer the one beyond it. After consolidating his conquest, he then squeezes the bypassed area between his two armies. This is an excellent method, but it wouldn't work if the other states would ally against him. Unfortunately, they're too jealous of their own prerogatives to submit to being lead by another state. Besides which, they don't trust each other. So Kramer has been having his own way.

"But I think that if we could deliver at least a crippling blow, the other states would then jump in like a pack of wolves and finish him off. So my idea is to make a night raid—by boat, of course—and burn his fleet. Maybe even a landing and a suicide force to try to kill Kramer. Knock him off, and his state will fall apart."

"I've already sent assassins after him, and they've failed," Stafford replied. "I like your aggressiveness, but I don't see how we could carry the attack off. There are two states to the south of us, and a stretch of twenty miles of river. We have to sail or row upriver, so we couldn't reach Kramer's land before morning if we left at dusk. Moreover, we'd be observed by his spies in the other states long before we got there, and Kramer'd be ready for us."

"Yeah, but you've forgotten the savages, the Huns, that live 'cross the river. So far, there's been an unspoken agreement that the middle of the river is the dividing line, and each stay on his side of the line. But I've got an idea. Here's what we could do."

They talked for another hour, at the end of which Stafford said that they would follow Mix's plan. It was better to take a chance, no matter how desperate, than *to let Kramer call the shot.* Stafford was beginning to pick up some of Mix's twentieth-century phrases.

VI

During the three-day preparation, Mix was busy. But he had some time in the afternoon for himself, and he decided to visit the man who could be his twin.

First, he stopped at Bithniah's. She was now living with one of the men whose mate had been killed during the river-fight, and she seemed fairly happy with him. No, she had not seen the "crazy monk," as she called him. Mix informed her that he had gotten glimpses of Yeshua now and then. He had been cutting down pine trees with his axe, preparatory to fashioning some furniture for Stafford.

Following her directions, Mix crossed the hills at a

southward angle and presently came to the foot of the mountains. He began climbing up a not-too-difficult path. In a few minutes, he heard a wild skirling of music. It sounded to him like a bamboo syrinx, of which there were many in this area.

The climbing became steeper. Only a mountain goat or a "crazy monk" would have daily used the so-called path; Mix decided that he was not going to make many calls on Yeshua. But there was something about the man— aside from his physical appearance—that intrigued him.

Sweating despite the shade, he pulled himself over the edge of the rock and found himself on a small plateau. A building that was more of an enclosed lean-to than a hut was in the middle of the tablerock. Beyond it was a small cascade, one of the many waterfalls that presumably originated from unseen snows on top of the mountains. The cascades were another mystery of this planet, which had no seasons and thus should rotate at an unvarying 90 degrees to the ecliptic. If the snows had no thawing period, where did the water come from?

Yeshua was by the waterfall. He was naked and blowing on the pan's pipe and dancing as wildly as one of the goat-footed worshippers of The Great God. Around and around he spun. He leaped high, he skipped, he bent forward and backwards, he kicked, he bent his legs, he pirouetted, he swayed. His eyes were closed, and he came perilously close to the edge of the plateau.

Like David dancing after the return of the ark of God, Mix thought. But Yeshua was doing this for an invisible audience. And he certainly had nothing to celebrate.

Mix was embarrassed for he felt like a window-peeper. He almost decided to retreat and leave Yeshua to whatever was possessing him. But the thought of the difficulty of the climb and the time he had taken made him change his mind.

He called. Yeshua stopped dancing and staggered backward as if an arrow had struck him. Mix walked up to him and saw that he was weeping.

Yeshua turned, kneeled and splashed the icy water from a pool by the side of the cataract, then turned to face Mix. His tears had stopped, but his eyes were wide and wild.

"I was not dancing because I was happy or filled with the glory of God," he said. "On Earth, in the desert by the Dead Sea, I used to dance. No one around but myself and The Father. I was a harp, and His fingers plucked the ecstasy. I was a flute, and He sounded through my body the songs of Heaven.

"But no more. Now I dance because, if I do not, I would scream my anguish until my throat caught fire, and I would leap over the cliff and fall to a longed-for death. What use in that? In this world, a man cannot commit suicide. Not permanently. A few hours later he must face himself and the world again. Fortunately he does not have to face his god again. There is none left to face."

Mix felt even more embarrassed and awkward. "Things can't be that bad," he said. "Maybe this world didn't turn out to be what you thought it was going to be. So what? You can't blame yourself for being wrong. Who was right? Who could possibly have guessed the truth about the unguessable? Anyway, this world has many good things that Earth didn't have. Enjoy them. It's true it's not always a picnic here, but when was it on Earth? At least, you don't have to worry about growing old, there are plenty of good-looking women, you don't have to sit up nights wondering where your next meal is coming from or how you're going to pay your taxes or alimony. Hell, even if there aren't any horses or cars or movies here, I'll take this world anytime! You lose one thing; you gain another."

"You don't understand, my friend," Yeshua replied. "Only a man like myself, a man who has seen through the veil that the matter of this physical universe presents, seen the reality beyond, felt the flooding of the Light within . . ."

He stopped, stared upwards, clenched his fists, and uttered a long ululating cry. Mix had heard only one cry like that—in Africa, when a Boer soldier had fallen over a cliff.

"Maybe I better go," Mix said. "I know when there's nothing to be done. I'm sorry that—"

"I don't want to be alone!" Yeshua said. "I am a human being; I need to talk and to listen, to see smiles and hear laughter, and know love! But I cannot forgive myself for being . . . what I was!"

Mix wondered what he was talking about. He turned and started to walk to the edge of the plateau. Yeshua came after him.

"If only I had stayed there with the Sons of Zadok! But no! I thought that the world of men and women needed me! The rocks of the desert unrolled before me like a scroll, and I read therein that which must come to pass, and soon, because God was showing me. I left my brothers in their caves and their cells and went to the cities because my brothers and sisters and the little children there must know, so that they would have a chance to save themselves."

"I got to get going," Mix said. "I feel sorry for whatever's riding you, but I can't help you unless I know what it is. And I doubt that I'd be much help then."

"You've been sent to help me! It's no coincidence that you look so much like me and that our paths crossed."

"I'm no doctor," Mix said. "Forget it. I can't straighten you out."

Abruptly, Yeshua dropped the hand held out to Mix, and he spoke softly.

"What am I saying? Will I never learn? Of course you haven't been sent. There's nobody to send you. It's just chance."

"I'll see you later," Mix said.

He began climbing down. Once he looked upwards, and he saw Yeshua's face, his face, staring down at him. He felt angry then, as if he should have stayed and at least given some encouragement to the man. He could have listened until Yeshua talked himself into feeling better.

By the time he had reached the hills and started walking back, he had a different attitude. His story that he had to be back soon was true, for Stafford was holding a council of war. Mix, although technically a private, was actually an important man.

Moreover, he doubted that he could really aid the poor devil.

Yeshua must be half-cracked. Certainly he was half-baked. And that was a peculiar thing about this world and the resurrection. Everybody else had not only been awakened from the dead with the body of a 25-year-old—except, of course, for those who had died on Earth before that age—but all who had suffered a mental illness on Earth had been restored mentally whole.

However, as time passed, and the problems of the new world pressed in, many began to sicken again in their minds. There wasn't much schizophrenia; but he understood from talking to a twentieth-centurian that at least three-quarters of schizophrenia had been proved to be due to a physical imbalance and was primarily genetic in origin.

Nevertheless, five years of life in the rivervalley had

produced a number of insane or half-insane people, though not in the relative proportions known on Earth. And the resurrection had not been successful in converting the majority of the so-called sane to a new outlook.

As before, most of humanity acted irrational and was impervious to logic. Mix was not affected. He had always known the world was half-mad and behaved accordingly, usually to his benefit.

But Yeshua, miserable fellow that he was, could not forgive himself for whatever it was he had been or done on Earth.

VII

That evening, immediately after the copias were filled the fleet of Albion set sail. It consisted of five men-of-war, twenty frigates, and forty cruisers. The so-called men-of-war were huge single-hulled ships, two-masted, fore-and-aft rigged, the bamboo reinforced with pine and oak. The crew of each was fifty men. The other classes were smaller, swifter catamarans.

The fleet had no sooner rounded the bend that took them alongside the state of Anglia than the shores on both sides of the river boomed with the roar of big drums. The Anglians, perhaps fearing an invasion, were summoning their own forces. The second set of drums were those of Kramer's spies, hidden up in the mountains, and signalling in relay to their home base. Across the river, the Huns, aroused because of fears that the two-year-old treaty was to be broken, burst into a frenzy of drumming.

Stafford directed his fleet to sail in close to the Anglian shore, run along it for a mile and then cut to the Hunnish side. By the time the Anglians had boarded their vessels and were ready to fight, the Albion fleet was close to the opposing Hunnish bank and a mile ahead. Now the Huns put out their boats.

All that night, tacking back and forth, the Albion ships sailed with an increasing number of pursuers. There came the time when ships ahead of them put out to intercept them. Then, the fleet cut back and forth in the middle of the river and managed to keep from close quarters because of a desire by both the Huns and the English Anglians and New Cornwallians to avoid conflict with each other.

Neither wanted to pursue the Albions into the others' waters.

Besides, by now, it was becoming apparent that the Albions did not intend to land on either bank. Kramer's capital city, Fides, must be his goal. Stafford and Mix were betting that Kramer, on hearing of the approaching fleet, would advance his own campaign plan ahead of time. He would order his huge fleet, larger than the combined ships of Albion, Anglia, and New Cornwall, to set out at once. Stafford had timed his sailing very carefully, and events worked as if he had been clocking them. The clouds, which always appeared at two o'clock after midnight covered the skies and blackened the land and the river. The rains torrented to reduce visibility to almost zero.

But, just before the clouds began to form, Stafford saw the starlight on the sails of Kramer's fleet. By then, the Anglianships had dropped back to protect their own coasts, and the New Cornwallians were beginning to turn. The Huns, however, were still following. Some of them had closed in with each other, for there was great hostility between differing tribes, and these could not resist the chance to attack.

Just before the starlight was cut off by the clouds, Stafford commanded his flagship to sail toward the Hunnish coast. The Fidean fleet immediately changed its course to go toward the same point. Stafford maintained the line of direction for half a mile, then had his signalman, using a hooded fish-oil lamp, transmit the code ordering the fleet to head for the western bank.

The plan worked to the extent that the two fleets sailed on by each other without any contact. Whether or not Kramer's ships then encountered the Hunnish ships was something that could not be determined. An hour after daybreak, the Albion vessels beached at the capital of Fides. The city was well fortified with earthen ramparts and great bamboo logs and stones hauled down from the mountain. Nor had Kramer stripped Fides of fighting men to crew his fleet.

Stafford did not attack the city at once. He sent ships to land their personnel further along the bank. These overcame the relatively small garrisons guarding the slave stockades. The freed men were given weapons and set to liberating other stockades. At noon the onslaught against the capital began.

Two small catapults threw large stones to batter down two widely separated spots. The forces that sallied out to destroy the catapults were themselves destroyed. Fires were built against the two salient spots, and more stones were cast. Finally, men protected from fire in armor of riverserpent hide and drenched with water drove battering rams against the wall. The walls crumbled, the ram-men stepped aside and the Albions poured in.

A half hour later, the capital was taken and all defenders killed.

Mix, blackened with smoke and bleeding slightly from two wounds in an arm and leg, climbed a tree on top of a hill. The fleet of Kramer was not in sight. So far, so good.

However, Kramer could not be found. Either he had escaped or else, as seemed unlikely but was possible, he had sailed with his ships. Stafford became alarmed. If the Fidean fleet had missed contact with the Hunnish fleet or had bulled its way through, Kramer could be doing the same thing in Albion that he, Stafford, had done here. Although his men were tired from the voyage and the fighting, he ordered them aboard. Sail was set immediately. At least, the trip down would be faster than that up.

Shortly after the rainfall of the next night, they came to the banks of Albion. All was quiet—but it was not normal.

No lanterns signalled back. Stafford had no time to hesitate. The Fidean fleet appeared from its hiding place on the opposite bank.

Outnumbering the Albion ships two to one, they drove them towards the home bank. Stafford's men fought more than well, and many a ship drifted down the river without a steersman at the helm and none but dead or seriously wounded on the decks.

Nevertheless, the survivors of Albion had no choice but to make a stand on the plains. They beached their vessels and grouped to attack the sailors of Kramer as they debarked. Then the trap closed. Land troops, hiding in the trees among the hills, rushed across the plain. The Albions resisted until they died or were too wounded to continue battling.

Stafford was one of the last to go down, but a spear through his eye and into his brain took his life.

Mix was not so lucky. A club knocked his leather helmet off, and another club tore him loose from his wits.

When he awoke, he had a large lump on the side of his head, a throbbing sickening ache in his brain and stomach and a thong around his wrists, tied behind his back.

He was lying on the grass floor of a bamboo stockade with a number of other prisoners. The morning sun was a few degrees above the mountains.

Near him sat Yeshua. His knees were drawn up to his chest, and he stared downward, his cheeks propped against the inside of his knees. Dried blood caked his right ribs and the hair on the left side of his head.

Groaning and wincing, Mix raised himself to a sitting position. The effort dizzied him, and his eyes had a tendency to cross. But, during the intervals he could see straight, he counted thirty prisoners, twenty-one men and nine women.

"Where's Bithniah?" he said to Yeshua.

Yeshua did not look up. He said, hollowly, "She was being raped by many men the last I saw her. She should be dead by now. At least I haven't heard her screaming. The other women have stopped screaming. They must be dead, too."

Mix gestured at the female prisoners. "How'd they escape it?"

"Kramer saved them. He said he wanted some alive . . . to burn."

Mix grunted and said, "I was afraid that was the reason they didn't kill me."

He looked along the tops of the walls. The guards were many and alert. They would be down and on him at once if he tried to ram his head on the wall. Still, he might be able to do it once. He felt as if he had suffered a concussion of the brain. One more hard blow might remove him from the fire and restore him whole somewhere else, far away on the riverbank.

He said, "If we started a ruckus, they might have to kill some of us to quiet us down. We'd be lucky if we could die now."

Yeshua raised his head. His eyes were wild and staring as when Mix had last seen him. They were also red and puffy, as if he had wept much.

"If only a man did not have to live again! If he could be dust forever, his thoughts and agonies dissolved into the soil, eaten by the worms as his flesh is eaten! But no, there's no escape. He must live again. And again. God will not permit him release."

Mix did not reply. He was thinking that if he could

muster enough strength, he could run at full speed across the 30 yards of the stockade floor.

When he drove his skull into the bamboo wall on the other side, he might crack his head open.

Now was the time.

"So long, Yeshua, you poor devil," he said. "Maybe you will be happy again some day."

He rose to his feet. A guard shouted at him to sit down. The stockade whirled, his knees buckled. When he regained consciousness, he was even more sick.

Yeshua said, "There was a time when I might have rid you of your pain, driven the demons from your body. But no more. You have to have faith—and now I do not have it."

VIII

The gates swung open. Spearmen entered first and took positions around Yeshua. Kramer followed.

He was a short fat youth with dark-brown hair and pale blue eyes. His face was piggish. He wore a black kilt and a long black towel as a cloak.

With Kramer were two prisoners. Both were short dark men with Levantine faces. Both were bloody and bruised. Mix, who had managed to sit up again, recognized one of the prisoners. He was Mattithayah, the little man who had mistaken Mix for Yeshua.

Kramer pointed at Yeshua. He spoke English with a heavy German accent. "Is that the man?"

Mattithayah broke into a storm of unintelligible words. Kramer sent him staggering with a blow of his fist against the jaw. He spoke to the other prisoner. This one answered in English as heavily accented as Kramer's, but his native tongue was obviously different.

"Yeshua!" he cried. "Rabbi! Master! We have looked for you for many years. And now *you* are *here*, too!"

He began to weep and tried to walk to Yeshua, but spears forced him back.

Yeshua had looked once at the two prisoners, groaned, and let his head sink back to its resting place on his knees.

Kramer, scowling, muttering strode up to Yeshua and seized his long hair. Jerking it upward, he forced Yeshua to look at him.

"Madman! Anti-Christ!" he shouted. "You'll pay for your blasphemies! Just as your two crazed friends will pay!"

Yeshua closed his eyes. His lips moved soundlessly. Kramer struck him in the mouth with the back of his hand, and blood flowed from the right corner of Yeshua's lips.

Kramer screamed at him. "Speak, you filth! Do you claim to be Christ?"

Yeshua opened his eyes. He spoke in a low voice. "I claim to be only a man named Yeshua. If this Christ of yours did exist and He were here, He would be horrified, driven to madness with despair, at what has happened to His teachings."

Kramer hit Yeshua so hard that he fell upon his back. Kramer drove the toe of his hard leather sandal against Yeshua's ribs.

"Renounce your blasphemies! Recant your Satanic ravings! You will escape much pain in this world if you do, and you may save your soul in the next!"

Yeshua said, "Do what you will to me, you unclean Gentile!"

Kramer shouted, "Shut your dirty mouth, you insane monster!"

Yeshua grunted as Kramer's sandal drove into his ribs again, and he moaned for a while thereafter.

Kramer strode to the two prisoners. "Do you still maintain that this lunatic is the Blessed Son of God?"

The two prisoners were pale beneath their dark skins and their faces looked as if fashioned from wax. Neither replied to Kramer.

"Answer me, you swine!" he cried. He tore a spear from a soldier's hands and began to beat them with the butt. They tried to run but were held by soldiers.

Yeshua, who had struggled to his feet, said, "He is so savage because he fears that they may speak the truth."

Mix said, "What is the truth?" He was getting sicker and beginning to lose his interest in the situation. God, if only he could die before he was tied to the stake and the pile set aflame!

"I've heard that question before," Yeshua said.

When Kramer had beaten the two prisoners into unconsciousness, they were dragged out through the gates by their legs, their heads bobbing on the grass and their arms trailing behind. Kramer started to walk toward Yeshua, but he stopped as a man ran through the gates and shouted at him.

Mix was close enough to hear them talking. The messenger brought news of the approaching enemy. The Fideans would have to board their ships soon and set sail for home. Otherwise, they would be trapped on land by a superior force.

Apparently the states on both sides of Albion had decided to band together and attack. Moreover, the Huns across the river had joined them.

Kramer replied that the Fidean fleet must return to its home base at once. Before doing so, however, they would burn the heretics.

Mix knew then that Kramer had not heard of the destruction of his capital city and the uprising of the slaves. Despite his pain and the knowledge of the fire waiting for him, he managed a smile. Kramer was doomed. If he were captured alive, he would undoubtedly be tortured and then burned. Mix hoped that he would be. Perhaps if Kramer himself experienced the flames, he might not be so eager to burn others when he rose again. But Max doubted it.

Kramer had quit giving orders and had resumed his course toward Yeshua. Mix called to him.

"Kramer! If Yeshua is who those men claim he is, and they've no reason to lie, then what about you? You've killed and tortured for nothing; you've put your own soul in the gravest of jeopardy."

Kramer reacted as Mix had hoped he would. He shouted and ran at Mix with the butt-end of the spear raised. Mix saw it come down on him. Then he knew nothing.

But he was not completely successful. He regained consciousness to find himself upright and tied to a great bamboo stake. Below him was a large pile of small bamboo sections and pine needles.

His eyes crossed, and all became blurred. But he could smell the torch as it was applied to the pile, and set him to coughing. Agony struck like a fist. Vision faded; he fell into oblivion.

But he heard Yeshua's voice, distorted, far away, like thunder on the mountains.

"Father, they *do* know what they're doing!"

A Few Miles

Brer John Carmody was bent over, pulling out the carrots from the garden soil, when he heard his name called.

He straightened up, saying "Ough!" as he did so and putting the palm of his hand to his aching back. He waited for Brer Francis because Brer Francis had not told him to come but had merely named him.

Brer John was a short heavily built man with a square face, one drooping eyelid and a shock of blueblack hair that bristled like porcupine quills. Lay brothers of the order of St. Jairus, to which he belonged, did not shave their heads. He wore an ankle-length robe of maroon fiberglass and maroon plastic sandals. A broad plastleather belt circled his bulging stomach, and from it hung a cross and a small maroon book.

Brer Francis, a tall thin man with narrow face and a ski-slope nose, halted before the fat man. He pointed at the bunch of carrots in the fat man's hand and said, "What happened to those, Brer?"

"Rabbits," said Brer John. He looked upwards and gestured furiously, though it was evident by his half-grin that his anger was mock.

"Rabbits! How do you explain that, heh? We live in cities that are completely roofed over and walled, and the walls go deep into the ground. Yet rabbits and mice and rats manage to get under the walls and raid our gardens and pantries. And squirrels somehow climb into our trees, and birds, who must squeeze themselves through the interstices of the molecules of the roof, nest on every tree. And insects, who don't know how to burrow, only to fly or hop, are here at hand."

He swatted at a fly and said, "And on my nose, too. That pesky creature of Satan has been tickling my bulbous proboscis for the last past hour. However, I have

105

refused to kill it on the grounds that it might have been sent to tempt me to anger and violence. And it has nearly succeeded, too, I might add."

"Brer John, you talk too much," said Brer Francis. "Far too much. However, I did not come here to reprimand you for that . . ."

"Though you have stayed to do so," said Brer John; and then, quickly, before Brer Francis' reddening face exploded into words, "Forgive me for that last remark. And the previous ones, too. As you said, I talk too much. It is a very grave fault, or, if not a fault, at least a characteristic to be frowned upon, and . . ."

"Brer John!" said Brer Francis. "Will you keep quiet long enough to allow me to tell you why I am here? I did not come out here to satisfy my curiosity, you know."

"Forgive me," said Brer John. "I'm all ears."

"The bishop wishes to see you. At once," said Brer Francis very quickly as if he were afraid Brer John would interrupt if he breathed between words.

Brer John turned and threw the rabbit-damaged carrots into a cart and the good carrots into another. Then he set off towards the main building, a long low structure of pressed earth-blocks painted a dark maroon. Its high-pitched roof was raised several feet above the walls by thin poles, and a grillework of maroon metal filled the space between roof and wall. The entrances had no doors, for it was the tradition of the order never to have a locked door, and here in the controlled environment of the enclosed city, it was not necessary to keep out the weather. The roof was there only to give privacy from people flying overhead.

Brer John entered the main building and, without bothering to clean his dirty hands and face, went straight to the office of the Father Superior. When the chief called, no man loitered.

The rooms within the building did have doors, though they were unlocked. As the door to the Father Superior's office was closed, Brer John knocked.

"Come in!" said a voice within, and Brer John, not for the first time since he had joined the order as a lay brother, entered the large triangular room. He stood at the base of the triangle, and the Father Superior sat behind a large translucent desk at the apex of the triangle. The top of the desk was loaded with piles of tapes, a stenowriter, and a vuephone. The Father Superior, however, was not dwarfed by the mountainous mass before him; he was a very tall man.

He was broad-faced with long rusty-red hair and a full rusty-red beard, which he and only he in the "inn" was entitled to wear. He was puffing on a huge Havana cigar.

Brer John, who had given up smoking for a month as a penance for one of his several sins, sniffed hungrily at the green smoke roiling around him.

The Father Superior flicked off the toggle of the steno-writer into which he had been dictating.

"Good-morning, Brer John," he said. He waved a cartridge at the fat man.

"I have here an order which just came in via space-ship. You are to go to the planet of Wildenwooly at once and report to the Bishop of Breakneck. We will miss you in more ways than one, but we love you. God speed you, and our blessing."

Brer John's blue eyes widened. He did not move, and for the first time in a long time he could not talk.

The Father Superior, however, had closed his eyes and leaned back on his tilting chair while he dictated out of one corner of his mouth and puffed cigar smoke out of the other. It was evident that he considered that he had given all orders necessary.

For a moment Brer John stared at the long ash on the end of the Father Superior's cigar. Obviously, the ash was just about to fall, and he wondered if it would fall on the long red beard beneath it.

However, the Father Superior, without opening his eyes, removed the cigar and flicked the ashes onto the stone floor.

Brer John shrugged and left the room, but the wonder was still on his face.

Outside the room, he hesitated for a few minutes. Then, sighing, he walked outside and crossed the garden to Brer Francis.

"Brer Francis, may I speak?"

"Yes," said the thin man. "If you confine yourself to the matter at hand and do not take the opportunity to run off at the tongue as usual."

"Where is Wildenwooly?" said Brer John with a tone that bordered on the pathetic.

"Wildenwooly? It is, I believe, the fourth planet of Tau Caesari. Our order has a church and an inn there," he said.

Brer John did not think that the order had a tavern

on the planet. The dwellings of the order were customarily called inns because they had been so designated by the founder, St. Jairus.

"Why do you ask?" continued Brer Francis.

"I have just been ordered to go to Wildenwooly by the Father Superior." He looked hopefully at the other man.

But Brer Francis merely said, "Then you must go at once. God speed you, Brer John. Go with my love. I may have reprimanded you many times, but it has been for your good."

"I thank you for your love," said Brer John. "But I am at a loss."

"Why?"

"Why? To whom do I go to get a ticket for berth on a spaceship? Who gives me a draft on the order for travel expenses? What about a letter of introduction to the Bishop at Breakneck? I don't even know his name. I don't even know when a spaceship might leave for Wildenwooly or how long I might have to wait for it or where to wait for it. I don't even know where the spaceport is!"

"You talk too much," said Brer Francis. "You have been given all the orders you will get. Or need. As for the spaceport, it's only a few miles outside the city. And the inn on Wildenwooly is only a few miles outside the city of Breakneck. With good luck you might be there by this afternoon."

"That's all you have to say?" said Brer John unbelievingly.

"Only a few miles," repeated Brer Francis. "You must leave at once. Orders, you know."

Brer John looked hard at Brer Francis. Was he imagining or was a grin about to break out on that long lean rarely smiling face? No, he must be mistaken. The face was grim and unmoving.

"Don't be distressed," said Brer Francis. "I was once given just such an order. And so have others."

Brer John's eyes narrowed. "This is a test of some sort?"

"The order wouldn't send you forty thousand light-years away just to test you," said Brer Francis. "You are wanted and needed at Wildenwooly. So go."

Brer John Carmody seldom hesitated. Once he had decided upon a course, and it did not customarily take

him long to decide, he acted. Now he walked swiftly to
the communal shower, entered the room, removed his
robe, revealing a white body and legs painted black to the
groin. He inserted the robe into a rectangular hole in the
wall, and then he entered the shower. He did not stay
long, for though the order had installed an entirely automatic shower, it had insisted that only cold water would
be provided for the discomfort of its members. Once a
month the order was treated to a warm shower.

He stepped out, shivering, and dried off in a blast of
air, also cold, which blew from vents in the wall. Then
he took out his robe from a receptacle below the one in
which he had inserted the robe and put it on. And he
gave a short thanksgiving that the order had at least
installed a cleaning apparatus. When he got to the
frontier planet of Wildenwooly, he would have to wash
his clothes by hand. And probably, considering his humble
position, the robes of the other members, too.

Putting on his robe, he went to his cell. This was a
room, six feet by seven feet, with luminescent walls, a
crucifix attached to the wall, a hammock which was
rolled into a bag during the day, a desk which folded
down from the wall, and a niche in the wall where he
kept all his worldly possessions. These, a missal, a history
of the Church from 1 A.D. to 2260 A.D., a Latin
grammar, and a Life of Saint Jairus, he put into the sack
formed by the hood hanging down over his shoulders.
Then he got down onto his knees before the crucifix, said,
"Lord and Master, let me know what I am doing. Amen,"
rose and walked to the door of his cell. Just before
leaving, and without breaking his stride, he reached out
and took a long shepherd's staff from its peg on the
wall. All lay brothers were required to take that crook
with them when they went into the outside world, if the
encapsulated city of Fourth of July could be called the
outside world.

It was past noon, and the Arizona summer sun was
sliding downhill. Brer John found the temperature only
a little warmer than inside the inn. The plastic roof over
the city was, at this time of the day, opaqued enough to
reflect most of the rays. Even so, Brer John looked forward to getting outside the walls, even if it meant being
immersed in the staggering heat of midsummer Arizona.
He had long felt cooped up, and, though he had never
openly complained, he had felt the urge to do so. And
had accordingly confessed and made his penance.

For a moment he paused. He knew there was a space-port near Fourth of July, but he had no idea in which direction. So he went to a cop.

The cop was one of the new types, a Mark LIV. Its face and body were made of a tantalum alloy, but the eyes were of protoplasm, copied from those of some long-dead corpse and grown in the laboratory. And it had a semi-independent action, for the brain in its metallic belly was not a mechanism controlled remotely from head-quarters below the ground. Its brain was a grey proto-plasmic shape like a man's, twice as large and half as intelligent. It could not carry on a decent conversation, much less an indecent one, but it could handle its job quite well, and it could not be bribed or influenced. And, unlike its predecessors, it got around on legs in-stead of wheels. Its feet were flat.

Brer John looked at the name on its chest, and then said, "Officer O'Malley, where is the spaceport?"

"What spaceport?" replied the cop. The voice was loud and toneless and sent shivers down Brer John's spine. It was like talking with a man deprived of his soul.

"Ah, yes, I forgot," said Brer John. "It's been so long since I talked to a cop. And they were usually shooting at me. I must ask direct questions, *n'est-ce pas?*"

"*N'est-ce pas?*" echoed the cop. "What language do you speak? I will refer you to Headquarters," and the cop reached with a huge grey-scaled hand for the microphone attached to the side of its head.

"I speak American," said Brer John hastily. "I wish to know how to get to the Fourth of July Spaceport from here."

"Are you going by tubeway or private car?" said the cop.

Brer John put his hand into the huge pockets of his robe and then withdrew them, empty. "Shank's mare," he said sadly.

"You told me you spoke American," said the cop. "Please speak American."

"I mean, I am going to the spaceport on foot," said Brer John. "I am walking."

The cop stood silent for a moment. Its face was ex-pressionless as metal, but Brer John, who had a vivid imagination, thought he saw puzzlement film the features and then flit away.

"I can't tell you how to get there if you walk," said the cop. "Just a moment. I'll refer you to Headquarters."

"That won't be necessary," said Brer John hastily. He

could visualize himself going into a lengthy explanation to Headquarters just why he was *walking* to a city exit from this distant point. And perhaps being delayed to wait while a human cop was sent to investigate him on the spot.

"I can follow the tubeway to its end," he said. He pointed to a line of tall metal rods, each of which was surmounted by an enormous loop of metal.

"Which way do I go to the exit closest to the spaceport? Fourth of July," he added.

The cop was silent for two seconds. Then it said, "You don't mean on the date of the Fourth of July? You mean the spaceport called Fourth of July, right?"

"Right," said Brer John.

The cop pointed to the closest tubeway. "Take a North car on Number Ten Tubeway. Get off at the exit to the city. Go outside the city. Take a taxi from there to the spaceport of Fourth of July."

"Thank you," said Brer John.

"You're welcome to the services of the city," said the cop.

Brer John hurried away. The living eyes of the dead face made him uncomfortable. But he could not help wondering if the cop was truly incorruptible. Ah, if it had been the old John Carmody talking to the cop, then things might have been different! Not a humble lay brother of St. Jairus asking directions, but the cleverest crook in the cosmos trying to see if finally here was a cop who couldn't be bribed, tricked or coerced.

"John Carmody," said Brer John to himself, "you're a long way from being pure in thought. And you've just added another penance to suffer. God preserve you! You've barely left the cloister, just ventured into the outside world, and already you're thinking of the old days as the good old days. Yet you were a monster, John Carmody, a hideous monster who should have been obliterated. Not at all the lovable rogue you were picturing yourself as."

He walked below the tubeway. Overhead, a bus shot through the loops at the ends of the poles, then paused a hundred yards ahead of him and sank down to the ground to discharge its passengers. He wished he had a decicredit, vulgarly called "dessy," as fare. One decicredit would take him to the city exit and spare him the ten miles of shank's mare he had ahead of him.

He sighed, and said, "John, if wishes were horses . . ." and then he chuckled, visioning himself on a horse in this city. What a panic that would create! People running to stare at this monster seen now only on tridi or in the zoo! People running away in fright, the cops being called, and he . . . hauled off to jail. And guilty not only of secular crime but of ecclesiastical. A humble lay brother anything but humble, prancing pridefully on a horse, or was it a horse that pranced? Guilty of public display, inciting to riot and God knew what else.

He sighed again and began walking. Fortunately, he thought, a man was able to walk from one end of the city to the other if he followed the narrow path created by the poles of the tubeway. Unlike the old days, when there had been streets for a man to walk on, the city was one maze of narrow yards with high fences and a single family room in the middle of each strip of fence and grass, the main quarters being underground. And underneath the houses, the factory or offices where the house dwellers earned their living. If you could call it living.

He walked and walked, while overhead the citizens traveled in the tubeway bus or flew in their private cars (rented to them by the clutch to which they belonged). Once a robin flew over him, and Brer John said, "Ah, John, if you believed in the pernicious doctrine of transmigration, you would wish to enter the cycle of karma again as a bird But of course, you don't so why sigh for the ecstasy of ⌐ .ings? It is your aching feet that make you think these dangerous thoughts. Go, John, go! Plod on like the weary ass that you are."

He walked for perhaps two more miles and then to his delight he saw a park open up before him. It was one of the two large parks afforded by the city, where the citizens flocked to get a facsimile of the outdoors world. Here were winding dirt paths and rocks heaped up to resemble small mountains and caves in the mountains and trees and birds and squirrels and lakes on which swans and geese and ducks swam and every now and then a fish leaped up from beneath the surface.

It was, compared to the geometric jungle from which he had just come, a paradise. Alas! this paradise had no snakes, but it had too many Adams and Eves. They swarmed everywhere with their little Abels and Cains, lolling, drinking, eating, shouting, running, screaming, bellowing, lovemaking, quarreling, laughing, scowling.

Appalled, Brer John halted. He had been shut up so long inside the walls of Our Lady of Fourth of July that he had forgotten the manswarm.

He paused, and at the same time he heard a sound

that shut up the uproar. A fire siren whooping in the distance.

He turned and saw the smoke pouring from an eathouse on the edge of the park. And overhead, shooting through the air, the red needle shape of a fire engine.

Brer John ran towards the eathouse. It was one of the aboveground dining places in the city, a building constructed to resemble an Early American loghouse. Here the picknickers could go to eat in "atmosphere" and get away from the vast and dismally clean and bright cafeterias of the clutches where they habitually ate.

The owner of the YE OLDE ARIZONA LOGHAUS stood in the doorway and barred Brer John's entrance.

"No looting!" he shouted. "I'll kill the first man that tries to come in!" He held in his big meaty hands a butcher's cleaver.

Brer John halted and said, between gasps, "I've no wish to loot, my friend. I ran to see if I could help."

"No help needed," said the owner, still holding his cleaver poised. "I had a fire a couple years ago, and the mob broke in and stole everything before the cops could get here. I'll ha~ no more of that."

Brer John himself pushed from behind. He looked over his ᴀ...der and saw that he was being u ged forward by the pressure of many men and wom n ehind him. Obviously, they wanted to burst in and stea everything they could lay their hands on and wreck the e house before the police arrived. It was the custom when anything broke down in the city, an expression of the resentment they felt at their hemmed-in lives and at the non-human representatives of the authorities.

The owner stepped back inside the doorway and shouted, "So help me, I'll split the skull of the first man or woman who tries to get in!"

The mob yelled with fury, and it snarled at him for having the effrontery to spoil their sport. It thrust forth a pseudopod of force, and Brer John found himself, willy-nilly, the vanguard and vicar of violence.

Luckily, at that moment, the shadow of the fire engine fell on the crowd, and the next moment a spray of foam drenched them. They fell back, panting, the oxygen suddenly cut from around their noses and mouths. Brer John himself almost strangled before he could fight his way out of the foam that roiled hipdeep around him.

Immediately afterwards, the copcars, sirens screaming, slid down out of the sky. And the cops poured out of the cars, light gleaming from the metal rings of their legs and round metal chests and the living black eyes, wet in the dead metal faces, moving back and forth. Their voices roared above the crowd's, and in a short time they had returned order to the park. The firemen walked into the eathouse, and in ten minutes came out. Most of them took off their fire engines; one company stayed behind to clean up the foam. A lone cop recorded a report from the owner, and then he, too, left.

The owner was a short dark beefy man of about fifty. He had a thick black walrus moustache, through which he cursed fluently and loudly in American, Lingo, and Mexican for five minutes. Then he began locking the doors of the eathouse.

Brer John, one of the few people who had remained to watch, said, "Why are you closing? Hasn't the place been cleaned up?"

He was not really worried about *why*; he hoped that somehow he would be able to get a meal from the man. His stomach had been growling like a starving dog for half an hour.

"Oh, it's clean enough," said the man. "But the autochef is out of order. It started smoking; that's why I called the firemen."

"Can't you have it repaired?" said Brer John.

"Not until I sign a new contract with the Electrical Maintenance Union," growled the man. "And that I won't do. They're on strike now for higher wages. Well, I don't give a damn. I'll go out of business before I deal with them. Or wait until my brother Juan gets here from Mexico. He's an electronics tech; he's going into business with me, and he can keep the autochef going. But he won't get here until next week. When he does, we'll show the bastards."

"It just so happens," said Brer John, grinning, his mouth watering at the thought of all the goodies within, "that I am an electronics expert, among other things. I could repair the chef for you."

The man looked at him from under thick brows. "And just what's in it for you?"

"A good meal," said Brer John. "And enough busfare and taxi fare to get me to the spaceport."

The man looked around, then said, "Ain't you worried about the union? They'll be down on us like a bus whose antigrav has given out."

Brer John hesitated. The growling of his belly was loud.

He said, "I don't wish to be called a scab. But if it is true that your brother is going to fix it anyway, then I seen no harm in repairing the machinery a few days before he gets here. Besides, I'm hungry."

"O.K." said the owner. "It's your funeral. But I oughta warn you that there's a picket stationed in the kitchen."

"Will he resort to violence?" asked Brer John.

The owner took the cigar out of his mouth and stared at the brother. Then he said, "Where you been all your life?"

"I was gone from Earth quite a few years," said Brer John. "And my life here on Earth has been quite cloistered since my return."

He did not think it necessary to add that the first year had been spent at John Hopkins, where he had been undergoing rehabilitation therapy after surrendering himself to the police.

The owner shrugged and led Brer John through the dining rooms into the kitchen. There he pointed at a large painting hanging from the wall, Trudeau's *Morning on Antares II*. "Looks like a picture," he said. "It's the picket. A TV receiver. The union monitors it from its headquarters. Once they see you working on the chef, they'll be down on us like the wolf on the fold."

"I don't wish to suggest anything illegal or unethical," said Brer John. "But what would happen if we—I—turned off the picket's power?"

"You can't turn it off unless you was to smash it," said the owner gloomily. "The power switch is remote-controlled by the union."

"What about hanging a sheet over it?" said Brer John.

"An alarm would go off at union headquarters," replied the owner. "And I'd be hauled off to jail by one of those stinking zombie cops. It's against the law for me to interfere with the vision of the picket in any way. I even have to keep the lights on in the kitchen day and night. And what's worse, *I* have to pay the light bill, not the——ing union."

The use of the four-letter word did not bother Brer John. Such words had long ago ceased to be equated with vulgarity or immorality; it made no difference whether one used words of English or Latin origin in describing bodily functions or as expletives. Twenty-third century culture, however, did have other taboo words, and the owner could have offended Brer John by using them.

The brother asked for pliers, cutters, a screwdriver, and

insulating tape. Then he stuck his head into the hole left by the removal of the wall-panels by the firemen. The owner began pacing back and forth, his big cigar puffing like signals sent by an Indian frantically asking for money from home.

"Maybe I shouldn't ought to of let you start doing this," he said. "The union'll have its goon squad on the way. Maybe they'll try to wreck the place. Maybe they'll start a lawsuit against me. It ain't as if you was my brother fixing that damn chef. They can't do nothing if the repairman is part-owner of the place."

Brer John wished he had insisted upon being fed before beginning work. His stomach rumbled louder than ever, and his intestines felt as if they had turned cannibal.

"Why not call a cop?" he said. "He can maintain order."

"I hate those metal-bellied zombies," said the owner. "So does any decent man. It's got so people won't call a cop unless they absolutely have to. People are beginning to take the law in their own hands 'cause they hate to deal with the cops. I'd rather have the joint wrecked and pay for it than ask them damn zombies for help."

"Impersonal uncorruptible law enforcement has always been an ideal," said Brer John. "So, now we have it . . ."

"Brer, if you wasn't a man of the cloth, I'd tell you where to stick it," said the owner. "But you get the message. Say, tell me, how come you monks are called Brer instead of Brother?"

"Because that is the way our founder, St. Jairus, pronounced brother," said Brer John. "He was born on the planet of Hawaiki, where the Polynesian colonists developed their own brand of American. Ah, here's the trouble! Burned-out transformer in the high voltage power supply. Lucky for us the malfunction is so obvious. Maybe not so lucky unless we can replace the transformer. Do you have spare parts? Or do you, I suppose, depend upon the maintenance men to supply the parts?"

The owner grinned and said, "Usually I do. But my brother phoned me and said to lay in all the parts I'd need before the union caught on he was coming. You see once they knew I was using him, the union'd fix it up with the suppliers in L.A. not to sell me any stuff. Oh, those bastards! One way or another, they'll turn off your switch!"

"Ah well, they must ensure their living, too," said Brer John. "There's something to be said for both sides in a labor-management dispute."

"The hell there is!" said the owner, clamping down on his cigar. "Besides, I ain't no management. I'm a proprietor who has to pay highway robbery prices to keep my electronic stuff going, that's what."

"Show me where you keep those parts," said Brer John.

He paused. A loud knocking had penetrated the kitchen from the front of the eathouse.

The owner scowled and said, "They're here. But they can't get in unless I unlock the doors. Or they bust 'em down."

He hurried into a room behind the kitchen. Brer John followed, and there he picked out the transformer he needed. When he came back into the kitchen, the knocking was louder and more furious.

"Do you intend to let them in?" asked Brer John.

"If I don't, they'll kick the door open," said the owner. "And I can't do a damn thing about it. According to the law, they got a perfect right to make sure nobody except the owner fixes up the electronic equipment. And they're trying to get a law passed to keep a man from doing that."

"Yes, it's true that a man has increasingly little liberty and rights," said Brer John. "On Earth, that is. That is why the individualist and nonconformist leave Earth in such great numbers for the frontier planets."

He paused, frowned as if he were thinking deeply, and said, "Perhaps that is why I am being sent to Wildenwooly." He sighed and added, "Though it looks as if I may not be getting there."

He turned to the open panel and said, "You keep them out as long as you can without resorting to violence. Perhaps, by the time they get here, I can have this repaired."

It did not take him long, for the transformer needed only to be clipped onto the circuit board and the terminals plugged in. He laughed. It was so simple that the owner, if he had taken the time to examine the situation, could easily have done the repair work himself. But he, like many, thought of electronics as being such a highly mysterious and complex science, that he needed an expert. Though there were many things that only a highly trained technician could troubleshoot, this was not one of them.

He withdrew the upper part of his body from the opening just in time to see the owner being pushed by four maintenance men into the kitchen. These were dressed in scarlet coveralls and electric-blue caps and wore their emblems on their chests and backs, a lightning streak crossed by a screwdriver.

On seeing Brer John they halted in astonishment; apparently they had not seen him on the picket but had been told to go to Ye Olde Arizona Loghaus and stop the scab.

Their leader, a six-foot-six man with the protruding brows and thick jaw of a pugilist, stepped forward. "I don't know what you're doing here, brother," he said. "But you better have a good reason."

Another man, shorter than the first but broader, said, "Perhaps the Father didn't know what he was doing?"

The big man whirled on the broad man. "He ain't no Father!" he snarled. "If you was one of our faith, you'd know that. He's a monk or a friar or a lay brother, something like that. But he ain't no priest!"

"I'm a lay brother of the Order of St. Jairus," said Brer John. "Brer John is the name."

"Well, Brer John," said the big man. "Maybe you've been shut up behind those walls so long meditating that you don't know that you're scabbing on us, taking the bread out of our mouths."

"I knew what I was doing," said Brer John. "By not fixing the autochef, I was taking the bread out of this man's mouth—," he pointed to the owner. "And I was also depriving many people of the chance to get away from those ghastly soulless clutch cafeterias."

"All this capitalist has to do is pay us what we want, and he can feed as many people as he can handle," snarled the big man.

"Well," said Brer John, "the trouble has been fixed."

The big man turned purple and clenched his fists.

"Shame on you," said Brer John. "You are ready to strike a man of your own faith, a member of a holy order, too. And yet that man"—he pointed to the broad man— "a man of another faith, if any, is ready to take a reasonable attitude."

"He's one of them damn Universal Light people," said the big man. "Always ready to consider the other fellow's side, even if it's to his own injury."

"Then the more shame to you," said Brer John.

"I didn't come here to be shamed!" roared the big man. "I came here to get rid of a sneaky little scab hiding behind a robe! More shame to you, I say!"

"And just what do you propose to do?" said Brer John. He was shaking all over, not from fear of injury but from the fear that he might lose his self-control and attack the big man. And thus betray his own principles. Not to mention the principles of the order to which he belonged. What if they heard of this incident! What would they say, what action take?

"I propose first to throw you out," said the big man. "And then I propose to take out that transformer you put in."

"You can't do that!" bellowed the owner. "What's done is done!"

"Wait a minute," said Brer John to the owner. "No use getting upset. Let them take the transformer out. You can put it back in yourself, and there's not a thing they can do."

Again the big man purpled, and his eyes bulged out. "He will like hell!" he said. "If the picket sees him do anything like that, or even try to, we'll be down on him like the roof of the city fell in!"

"There ain't a thing you can do about it," said the owner, smiling smugly. "Go ahead. Take the transformer out. I'll just stand here and watch how you do it so's I'll know how to, too."

"He's right," said the broad man. "We can't do a thing if the trouble's that simple."

"Say, whose side you on?" roared the big man. "You a scab?"

"No. I just want to be legal," said the broad man. "Anyway, we can hire human pickets to picket the place."

"Are you out of your skull?" said the big man. "You know the Human Picket Union just upped their hourly rates, and we can't afford to hire any. And we don't have enough men of our own to spare for picketing. Besides, them damn pickets are pushing through a law to make it illegal for anybody except a picket union member to picket. The nerve of them guys!"

Brer John smiled and shook his head and tsk-tsked.

"I'm warning you!" shouted the big man, shaking his fist in the direction of the owner and Brer John. "If you re-repair the autochef, you won't have an eathouse to run!"

The owner, whose own face had been purpling, suddenly jumped on the big man and bowled him over. The two went down together, locked in furious, if not deadly, combat. Another of the goon squad took a poke at Brer John. Brer John ducked, and before he could think, his reflexes took over. He threw up his left to block the fellow's punch, and seeing him wide open, slammed him in the belly with a hard right.

A fierce joy ran through him. Before he could recollect what he should be doing, he had done what he should not. Excellent student of karate, judo, sabate, *akrantu*, and *vispexwun*, and veteran of a hundred bar-room and back alley brawls, he went into action like a maddened lynx mother who thought her kittens were in danger. A chop of the palm-edge against a neck, a thrust of stiff fingers into a soft gut, a hard heel of a foot against a chin, a knee in the groin and an elbow in the throat, and all except the big man were out of the fight. Following the Biblical precept of saving the best for the last, Brer John incapacitated the big man by pulling him from the owner and working him over with palm, fingers, knee, foot, and elbow. The big man went down like a tree attacked by a thousand woodpeckers.

The owner struggled to his feet and was astonished to see Brer John on his knees, eyes closed, praying.

"What's the matter?" said the owner. "You hurt?"

"Not physically," said Brer John, getting to his feet. He did not believe in long prayers when they were informal. "I am hurt because I failed."

"Failed?" said the owner, looking around at the unconscious or groaning men. "Did one of them get away?"

"No," said Brer John. "Only it should be I who am on the floor, not they. I lost my temper, and also my self-respect. I should have let them do what they wanted to with me but never lifted a finger."

"——!" cried the owner. "Look at it this way. You saved these men from being murderers! Believe me, they'd have had to kill me before I would have let them mess up my autochef. No, you've done them, and me, a great service. Though I don't know what's going to happen once they go back to headquarters. There'll be hell to pay."

"There usually is," said Brer John. "What will you do?"

"Don't say that," said the owner. "The last time you asked that, we had a free-for-all. But I'll tell you what. I'm going to drag these goons out—and I could use some help from you—and then I'm going to lock the door, and then, much as I hate to have anything to do with those metal-bellies, I'm going to call the cops. They can station a flatfoot here and keep the goons from bombing or wrecking the place. I'll say that much for the zombies, they can't be scared by threats or influence."

Brer John began helping the owner carry the men out of the eathouse. They had, however, no sooner placed the four on the sidewalk and locked the door than they heard the siren of a police car.

"I have to go now," said Brer John. "I can't afford to have my name on the police records or in the papers. My superiors would frown on such unfavorable publicity. And it wouldn't do me any good either," he added, thinking of his pre-Christian days. It was possible that he might be taken back to John Hopkins for further observation.

"What will I tell the cops?" wailed the owner.

"Tell the truth," said Brer John. "Always tell the truth. I'm sorry I failed you so miserably. I have a lot to learn yet. And I'm still hungry," he said, but it was doubtful if the owner heard the last phrase, for Brer John was running in his shapeless maroon robe like a frightened bear for the shelter of a copse of trees in the park.

Once inside the grove, he stopped. Not because he had planned to, but because he ran across a picnic blanket and his feet slipped on a bowl of potato salad. He fell face forward in a plate of fish eggs. And lay there, half-stunned, vaguely aware of the howls and shrieks of laughter around him.

When he managed to sit up and look around, he saw that he was surrounded by six teen-age boys and girls. Luckily for him, they were in a holiday mood. If they'd been in an ugly mood, they might have been able to harm or perhaps even to kill him. They were dressed in the uniform of the "skunks" as others called them and as they called themselves. These were black-and-white striped jumpers with close-fitting hoods, and their legs were painted with vertical black and white stripes. The eyes of the girls were ringed with black paint, and the eyes of the boys were painted with black semi-circles.

"Gimp the high priest!" screamed one of the boys. He pointed with red-painted fingernails. "Ain't him a dudu!"

"A real dong-dong," said one of the girls. She bent over Brer John and pulled a little string hanging from the side of her jumper. Her breasts leaped out of the low-cut bodice and stared at him with two red-pupilled blue-rimmed eyes. The rest howled and screamed and threw themselves gasping on the grass.

Brer John averted his eyes. He had heard of the trick the juvinquent girls liked to play; the false breasts which leaped out at the startled stranger like a jack-in-a-box. But he wasn't sure that these were false.

The girl stuffed the device back into her grotesquely out-thrust bosom. She smiled at Brer John, and he saw that she would have been a pretty girl if it hadn't been for the absurdly painted face. "What's ionizing, Willie?" she said to him.

Brer John rose, and, while he wiped his face with a handkerchief he took from his pocket, he said, "I am running from the cops."

He couldn't have said anything else that would have more quickly gained their sympathy.

"Hophopping the deadpans? Ain't him a dudu? Don't him look some priest? Scratch one, him's some monk, nothing a priest, you short-cut to zero."

Home among my own, thought Brer John, and hot on the heels of that thought a fierce denial. No, they are not my own. My brothers and sisters, sons and daughters, sinners, too, but I am not home. I can understand them, how and why they are, but I will not be one of them. I will hurt no man with malice aforethought.

"Pink some me," said the girl who had popped out her bosom, false or otherwise. "Me'll straight you some hole." Brer John interpreted that to mean that he was to give her his hand and she would lead him to a hiding place.

"Me'll stick my nose along," said a youth who was distinguished from the others by his tallness and the closeness of his black eyes.

"Some poxy," said the girl, which seemed to mean that the boy was to come along. She led Brer John out of the grove and down a winding path and then through another grove where they stepped over couples in various degrees of passion, and then up over an artificial hill and under an artificial waterfall and into another collection of trees. Brer John looked overhead from time to time. A police car was still hanging in the air, but evidently they hadn't spotted him yet. Suddenly, the girl pulled him into a thick collection of bushes and sat down in the middle of them. The youth forced his body between the girl and Brer John and began drinking from the bucket of beer which he had brought along.

The girl handed Brer John a sandwich, and he devoured it. His stomach growled, and his mouth salivated. By the time he'd eaten it, the boy had put the bucket down, and the girl handed the bucket to Brer John. He drank it eagerly in great gulps. But the boy tore the bucket from his hands.

"Don't no road," he said, which freely translated meant, "Don't be a hog."

"Some you dudu," said the girl. "Frwhat you jet some?"

Brer John interpreted this to mean that she wanted to know from what he was running. He told them that he was a lay brother of the order of St. Jairus, one who had not yet taken his final vows. As a matter of fact, inside a week his year would be up, and if he then wished to quit the society, he could do so. He didn't even have to notify his superiors.

He did not tell them that he suspected that this order to go to Wildenwooly at the same time that his year was up had been authorized so he could make up his mind whether he wished to remain with the order of St. Jairus.

He told them that there was a possibility that he might go into the priesthood, but he wasn't sure that he wouldn't be happier by remaining a simple brother. He would get all the dirty menial tasks, true, but he also would not have the tremendous responsibilities that came with being a priest.

Also, though he did not say so, he did not want the humiliation of being refused permission to enter the priesthood. He was not sure that he was worthy.

There was silence except for the loud gulpings of the youth as he drank from the bucket. Brer John looked out through the bushes and saw that they were next to a fence. Just beyond the fence was a narrow strip of dirt and then a deep moat. On the other side of the moat was a large bare space of rock and, beyond it, a cave. Evidently this was the cage of some animal, and it had been prepared to resemble the natural habitat of the animal.

He looked for the animal but could not see it. Then, he saw a sign by the fence.

HOROWITZ
A fierce meat-eating giant bird
of the planet Feral.
Highly intelligent.
Named after its discoverer,
Alexander Horowitz.
Please do not tease.
This area monitored.

The girl reached out a hand and stroked Brer John's chin. "Some scratch," she said.

She turned to the youth and jerked her thumb in an invitation for him to leave.

"Whyn't some ionize?" she said.

He narrowed his eyes and said, "Me? Summun want rigor mortis?"

"Me never no monk-monk before," said the girl, and she laughed, while her blue eyes looked at Brer John with a look he knew too well.

The boy snarled, "Monk-monk?" and then Brer John understood that the girl was punning. Monk-monk, he remembered now, was an extremely vulgar word which had replaced one of the formerly tabooed four-letter words.

"Monk-monk the monk-monk," said the boy. "Me monk-monk summun if summun ain't getting the monk-monk off the pad."

He turned to Brer John. "Ionize, gutbutt!"

Suddenly, a knife was in the girl's hand, and the point was at the boy's throat. "Me seesaw rigor mortis," she said crooningly.

"Some?" said the boy amazedly, jerking his thumb at Brer John.

The girl nodded her head. "Me some. Never no monk-monk a monk-monking monk, comprendo? You ionize sooner than later. Some seesaw rigor mortis, no?"

The boy put his hands on the ground behind him and tried to back away from her. She followed him, the knife held to his throat.

As she did so, Brer John's hand flashed out and knocked the knife from her grasp. All three dived for it, and their heads came together. Brer John saw stars; by the time he'd recovered, the youth had grabbed him by the throat and was trying to strangle him. Brer John fought back; his stiff fingers plunged into the boy's stomach, the boy said, "Oof!" and released his hold. The girl, knife in hand, leaped at the boy. He turned and hit her on the jaw with his fist and knocked her unconscious to the ground. Then, before Brer John could move in close enough, the boy grabbed him by the front of the robe and lifted him high and helpless in the air. And the next Brer John knew, he was flying over the fence. He hit the ground hard, rolled over, felt the world slipping away beneath him, knew briefly that he was falling into the moat, fell backwards, and then . . . heard a voice shrieking, "Hey, John, hey, John! Here I am, John!"

He woke to hear the same voice calling, "Hey, John! Here I am!"

He was flat on his back, staring upwards past the grey walls of the moat and up at the roof of the city. The roof was no longer transparent, allowing the blue of the Arizona sky to come through undiminished. Night had fallen outside the roof, and now the roof itself was a glow bright as day, shining with energy stored during the day and released at sunset.

Brer John groaned and tried to sit up to see if he had any broken bones. But he could not move.

"Holy Mother!" he breathed. "I'm paralyzed! St. Jairus preserve me!"

But he was not totally paralyzed. He could move his legs and his arms. It was just that his chest felt as if it were crushed against the earth by a great weight.

He turned his head, and he almost fainted with fright. It was a weight that was holding him down. A huge bird . . .

It had been squatting by his side, its giant claw placed on his chest, pinning him to the ground. Now that it saw the man had his eyes open, it rose to one foot, still keeping the other placed on him.

"Hey, John!" it screamed. "Here I am, John!"

"So you are," said Brer John. "Would you mind letting me up?" But he did not expect anything, for it was obvious that the huge bird—if it was a bird—had a parrot's power to mimic.

Slowly, he moved his arms, not wishing to alarm the horowitz, for that must be what it was. It could have torn him open at any moment with its tremendous three-toed foot or with its moa-sized beak. Evidently it had leaped down into the moat after him, with what purpose, he didn't know.

His arms bent at the elbows, he lowered the upper parts to feel his chest. He had wondered what it was that lay on his chest, which was bare, probably because the big bird had ripped his robe open.

He felt sick. An egg lay on his chest.

It was a small egg, not much larger than a barnyard hen's. He couldn't imagine why a creature that large would lay such a small egg, why it would lay it on him. But it was and it had.

The horowitz, seeing the man's hands feel the egg,

screamed with protest. Its huge beak stabbed down at his face. Brer John closed his eyes, and breathed in the rotten breath of the meat-eating creature. But the beak did not touch him, and after a moment he opened his eyes. The beak was poised a few inches above his face, ready to complete its descent if he harmed the egg.

Brer John gave a longer than usual prayer, then he tried to think of a way to get out of his predicament.

And could not. He dared not try to escape by force, and he could not, for one of the few times in his life, talk his way out. He did turn his head to look up at the edge of the moat from which he had fallen, supposing that some spectators would notice him. But there were none. And in a moment he realized why. The people who had been in the park probably had gone home to supper or to work, and the second shift at the clutches had not yet come into the park. And, of course, it was possible that nobody would come by for a long time. Nor did he dare to shout for fear of alarming the horowitz.

He was forced to lie motionless on his back and wait until the big bird left him. If it intended to leave him. It did not seem likely that it would. For some reason it had jumped into the moat to lay its egg on him. And it could not jump back out. Which meant that in time it would get hungry.

"Who would have thought that when I was told to go to Wildenwooly that I might perish in the city zoo only halfway out of the city. Strange and wondrous are the ways of the Lord," he muttered.

He lay, staring upwards at the glowing roof, at the huge beak and black red-rimmed eyes of the bird, and occasionally at the top of the moat, hoping for a passerby.

After a time he felt his chest tickling beneath the egg. The tickling grew stronger with every minute, and he had an insane desire to scratch, insane because to indulge would be to die.

"Holy Mother," he said, "if you are torturing me to make me think on my sins before I die, you are certainly succeeding. Or would be if I weren't so concerned with the tickling and itching itself. I can barely think of my most grievous faults because of the disturbing everlasting damnable itching. I have to scratch! I must!"

But he did not dare. To do so would have been to commit suicide, and that, the unpardonable sin because it could not be regretted, was unthinkable. Or perhaps not unthinkable because he *was* thinking of it; what *was* the correct word—undoable? No, but it did not matter. If he could only scratch!

Presently, after what seemed hours but probably was not more than fifteen minutes, the itching quit. Life again became endurable, even if not pleasant.

It was at that precise minute that the youth who had thrown him into the moat appeared above him.

"Grab time!" called the youth. "Me'll drop a rope!"

Brer John watched the boy tie one end of a rope to the fence and then throw the other end down into the moat. He wondered if the youth expected him to walk over and draw himself up, meanwhile blithely ignoring the huge bird. He wanted to call out and tell him he couldn't even sit up, but he was afraid his voice might alarm the creature.

However, he did not have to initiate any action. The second the rope touched the floor of the moat the horowitz released its hold on the man and ran to the rope. It seized it in its two small hands and, bracing its feet against the side of the moat, swarmed up.

Brer John jumped up and shouted, "Don't let it get out of the moat, son! It'll kill you!"

The youth stared at the creature coming swiftly up the rope. Just as the bird's head came over the edge of the moat, the youth came out of his paralysis. He stepped up to the bird and kicked savagely at the beaked head. The bird gave a cry, loosed its hold on the rope, and fell backwards. It struck the earth, rolled a few feet, and lay stunned, its eyes glazed.

Brer John did not hesitate. He ran to the rope and began hauling himself up hand over hand on it. Halfway up, he felt the rope straighten out beneath him. Looking down, he saw the horowitz had recovered and was following him up the rope. It began squawking furiously, intermingling its cries with screams of "Hey, John! Here I am, John!"

Brer John climbed a few feet higher, then hung there while he kicked at the crested head beneath him. His foot drove solidly into the creature's skull, and once again the bird lost its hold and fell backwards to the ground. Gasping for breath, it lay there long enough for Brer John to pull the rope out of its reach.

"We must notify the zoo personnel," he said. "Otherwise, the poor creature might starve to death. Besides, I have something that is the property of the zoo."

"Me don't scratch you," said the youth. Brer John

interpreted this to mean that he didn't understand him. "Dum-dum some rigor mortised summum."

"The bird was only obeying the dictates of its nature," said Brer John. "Unlike you or me, it doesn't have free will."

"Will-swill," said the youth. "Gimp the baldun."

"You mean, look at the egg?" replied Brer John. He looked down to examine the strange situation of the egg. It had not fallen off his chest when he rose but had clung to his skin as if glued on. He pulled it away from his chest, and the skin stretched with it.

"Curioser and curioser," he said. "Perhaps the bird secretes an adhesive when it lays an egg. But why should it?"

Then he thought of his manners and his gratitude, and he said, "I thank you for coming to my rescue. Though I must admit I was surprised since—forgive me for mentioning it—you were the one who threw me down there."

"Goed out of me frying-pan," said the youth, meaning that he had lost his head. "Goed monk-monk gimping the trangle smack-smacking summun. Her's no monk-monking good. Gived her the ivory-doctor."

"Knocked her teeth out?" said Brer John.

"Scratch," said the youth. "Telled the trangle ionize. Daily dozen gived me cross-gimps."

"You told the girl to get lost because she was always getting you in trouble?"

"Scratch. Rigor mortis summun; me get sing-singed grey fat fried."

"You might kill someone and get sent to an institution where your personality would be changed? Possibly. However, your act in coming back shows you have promise. I wish I could repay you, but I have nothing to give you."

Suddenly, he began scratching furiously, and he added, "Except for these monk-monking lice that bird gave me. Is there anything I could do for you?"

The youth shrugged hopelessly. "Round-round. You going to Wildenwooly?"

Brer John nodded. The youth looked up at the glowing roof overhead.

"Bye-bye, maybe me go some there. Nothing but daily dozen in-and-out on The Antheap. Is a different dummy out in deep space."

"Yes, getting off Earth and on a frontier planet might

make a new man of you," said Brer John. "And you might learn to speak American, too. Well, God bless you, my boy. I must go. And if you should get to Wildenwooly before I do, tell them I'm doing my best to get there. Holy Mary, it's only a few miles, said Brer Francis!"

He began walking away. Behind him rose a harsh wail of "Hey, John! Here I am, John! Your old buddy, John!"

He shuddered and crossed himself and continued walking. But he could not forget the monster in the moat. The vermin that now swarmed under his robe and drove him almost frantic would not allow him to forget. Neither would the egg attached to his chest.

It was the combination of the two which decided him to find a secluded spot on the lagoon and bathe. He had hopes he could drown the bird-lice and unglue the adhesive which made the egg stick so tightly. Finding a place where he would not be seen was not, however, so easy. The first shift was streaming from the clutches into the park and was lying on the sandy beaches or swimming. Brer John did his best to avert his eyes from the naked as he passed through them. But it was impossible not to catch more than a glimpse of the women as they lay on the sand or ran before him. And, after a while, he quit trying. After all, he told himself, he had been accustomed all his life to seeing them all undressed at the beach and in his own home before he had gone into the order of St. Jairus. And all the fulminations of the Church had not been able to stop the faithful from following the custom any more than it had been able in the previous centuries to keep them from swimming in the abbreviated bathing suits. The Church had long ceased protesting against nude public bathing, but it still denounced the appearance of nudes in the streets. Though what its policy would be twenty years from now was unpredictable. Occasionally, a nude did venture on the street or in the markets and was arrested for indecent exposure, just as women in shorts or bathing suits outside of the beach had been arrested in the early part of the Twentieth Century? The laity might go undressed in the public bathing places, but the clergy did not. In fact, they were forbidden even to be at such places. And he, Brer John, was disobeying the rules of his order, not to mention the Church as a whole, by being here.

But expediency sometimes dictated the breaking of rules, and the bird-lice biting madly into him demanded that he get rid of them at once before he made a spectacle of himself.

Brer John went halfway around the lagoon before he found what he was looking for. This was a high bank which was shielded from view by a group of bushes. He pushed through the foliage, and almost put his foot on a couple who must have thought they were alone in the Garden of Eden. He stepped over them and plunged on until he could not see them, though he was still distressed by the sounds.

Quickly, he slid his robe off and then let himself down the high bank of mud into the water. He shivered as the relatively cold water hit him, then after a moment he felt quite comfortable. Remembering the fable of how the fox rid himself of fleas, he slowly immersed himself. He had a hope that the insects would climb up his body as the water came towards them and that when he had ducked his head, they would be left to shift for themselves.

His head went under, and he held his breath while he counted one hundred and eighty seconds. Then he lifted his head above the water. He didn't see the collection of insects floating before his nose that he had expected. But the lice must have gone somewhere, for he no longer was being bitten.

Then he tried to pull the egg away from his skin and allow the water to soften the glue. But he had no success.

"It's as if it had put out tendrils into my skin," he said.

His eyes widened, and he paled. "Good St. Jairus! Maybe that's what *did* happen!"

He forced himself to push back the rising panic and to think, if not calmly, at least coherently. Perhaps the horowitz had egg-laying habits analogous to that of the wasp. It might be its instinct to place the egg on a corpse or even living creature. And the egg might send forth small fleshy roots to hook into the bloodstream of its host. And through the roots it would draw the nourishment it needed to grow larger and to develop into an embryo. The horowitz might have taken an evolutionary step which would place it among placental creatures, the difference being that the embryo would develop on the *outside* of the body of its host instead of *inside*.

Brer John didn't feel much like taking a strictly biological and zoological attitude. This thing attached to his body was a monstrous leech, and it was sucking the blood from him.

It might not be necessarily fatal. And he could kill the egg now, and, presumably, the roots would dissolve.

But there was the ethical view to consider. The egg was not his property to dispose of as he wished. It belonged to the zoo.

Brer John squelched his desire to rip out the thing by the bloody tendrils and to throw it away as far as possible. He must return it to the zoo authorities. Even if that would involve much time while he told the long and complex story of just how he had happened to be in a situation where he could have an egg laid on him.

He scrambled back up the bank. And stood dismayed. His robe was gone.

Brer John had always thought of himself as a strong man. But tears ran down his cheeks, and he groaned, "Worse and worse! Every step I take towards Wildenwooly puts me back two steps! How will I ever get out of this mess?"

He looked up at the sky. No sky, just a blaze of light from a man-made roof. Light but no revelation.

He thought of the motto of the order of St. Jairus. *Do as he would do*.

"Yes, but he was never in such a situation!" he said aloud.

However, he thought, consideration of the life of St. Jairus did show that he had always taken the lesser of two evils, unless doing so might lead to an evil even greater than the one rejected. In which case one chose the greater evil, if one had to choose.

"John," he said to himself, "you are not a philosopher. You are a man of action, however ill-advised that action may be. You have never really thought your way out of a mess. Which is why you may be in this particular one. But you have always trusted to the wisdom of your feeling to extricate yourself. So, act!"

The first thing he had to do was to clothe himself. He could remain nude while he searched the beach for whoever might have stolen his clothes. But he did not think it likely that the thief, or prankster, would be in evidence. And he had no means for covering the egg on his chest. That would lead to an intense curiosity and probable trouble for him before he had gotten far. The cops might be called, he might go to jail. And he would have much explaining to do, not only to the secular authorities but to his superior.

No. He must find clothing. Then he must get money

to call the director of the zoo and get rid of the egg. Then, somehow, he must get the money for fare to Wildenwooly.

Cautiously, he pushed back into the bushes. The couple over whom he had stumbled were still there, but they now seemed to be asleep in each other's arms. Muttering under his breath, "Only a loan. I will see you get it back," he reached out and took the man's clothes from the bush on which they hung. Then he retreated to the edge of the bank and put them on.

He found the experience distasteful for several reasons. One, he was giving the police another reason to look for him. Two, when the man woke up, he would be in Brer John's difficult position of getting off the beach and home without his clothes, though, doubtless, he could send the woman after some. Three, the puffkilt he was putting on was covered with garish mustardyellow circles and pink dots. This was not only an esthetic crime in itself but, four, the puffkilt was soiled and smelly. Five, the dickey which he put on his chest was an electric-blue with crystal sequins.

"Horrible taste," said Brer John, shuddering. He was aware that he made a ridiculous figure.

"Better than having an egg hanging from our chest," he said, and he set off across the part towards the city.

He intended to enter a public phone booth and there find out the address of the zoo director. Then he would walk to the zoo director's house and tell him about the egg. What would happen then, he told himself, would be up to God and the agile (?) wits of Brer John. But somehow, he must also contrive to get the stolen (borrowed) clothes back to the owner with some recompense.

Brer John walked swiftly towards the edge of the park. He did not look behind him as he passed the white-fleshed bodies and many-colored legs of the beachpeople. But he felt what he had not felt for a long time, the prickling frightening half-exhilarating sensation that at any moment the cry of "Stop, thief!" would ring out. And he would be in full flight ahead of the pack.

Not that there was much chance of that. The man had been sleeping too deeply.

"Stop, thief!" rang the cry.

Automatically, Brer John increased his pace, but he did not start running yet. Instead, he pointed dramatically to one side at a man who was running by a happy coincidence away from those beside him.

"There he goes!" he yelled. And the crowd surged around him, running after the innocent who fled when every man was pursuing. Unfortunately, the crowd by Brer John ran into the crowd behind the man who was running after Brer John and the stolen clothes. Somebody pushed somebody, and within two seconds a full-scale brawl had spread through this section of the park.

A cop's whistle blew; a number of men piled upon the cop and bore the metal man under by sheer weight. Brer John decided that now was as good a time as any to run.

He reached the edge of the park and began running through a narrow alley formed by the fences around the small yards of private houses. It was a twisting labyrinthian alley in which he could easily lose any ground pursuit. But a cop's car was scooting overhead towards the riot in the park, so Brer John vaulted over a fence lithely as a cat despite his round-stomached bulk. He landed easily and crouched against the fence, hugging it to avoid observance from the air.

The footsteps of a man running went by the fence and faded into the distance. Brer John smiled, then the smile froze as a low growl came from behind him.

Slowly, he turned his head. He was inside the yard of a typical house. The fence encircled a small plot of grass in the center of which was a roofed patio. The patio held a table and a few chairs and a *chaise-longue* and the entrance to the house underneath the ground. No human beings were in evidence, but a dog was very much so. It was a huge Doberman-Pinscher, and it was ready to charge.

Back over the fence went Brer John, the dog so close to him that he felt its jaws clash at the edge of his puffkilt. Then he was running again.

However, after he had spurted for a hundred yards and looked behind him to make sure that the dog hadn't come over the fence after him, he slowed to a fast walk. He saw a public phone booth and made for it. Before he was at its door, a man stepped up to him and seized his elbow.

"Wanta talk to you," he said. "Me can solve all your problems for you in a micro."

Brer John looked at the man closely. He was small and thin and had a ratty face. His legs were painted

barber-pole fashion with red and white stripes, his kilt
and dickey were sequined with imitation diamonds, and
he wore a tricorne hat with a long plume. These were
enough to identify him as one of the lower classes;
the plastic imitation bone stuck through the septum of
his nose marked him at once as a lower-class criminal.

"Me got switches," the man said, meanwhile darting
glances from side to side and turning his head like a
robin afraid the cat was sneaking up on him. "Heard
'bout ya quick as ya robe was snatched. Heard 'bout
the egg, too. That's what wanta talk ta ya 'bout. Ya sell
the egg ta me; me sell the egg to a rich beast in Phoenix.
Him's queer, get it? Eats, uh, rare delicacies, gets his
rockets off. Been vine out long time good zoola horowitz
egg. Scratch?"

"Scratch," said Brer John. "You mean a rich man
in Phoenix pays big prices for food hard to get, like
the ancient Chinese paid high for so-called thousand
year old eggs?"

"Scratch. Know ya need ticket to Wildenwooly. Can
finger."

"I'm tempted, *friend*," said Brer John. "You would solve
my temporal difficulties."

"Do? Buzz-buzz. Only drag is, have to go ta Phoenix
first. Slice egg off here, no buzz-buzz. Egg rigor mortis;
no carry from fat beast."

"You tempt me, *friend*," said Brer John. "But,
fortunately I remember that I will also have eternal
difficulties if I deal with you. Moreover, this egg so
fondly clutching my breast is not my property. It belongs
to the zoo."

The man's eyes narrowed. "No buzz-buzz. Come
anyway."

He pulled a whistle from a pocket on his puffkilt
and blew. No sound issued, but three men stepped out
from the corner of a tavern. All three held airguns,
which doubtless contained darts whose tips were smeared
with a paralytic.

Brer John leaped like an uncoiling rattler striking.
The ratty little man squawked with terror, and his hand
darted towards his pocket. But Brer John chopped him
into unconsciousness with the edge of his palm, and
he thrust the man before him. There was a whacking
sound as two darts hit the sagging form. Then Brer
John, holding the man into the air before him, managed

to run towards the three gunmen. Another dart thwacked into the flesh of his shield, and then he was on them. Or they were on him; it was hard to tell. He went down; he was up; airguns hissed in the air and missed; one man cried out as a dart hit him; another folded as stiff fingers drove into his soft belly; then the butt of a gun came down on Brer John's temple.

Stars . . . blackness.

He woke to find himself lying on a couch in a strange room. And a strange man was looking down at him.

"I protest against this high-handed misuse of a fellow human being," said Brer John. "If you think you can get away with this, you're mistaken. I was once known as John Carmody, the only man who ever gave the famous detective Leopardi the slip. I'll hunt you down and I'll . . . turn you over to the authorities," he ended mildly.

The man smiled and said, "I'm not what you think, Brer John. The crooks who tried to snatch you were caught by a police car immediately after you were knocked out. They were injected, and they made a full confession. And you were injected, too. We know the full story. A most amazing one, too, and I've heard some weird ones."

Brer John sat up and felt dizzy. The man said, "Take it easy. Allow me to introduce myself. I'm John Richards, the director of the zoo."

Brer John felt at his chest. The egg was still attached.

"Wait a minute," he said. "The horowitz has a parrot's mimicking powers. Just as a guess, you taught it to call you by your name, John? Scratch? I mean, right?"

"Right," said John Richards. "And if it'll make you feel any better, I can solve your problem."

"The last time I heard that, I almost got kidnapped," said Brer John. But he smiled. "All right. What is this solution?"

"Just this. We have been waiting for a long time for the horowitz to lay its egg; we even had a host animal ready. Your appearance upset everything. But it doesn't necessarily ruin everything. If you would be willing to sign a contract to go to Feral, the native planet of the horowitz, and there allow yourself to be studied until the egg fully develops, then—"

"You give me hope, Mr. Richards. But there is something about your tone I don't like. What will this involve? Especially how much time will it take?"

"We—the Feral Study Grant group—would like you to go to Feral and there live as one of them while—"

"As one of them? How? They'd kill me!"

"Not at all. They don't kill the host animal until after the embryo is—uh—born. But we would step in just before that time. You'll be under close observance all the time. I wouldn't try to deceive you into thinking it couldn't involve danger. But if you agree, you'll be doing science a marvelous service. You can give us a much more detailed, and personal, account than we could get by watching through long-distance scopes.

"And, Brer John, at the end of your service, we'll guarantee you immediate passage to Wildenwooly. Plus a substantial contribution to your order there."

"How long will it be before I get to Wildenwooly?"

"About four months."

Brer John closed his eyes. Richards could not tell if he were praying or thinking. Probably, he decided, it was both.

Then Brer John opened his eyes, and he smiled. "If I took a job on Earth, I'd have to work two years to pay for the passage. I might be able to do something else, but offhand I can't think of anything. And from the strange course of events, I think I was *led* into that moat and thence into your hands. At least, I choose to think so.

"I'll go to Feral for four months. The best route is not necessarily the straightest one. Success in circuit lies."

Brer John was sitting in the waiting room of the spaceport, meditating and also thanking God that the loose robe of his order allowed the egg attached to his breast to be well hidden. Within a few minutes a bell would sound, and it would be time to board the *Rousehound*.

A man came in, placed his traveling bag on the floor, and sat down next to him. The man fidgeted a while, looking at Brer John every now and then. Brer John smiled whenever his eye was caught, and he said nothing. He was learning the value of silence. Presently, the man said, "Going frontier, Father?"

"Call me Brer," said Brer John. "I am not a priest but a lay brother. Yes, I am going frontier. To Wildenwooly."

"Wildenwooly? Me, too! Thank God, I'll be off Earth! What a dull restricted place! Nothing exciting ever happens here. Same old in and-out, up-and-down, day after day. Now, you take Wildenwooly! There's a place calling to every red-blooded freedom-loving adventurous man! Why, I understand you can't walk more than a mile or two before more strange and wonderful things happen to you than in a lifetime on this gray globe."

"Bless you!" said Brer John.

The man looked at the brother and moved away. He never did understand why Brer John's face turned red and his hand doubled up as if to strike a blow.

Prometheus

The man with the egg growing on his chest stepped out of the spaceship.

In the light of dawn the veldt of Feral looked superficially like an African plain before the coming of the white man. It was covered with a foot-high brown grass. Here and there were tall thick-trunked trees standing alone or in groves of from five to thirty. Everywhere were herds of animals. These were cropping the grass or drinking from a waterhole a quarter of a mile away. At this distance, some resembled antelopes, gnus, giraffes, pigs, and elephants. There were other creatures that looked as if they had come out of Earth's Pliocene. And others that had no Terrestrial parallels.

"No mammals," said a voice behind the man with the egg attached to his chest. "They're warm-blooded descendants of reptiles. But not mammals."

The speaker walked around John Carmody. He was Doctor Holmyard, sapientologist, zoologist, chief of the expedition. A tall man of about sixty with a lean body and leaner face and brown hair that had once been a bright red.

"The two previous studies established that mammals either never developed or were wiped out early. Apparently, the reptiles and birds jumped the gun in the evolutionary race. But they have filled the ecological niche the mammals occupied on Earth."

Carmody was a short rolypoly man with a big head and a long sharp nose. His left eye had a lid that tended to droop. Before he had gotten off the ship he had been wearing a monk's robe.

Holmyard pointed at a clump of trees due north and a

mile away. "There is your future home until the egg hatches," he said. "And, if you want to stay after that, we'll be very happy."

He gestured at two men who had followed him out of the ship, and they approached Carmody. They removed his kilt and fastened a transparent belt around his protruding stomach. Then they attached it to a sporran of feathers, barred red and white. Over his shaven head went a wig with a tall crest of red and white feathers. Next, a false beak edged with teeth was fitted over his nose. His mouth, however, was left free. Then, a bustle from which projected a tail of red and white plumage was fitted to the belt.

Holmyard walked around Carmody. He shook his head. "These birds—if they are birds—won't be fooled one bit when they get a close look at you. On the other hand, your general silhouette is convincing enough to allow you to get fairly close to them before they decide you're a fake. By then, they may be curious enough to permit you to join them."

"And if they attack?" said Carmody. Despite the seriousness of what might happen, he was grinning. He felt such a fool, togged out like a man going to a masquerade party as a big rooster.

"We've already implanted the mike into your throat," said Holmyard. "The transceiver is flat, fitted to curve with your skull. You can holler for help, and we'll come running. Don't forget to turn the tranceiver off when you're not using it. The charge won't last for more than fifty operational hours. But you can renew the charge at the cache."

"And you'll move camp to a place five miles due south of here?" said Carmody. "Then the ship takes off?"

"Yes. Don't forget. If—after—you've established yourself, come back to the cache and get the cameras. You can put them in the best locations for taking films of the horowitzes."

"I like that *if*," said Carmody. He looked across the plains at his destination, then shook hands with the others.

"God be with you," said the little monk.

"And with you, too," said Holmyard, warmly pumping his hand. "You're doing a great service for science, John. Perhaps for mankind. And for the horowitzes, too. Don't forget what I've told you."

"Among my many failings, a bad memory is not numbered," said John Carmody. He turned and began walking off across the veldt. A few minutes later, the great vessel lifted silently to a height of twenty feet, then shot off towards the south.

A lonely little man, ridiculous in his borrowed feathers, looking less like a man than a rooster that had lost a fight, and feeling like one at the moment, John Carmody set off through the grass. He was wearing transparent shoes, so the occasional rocks he stepped on did not hurt his feet.

A herd of equine creatures stopped feeding to look at him, to sniff the air. They were about the size of zebras and were completely hairless, having a smooth yellowish skin mottled with squares of a pale red. Lacking tails, they had no weapons of defense against the flies that swarmed around them, but their long nonreptilian tongues slid out and licked the flies off each other's flanks. They gave horsy snorts and whinnied. After watching Carmody for about sixty seconds, they suddenly broke and fled to a position about a hundred yards away. Then, they wheeled almost as a unit and faced him again. He decided that it must be his strange odor that had spooked them, and he hoped that the horowitzes would not also be offended.

At that moment, he was beginning to think that he had been foolish to volunteer for this job. Especially, when a huge creature, lacking only long tusks to resemble an elephant, lifted its trunk and trumpeted at him. However, the creature immediately began pulling down fruit from a tree and paid no more attention to him.

Carmody walked on, not without many sidewise glances to make sure it was keeping its air of indifference. By now, however, his characteristic optimism had reasserted itself. And he was telling himself that he had been guided to this planet for a very definite purpose. What the purpose was, he didn't know. But he was certain of Who had sent him.

The chain of events that had dragged him here was made of too strange a series of links to be only coincidences. Or so, at least, he believed. Only a month ago he had been fairly happy to be a simple monk working in the garden of the monastery of the Order of St. Jairus in the city of Fourth of July, Arizona, North America Department. Then, his abbot had told him that he was to transfer to a parish on the planet of Wildenwooly. And his troubles had begun.

First, he was given no money with which to buy a ticket for passage on a spaceship, no letters of introduction or identification or any detailed orders at all. He was just told to leave at once. He did not even have enough money to buy a bus ticket which would take him to the spaceport outside the domed city. He began walking and, as seemed to be his fate wherever he was, he got into one trouble after another. He finally found himself in the city park, where he was thrown by a hoodlum into a moat in the city zoo. Here a female horowitz, a giant bird of the planet Feral, had leaped into the moat and, holding him down with one foot, proceeded to lay her egg on his chest. Later, Carmody had escaped from the moat, only to find that the egg had put out tendrils of flesh and attached itself permanently to his chest.

When the zoo authorities located Carmody, they told him that the female horowitz, when she had no available male or other female on whom to attach her eggs, would attach it to a host animal. Carmody had been unlucky enough—or, from the viewpoint of the zoologists, lucky enough—to be a host. Lucky because now they would have an opportunity to study closely the development of the embryo in the egg and the manner in which it drew suste-nance from its host. Moreover, if Carmody would go to Feral and attempt to pass as a horowitz, he would be the means for furnishing the zoologists with invaluable data about these birds. The zoologists believed the horowitzes to be the Galaxy's most intelligent nonsentient beings. There was even speculation they might be advanced enough to have a language. Would Carmody work with the zoologists if they paid for his trip to Wildenwooly after the study was made?

So, the lonely little man walked across the veldt with a leathery-skinned egg attached to his bloodstream. He was filled with apprehension which even his prayers did little to still.

Flocks of thousands of birds flew overhead. A creature large as an elephant, but with a long neck and four knobbly horns on its muzzle, browsed off the leaves of a tree. It paid no attention to him, so Carmody did not veer away but walked in a straight line which took him only fifty yards from it.

Then, out of a tall clump of grass stepped an animal which he knew at once was one of the great carnivores. It was lion-colored, lion-sized, and was built much like a lion. However it was hairless. Its feline face wrinkled in a silent snarl. Carmody stopped and made a half-turn to face it. His hand slid among his tailfeathers and closed around the butt of the gun hidden there.

He had been warned about this type of meat-eater.

"Only if they're very hungry or too old to catch fleeter prey will they attack you," Holmyard had said.

This creature didn't look old, and its sides were sleek. But Carmody thought that if its temperament was as catlike as its looks, it might attack just because it was annoyed.

The leonoid blinked at him and yawned. Carmody began to breathe a trifle easier. The creature sat down on its haunches and gazed at him for all the world like a curious, but oversize, pussycat. Slowly, Carmody edged away.

The leonoid made no move to follow. Carmody was congratulating himself, when, on his left, a creature burst loose from a clump of grass.

He saw that it was a half-grown horowitz, but he had no more time to look at it. The leonoid, as startled as Carmody, leaped forward in pursuit of the runner. The horowitz cried in fear. The leonoid roared. Its pace increased.

Suddenly, out of the same clump from which the young bird had run, an adult darted. This one held a club in its hand. Though it was not match for the carnivore, it ran towards it, waving its club in its humanlike hand and yelling.

By then Carmody had drawn the pistol from its holster, and he directed the stream of bullets at the leonoid. The first missile exploded in the ground a few feet ahead of the creature; the remainder raked its side. Over and over the animal turned, and then it fell.

The adult horowitz dropped the club, scooped up the young bird in its arms, and began running towards the grove of trees about a half a mile ahead, its home.

Carmody shrugged, reloaded the gun, and resumed his walk.

"Perhaps, I can put this incident to good use," he said aloud to himself. "If they are capable of gratitude, I should be received with open arms. On the other hand, they may fear me so much they might launch a mass attack. Well, we shall see."

By the time he had neared the grove, the branches of the trees were alive with the females and the young. And the males had gathered to make a stand outside the grove. One, evidently a leader, stood ahead of the group. Carmody was not sure, but he thought that this was the one who had run with the child.

The leader was armed with a stick. He walked stiff-leggedly and slowly towards him. Carmody stopped and began talking. The leader also stopped and bent his head to one side to listen in a very birdlike gesture. He was like the rest of his species, though larger—almost seven feet tall. His feet were three-toed, his legs thick to bear his weight, his body superficially like an ostrich's. But he had no wings, rudimentary or otherwise. He had well-developed arms and five-fingered hands, though the fingers were much longer in proportion than a man's. His neck was thick, and the head was large with a well-developed brain-case. The brown eyes were set in the front of his broad head like a man's; the corvine beak was small, lined with sharp teeth, and black. His body was naked of plumage except for red-and-white-barred feathers in the loin region, on the back, and on the head. There a tall crest of feathers bristled, and around his ears were stiff feathers, like a horned owl's, designed to focus sound.

Carmody listened for a minute to the sounds of the leader's voice and those behind him. He could make out no definite pattern of speech, no distinguishing rhythm, no repetition of words. Yet, they were uttering definite syllables, and there was something familiar about their speaking.

After a minute, he recognized its similarity, and he was startled. They were talking like a baby when he is at the stage of babbling. They were running the scale of potential phonemes, up and down, at random, sometimes repeating, more often not.

Carmody reached up slowly to his scalp so he wouldn't alarm them with a sudden movement. He slid the panel-switch on the skull-fitting transceiver under his crest, thus allowing the zoologists at the camp to tune in.

Carmody spoke in a low tone, knowing that the micro-phone implanted in his throat would clearly reproduce his voice to the listeners at the camp. He described his situa-tion and then said, "I'm going to walk into their home. If you hear a loud crack, it'll be a club breaking my skull. Or vice versa."

He began walking, not directly towards the leader but to one side. The big horowitz turned as the man went by, but he made no threatening move with his club. Carmody went on by, though he felt his back prickle when he could no longer see the leader. Then he had walked straight at the mob, and he saw them step to one side, their heads cocked to one side, their sharp-toothed bills emitting the infantile babblings.

He passed safely through them to the middle of the grove of cottonwoodlike trees. Here the females and young looked down at him. The females resembled the males in many respects, but they were smaller and their crests were brown. Almost all of them were carrying eggs on their chests or else held the very young in their arms. These were covered from head to thigh with a golden-brown chicklike fuzz. The older children, however, had lost the down. The female adults looked as puzzled as the males, but the children seemed to have only curiosity. The older children climbed out on the branches above him and looked down at him. And they, too, babbled like babies.

Presently, a half-grown horowitz, a female by her all-brown crest, climbed down and slowly approached him. Carmody reached into the pouch in his tail feathers, and he brought out a lump of sugar. This he tasted himself to show her it wasn't poisonous, and then he held it out in his hand and made coaxing sounds. The young girl—he was already thinking of these beings as human—snatched the cube from his hand and ran back to the trunk of the tree. Here she turned the sugar lump over and over, felt its texture with the tips of her fingers, and then barely touched the cube with the tip of her long broad tongue.

She looked pleased. This surprised Carmody, for he had not thought of the possibility that humanoid expressions could take place on such an avian face. But the face was broad and flat and well-equipped with muscles and able as a man's to depict emotion.

The girl put all of the cube in her bill, and she looked ecstatic. Then she turned to the big horowitz—who had neared the two—and uttered a series of syllables. There was evident pleasure in her voice.

Carmody held out another lump of sugar to the leader, who took it and popped it into his bill. And over his face spread pleasure.

Carmody spoke out loud for the benefit of the men in the camp. "Put a good supply of sugar in the cache," he said, "plus some salt. I think it's likely that these people may be salt-starved, too."

"People!" exploded the ghostly voice in his ear. "Carmody, don't start making anthropocentric errors regarding these creatures."

"You've not met them," said Carmody. "Perhaps you could maintain a zoologist's detachment. But I can't. Human is as human does."

"O.K., John. But when you report, just give a description, and never mind your interpretations. After all, I'm human, and, therefore, open to suggestion."

Carmody grinned and said, "O.K. Oh, they're starting to dance now. I don't know what the dance means, whether it's something instinctive or something they've created."

While Carmody had been talking, the females and the young had climbed down out of the trees. They formed a semicircle and began clapping their hands together in rhythm. The males had gathered before them and were now hopping, jumping, spinning, bowing, waddling bent-kneed like ducks. They gave weird cries and occasionally flapped their arms and leaped into the air as if simulating the flight of birds. After about five minutes, the dance suddenly ceased, and the horowitzes formed a single-file line. Their leader, at the head of the line, walked towards Carmody.

"Oh, oh," said Carmody. "I think we're seeing the formation of the first breadline in the nonhistory of these people. Only it's sugar, not bread, that they want."

"How many are there?" said Holmyard.

"About twenty-five."

"Got enough sugar?"

"Only if I break up the cubes and give each a slight taste."

"Try that, John. While you're doing that, we'll rush more sugar to the cache on a jeep. Then you can lead them there after we leave."

"Maybe I'll take them there. Just now I'm worried about their reaction if they don't get a complete lump."

He began to break up the cubes into very small pieces and to put one into each extended hand. Every time, he said, "Sugar." By the time the last one in line—a mother with a fuzzy infant in her arms—had stuck out her hand, he had only one fragment left.

"It's a miracle," he said, sighing with relief. "Came out just right. They've gone back to what I presume are their normal occupations. Except for their chief and some of the children. These, as you can hear, are babbling like mad at me."

"We're recording their sounds," said Holmyard. "We'll make an attempt to analyze them later, find out if they've a speech."

"I know you have to be scientific," replied Carmody. "But I have a very perceptive ear, like all people who run off at the mouth, and I can tell you now they don't have a language. Not in the sense we think of, anyway."

A few minutes later, he said, "Correction. They at least have the beginning of a language. One of the little girls just came up and held out her hand and said, 'Sugar.' Perfect reproduction of English speech, if you ignore the fact that it couldn't have come from a human mouth. Sounded like a parrot or crow."

"I heard her! That's significant as hell, Carmody! If she could make the correlation so quickly, she much be capable of symbolic thinking." He added, in a more moderate tone, "Unless it was accidental, of course."

"No accident. Did you hear the other child also ask for it?"

"Faintly. While you're observing them, try to give them a few more words to learn."

Carmody sat down at the base of a thick treetrunk in the shade of branches, for the sun was beginning to turn the air hot. The tree had thick corrugated bark like a cottonwood, but it bore fruit. This grew high up on the branches and looked from a distance like a banana. The young girl brought him one and held it out to him, saying at the same time, "Sugar?"

Carmody wanted to taste the fruit, but he didn't think it would be fair to receive it without giving her what she wanted. He shook his head no, though he didn't expect her to interpret the gesture. She cocked her head to one side, and her face registered disappointment. Nevertheless, she did not withdraw the fruit. And, after making sure she knew he was out of sugar, he took the gift. The shell had to be rapped against the side of the tree to be broken, and it came apart in the middle, where it creased. He took a small bite from the interior and reported to Holmyard that it tasted like a combination of apple and cherry.

"They not only feed on this fruit," he said. "They're eating the tender shoots of a plant that resembles bamboo. I also saw one catch and eat a small rodentlike animal which ran out from under a rock she turned over. And they pick lice off each other and eat insects they find around the roots of the grass. I saw one try to catch a bird that was eating the bamboo shoots.

"Oh, the leader is pounding a club on the ground. They're dropping whatever they're doing and clustering around him. Looks as if they're getting ready to go some place. The females and young are forming a group. The males, all armed with clubs, are surrounding them. I think I'll join them."

Their destination, he was to find out, was a waterhole about a mile and a half away. It was a shallow depression about twenty feet across filled with muddy water. There were animals gathered about it: gazellelike creatures, a giant porcine with armor like an armadillo, several birds that seemed at first glance and far off to be horowitzes. But when Carmody got closer, he saw they were only about two and a half feet high, their arms were much longer, and their foreheads slanted back. Perhaps, these filled the ecological niche here that monkeys did on Earth.

The animals fled at the approach of the horowitzes. These established guards, one at each cardinal point of the compass, and the rest drank their fill. The young jumped into the water and splashed around, throwing water in each other's face and screaming with delight. Then they were hauled out, protesting, by their mothers. The guards drank their fill, and the group prepared to march back to their home, the grove.

Carmody was thirsty, but he didn't like the looks or odor of the water, which smelled as if something had died in it. He looked around and saw that the dozen trees around the waterhole were a different type. These fifty-feet high slim plants with a smooth lightbrown bark and only a few branches, which grew near the top. Clusters of gourds also grew among the branches. At the bottom of the trees lay empty gourds. He picked up one, broke in the narrow end, and dipped it in the water. Then he dropped in the water an antibiotic pill which he took from the bustle under his tailfeathers. He drank, making a face at the taste. The young girl who had first asked him for sugar approached, and he showed her how to drink from the gourd. She laughed a quite human-sounding laugh and poured the water down her open beak.

Carmody took advantage of the curiosity of the others to show them that they, too, could fill their gourds and transport water back to the grove.

Thus, the first artifact was invented—or given—on Feral. In a short time, everyone had gourds and filled them. And the group, babbling like babies, began the march back to home.

"I don't know if they're intelligent enough to learn a language yet," said Carmody to Holmyard. "It seems to me that if they were, they'd have created one. But they are the most intelligent animal I've yet encountered. Far superior to the chimpanzee or porpoise. Unless they just have a remarkable mimetic ability."

"We've run off samples of their speech in the analyzer," said Holmyard. "And there's no distribution to indicate a well-organized language. Or even an incipient language."

"I'll tell you one thing," replied Carmody. "They at least have identifying sounds for each other. I've noticed that when they want the leader's attention, they say, 'Whoot!' and he responds. Also, this girl who asked for sugar responds to the call of Tutu. So, I'm identifying them as such."

The rest of the day Carmody spent observing the horowitzes and reporting to Holmyard. He said that, during times of danger or during a joint undertaking such as going for water, the group acted as a whole. But most of the time they seemed to operate in small family units. The average family consisted of a male, the children, and anywhere from one to three females. Most of the females had eggs attached to their chests or bellies. He was able to settle for Holmyard the question of whether, generally, the females laid their eggs on each other, and so raised fosterfamilies, or transferred the eggs to their own skin immediately after laying. Towards dusk he saw a female deposit an egg and then hold it against the chest of another female. In a few minutes, little tendrils crept forth from the leathery-skinned ovum and inserted themselves into the bloodstream of the hostess.

"That, I would take it, is the general course of action," Carmody said. "But there is one male here who, like me, carries an egg. I don't know why he was singled out. But I would say that, at the time the egg was produced, the female and her mate were separated from the others. So the female took the lesser alternative. Don't ask me why the females just don't attach the eggs to their own bodies. Maybe there's a chemical factor that prevents the egg from attaching itself to its own mother. Perhaps some sort of antibody set-up. I don't know. But there is some reason which, up to now, only the Creator of the horowitzes knows."

"It's not a general pattern for all the birds of this planet," said Holmyard. "There are oviparous, oviviparous, and viviparous species. But the order of birds of which the horowitzes are the highest in development, the order of Aviprimates, all have this feature. From highest to lowest, they lay their eggs and then attach them to a host."

"I wonder why this particular line of creatures didn't develop viviparism?" said Carmody. "It seems obvious that it's the best method for protecting the unborn."

"Who knows?" said Holmyard, and Carmody, mentally, could see him shrugging. "That's a question that may or may not be answered during this study. After all, this planet is new to us. It's not had a thorough study. It was only by a lucky accident that Horowitz discovered these birds during his brief stay here. Or that we were able to get a grant to finance us."

"One reason for the externalism may be that even if the embryo is injured or killed, the hostess is not," said Carmody. "If the embryo of a viviparous mother is destroyed, then the mother usually is, too. But here, I imagine, though the embryo may be more susceptible to death and injury, the bearer of the unborn is relatively unaffected by the wound."

"Maybe," said Holmyard. "Nature is an experimenter. Perhaps, she's trying this method on this planet."

He is, you mean, thought Carmody, but he said nothing. The gender of the Creator did not matter. Both he and the zoologist were talking about the same entity.

Carmody continued to give his observations. The mothers fed the very young in the traditional manner of birds, by regurgitating food.

"That seemed probable," said Holmyard. "The reptiles developed a class of warmblooded animals, but none of these have hair or even rudimentary mammaries. The horowitz, as I told you, evolved from a very primitive bird which took up arboreal life at the time its cousins were learning to glide. The fleshy fold of skin hanging down between arm and rib is a vestige of that brief period when it had begun to glide and then changed its mind and decided to become a lemuroid-type.

"Or so it seems to us. Actually, we haven't unearthed enough fossils to speak authoritatively."

"They do have certain cries which can be interpreted by the others. Such as a cry for help, a cry for pick-my-fleas, a rallying cry, and so on. But that's all. Except that some of the children now know the word for sugar and water. And they identify each other. Would you say that that is the first step in creating a language?"

"No, I wouldn't," said Holmyard firmly. "But if you can teach them to take an assemblage of independent words and string them together into an intelligible sentence, and if they become capable of reasoning these words in different patterns and for different situations, then I'd say they are in a definite lingual stage. But your chance for doing that is very remote. After all, they might be in a prelingual stage, just on the verge of becoming capable of verbal symbolism. But it might take another ten thousand years, maybe fifty thousand, before their kind develop that ability. Before they take the step from animal to human being."

"And maybe I can give them the nudge," said Carmody. "Maybe . . ."

"Maybe what?" said Holmyard after Carmody had been silent for several minutes.

"I'm confronted with the theological question the Church raised some centuries before interstellar travel became possible," said Carmody. "At what moment did the ape become a man? At what moment did the ape possess a soul, and . . ."

"Jesus Christ!" said Holmyard. "I know you're a monk, Carmody! And it's only natural you should be interested in such a question! But, I beg of you, don't start muddling around with something as divorced from reality as the exact moment when a soul is inserted into an animal! Don't let this—this how-many-angels-on-a-pinpoint absurdity begin to color your reports. Please try to keep a strictly objective and scientific viewpoint. Just describe what you see; no more!"

"Take it easy, Doc. That's all I intend to do. But you can't blame me for being interested. However, it's not for me to decide such a question. I leave that up to my superiors. My order, that of St. Jairus, does not do much theological speculation; we are primarily men of action."

"O.K., O.K.," said Holmyard. "Just so we understand each other. Now, do you intend to introduce fire to the horowitzes tonight?"

"Just as soon as dusk falls."

Carmody spent the rest of the day in teaching little Tutu the word for tree, egg, gourd, a few verbs which he acted out for her, and the pronouns. She caught on quickly. He was sure that it was not the purely mimetic speech ability of a parrot. To test her, he asked her a question.

"You see the tree?" he said, pointing at a large sycamore-like fruit tree.

She nodded, a gesture she had learned from him, and she replied in her strange birdlike voice, "Yes. Tutu see the tree."

Then, before he could frame another question, she said, pointing at the chief, "You see Whoot? Tutu see Whoot. Him horowitz. Me horowitz. You . . .?"

knives. I've been thinking that I ought to lead them to a site where they can find some. Do you know of any?"

"We'll go out in the jeep and look for some," said Holmyard. "You're right. Even if they are capable of learning to make tools and pottery, they're not in an area suited to develop that ability."

"Why didn't you pick a group which lived near a flint-rich area?"

"Mainly, because it was in this area that Horowitz discovered these creatures. We scientists are just as apt to get into a rut as anybody, so we didn't look into the future. Besides, we had no idea these animals—uh—people, if they do deserve that term—were so full of potential."

Just then Tutu, holding a mouse-sized grasshopper in her hand, came up to Carmody.

"This . . .?"

"This is a grasshopper," said Carmody.

"You burn . . . the fire."

"Yes. Me burn *in* fire. No, not burn. Me cook *in* fire."

"You cook in the fire," she said. "You give to me. Me eat; you eat."

"She's now learned two prepositions—I think," said Carmody.

"John, why this pidgin English?" said Holmyard. "Why the avoidance of *is* and the substitution of the nominative case for the objective with the personal pronouns?"

"Because *is* isn't necessary," replied Carmody. "Many languages get along without it, as you well know. Moreover, there's a recent tendency in English to drop it in conversational speech, and I'm just anticipating what may become a general development.

"As for teaching them lower-class English, I'm doing that because I think that the language of the illiterates will triumph. You know how hard the teachers in our schools have to struggle to overcome the tendency of their high-class students to use button-pusher's jargon."

"O.K.," said Holmyard. "It doesn't matter, anyway. The horowitzes have no conception—as far as I know— of the difference. Thank God, you're not teaching them Latin!"

"Say!" said Carmody. "I didn't think of that! Why not? If the horowitzes ever become civilized enough to have interstellar travel, they'd always be able to talk to priests, no matter where they went."

"Carmody!"

Carmody chuckled and said, "Just teasing, Doctor. But I

do have a serious proposition. If other groups should show themselves as capable of linguistic learning, why not teach each group a different language? Just as an experiment? This group would be our Indo-European school; another, Sinitic; another, our Amerindian; still another, Bantu. It would be interesting to see how the various groups developed socially, technologically, and philosophically. Would each group follow the general lines of social evolution that their prototypes did on Earth? Would the particular type of language a group used place it on a particular path during its climb uphill to civilization?"

"A tempting idea," said Holmyard. "But I'm against it. Sentient beings have enough barriers to understanding each other without placing the additional obstacles of differing languages in their way. No, I think that all should be taught English. A single speech will give them at least one unifying element. Though, God knows, their tongues will begin splitting into dialects soon enough."

"Bird-English I'll teach them," said Carmody.

One of the first things he had to do was straighten out Tutu concerning the word *tree*. She was teaching some of the younger horowitzes what language she'd mastered so far and was pointing to a cottonwood and calling out, "Tree! Tree!"

Then she pointed to another cottonwood, and she became silent. Wonderingly, she looked at Carmody, and he knew in that moment that she thought of that cottonwood as tree. But that word to her meant an individual entity or thing. She had no generic concept of tree.

Carmody tried by illustration to show her. He pointed at the second cottonwood and said, "Tree." Then he pointed at one of the tall thin trees and repeated the word.

Tutu cocked her head to one side, and an obvious puzzlement settled on her face.

Carmody further confused her by indicating the two cottonwoods and giving each their name. Then, on the spot, he made up a name for the tall thin trees and said, "Tumtum."

"Tumtum," said Tutu.

"Tumtumtree," said Carmody. He pointed at the cottonwood. "Cottonwoodtree." He pointed out across the veldt. "Thorntree." He made an all-inclusive gesture. "All tree."

The youngsters around Tutu did not seem to grasp his meaning, but she laughed—as a crow laughs—and said, "Tumtum. Cottonwood. Thorn. All tree."

Carmody wasn't sure whether she grasped what he'd

said or was just mimicking him. Then she said, swiftly—perhaps she was able to interpret his look of frustration—"Tumtumtree . . . Cottonwoodtree. Thorntree."

She held up three fingers and made a sweeping gesture with the other hand. "All tree."

Carmody was pleased, for he was fairly certain she now knew tree as not only an individual but a generic term. But he didn't know how to tell her that the last-named was not a thorn but was a thorntree. He decided that it didn't matter. Not for the time being, at least. But when the time came to name a thorn as such, he would have to give the thorn another nomenclature. No use confusing them.

"You seem to be doing famously," said Holmyard's voice. "What's next on the agenda?"

"I'm going to try to sneak away to the cache and pick up some more ammo and sugar," said Carmody. "Before I do, could you drop off a blackboard and some paper and pencils?"

"You won't have to take notes," said Holmyard. "Everything you say is being recorded, as I think I once told you," he added impatiently.

"I'm not thinking of making memos," said Carmody. "I intend to start teaching them how to read and write."

There was a silence for several seconds, then, *"What?"*

"Why not?" replied Carmody. "Even at this point, I'm not absolutely certain they really understand speech. Ninety-nine percent sure, yes. But I want to be one-hundred percent certain. And if they can understand written speech, then there's no doubt.

"Besides, why wait until later? If they can't learn now, we can try later. If they do catch on now, we've not wasted any time."

"I must apologize," said Holmyard. "I lacked imagination. I should have thought of that step. You know, John, I resented the fact that you had, through pure accident, been chosen to make this first venture among the horowitzes. I thought a trained scientist, preferably myself, should have been the contact man. But I see now that having you out there isn't a mistake. You have what we professionals too often too quickly lose: the enthusiastic imagination of the amateur. Knowing the difficulties or even the improbabilities, we allow ourselves to be too cautious."

"Oh, oh!" said Carmody. "Excuse me, but it looks as if the chief is organizing everybody for some big move. He's running around, gabbling his nonsense syllables like mad and pointing to the north. He's also pointing at the branches of the trees. Oh, I see what he's getting at. Almost all of the fruit is eaten. And he wants us to follow him."

"Which direction?"

"South. Towards you."

"John, there's a nice valley about a thousand miles north of here. We found it during the last expedition and noted it because it's higher, cooler, much better watered. And it not only contains flint but iron ores."

"Yes, but the chief evidently wants us to go in the opposite direction."

There was a pause. Finally, Carmody sighed and said, "I get the message. You want me to lead them north. Well, you know what that means."

"I'm sorry, John. I know it means conflict. And I can't order you to fight the chief. That is, if it's necessary for you to fight."

"I rather think it will be. Too bad, too; I wouldn't exactly call this Eden, but at least no blood has been shed among these people. And now, because we want to plumb their potentiality, lead them on to higher things . . ."

"You don't have to, John. Nor will I hold it against you if you just tag along and study them wherever they go. After all, we've gotten far more data than I ever dreamed possible. But . . ."

"But if I don't try to take over the reins of leadership, these beings may remain at a low level for a long long time. Besides, we have to determine if they are capable of any technology. So . . . the end justifies the means. Or so say the Jesuits. I am not a Jesuit, but I can justify the premise on which we're basing the logic of this argument."

Carmody did not say another word to Holmyard. He marched up to the big leader, took a stand before him, and, shaking his head fiercely and pointing to the north, he shouted, "Us go this way! No go that way!"

The chief stopped his gabbling and cocked his head to one side and looked at Carmody. His face, bare of feathers, became red. Carmody could not tell, of course, if it was the red of embarrassment or of rage. So far as he could determine, his position in this society had been a very peculiar one—from the society's viewpoint. It had not taken him long to see that a definite peck-order existed here. The big horowitz could bully anyone he wanted to. The male just below him in this unspoken hierarchy could not—or would not—resist the chief's authority. But he could bully everybody below him. And so forth. All the males, with the exception of one weak character, could push the females around. And the females had their own system, similar to the males, except that it seemed to be more complex. The top female in the peck-order system could lord it over all but one female, and yet this female was subject to the authority of at least half the other females. And there were other cases whose intricacy defied Carmody's powers of analysis.

One thing he had noticed, though, and that was that the young were all treated with kindness and affection. They were, in fact, very much the spoiled brats. Yet, they had their own give-and-take-orders organization.

Carmody had up to this time held no position in the social scale. They seemed to regard him as something apart, a *rara avis,* an unknown quantity. The chief had made no move to establish Carmody's place here, so the others had not dared to try. And, probably, the chief had not dared because he had been witness to Carmody's killing of the leonoid.

But now the stranger had placed him in such a position that he must fight or else step down. And he must have been the top brass too long to endure that idea. Even if he knew Carmody's destructive potential, he did not intend to submit meekly.

So Carmody guessed from the reddened skin, the swelling chest, the veins standing out on his forehead, the glaring eyes, the snapping beak, the clenched fists, the sudden heavy breathing.

The chief, Whoot, was impressive. He stood a foot and a half taller than the man, his arms were long and muscular, his chest huge, and his beak with its sharp meateater's teeth and his three-toed legs with their sharp talons looked as if they could tear the heart out of Carmody.

But the little man knew that the horowitz didn't weigh as much as a man his height, for his bones were the half-hollow bones of a bird. Moreover, though the chief was undoubtedly a capable and vicious fighter, and intelligent, he did not have at his command the sophisticated knowledge of infighting of a dozen worlds. Carmody was as deadly with his hands and feet as any man alive; many times, he had killed and crippled.

The fight was sharp but short. Carmody used a mélange of all his skills and very quickly had the chief reeling, bloody-beaked, and glassy-eyed. He gave the *coup de grace* by chopping with the edge of his palm against the side of the thick neck. He stood over the unconscious body of Whoot, breathing heavily, bleeding from three wounds delivered by the point of the beak and pointed teeth and suffering from a blow of a fist against his ribs.

He waited until the big horowitz had opened his eyes and staggered to his feet. Then, pointing north, he shouted, "Follow me!"

In a short time, they were walking after him as he headed for a grove of trees about two miles away. Whoot walked along in the rear of the group, his head hung low. But after a while he regained some of his spirit. And, when a large male tried to make him carry some of the water gourds, he jumped on the male and knocked him to the ground. That re-established his position in the group. He was below Carmody but still higher than the rest.

Carmody was glad, for the little Tutu was Whoot's child. He had been afraid that his defeat of her father might make her hostile to him. Apparently, the change in authority had made no difference, unless it was that she stayed even more by his side. While they walked together, Carmody pointed out more animals and plants, naming them. She repeated the words, sound-perfect, after him. By now she had even adopted his style of speaking, his individual rhythm pattern, his manner of saying, "Heh?" when a strong thought seized him, his habit of talking to himself.

And she imitated his laugh. He pointed out a thin, shabby-looking bird with its feathers sticking out all round and looking like a live mop.

"That a borogove."

"That a borogove," she repeated.

Suddenly, he laughed, and she laughed, too. But he could not share the source of his mirth with her. How could be explain *Alice in Wonderland* to her? How could he tell her that he had wondered what Lewis Carroll would think if he could see his fictional creation come to life on a strange planet circling around a strange star and centuries after he had died? Or know that his works were still alive and bearing fruit, even if weird fruit? Perhaps, Carroll would approve. For he had been a strange little man—like Carmody, thought Carmody—and he would consider the naming of this bird the apex of congruous incongruity.

He sobered immediately, for a huge animal resembling a green rhinoceros with three knobbed horns trotted thunderingly towards them. Carmody took his pistol out from his bustle, causing Tutu's eyes to widen even more than at the sight of the tricorn. But, after stopping only a few feet from the group and sniffing the wind, the tricorn trotted slowly away. Carmody replaced the pistol, and he called Holmyard.

"You'll have to forget about caching the stuff I ordered in that tree," he said. "I'm leading them on the exodus as of now. I'll build a fire tonight, and you can relocate about five miles behind us. I'm going to try to get them to walk past this grove ahead, go on to another. I plan to lead them on a two mile and a half trek every day. I think that's about as far as I can push them. We should reach the valley of milk and honey you described in nine months. By then, my child," he tapped the egg on his chest, "should be hatched. And my contract with you will be terminated."

He had less trouble than he thought he would. Though the group scattered as soon as they reached the grove, they reassembled at his insistence and left the tempting fresh fruits and the many rodents to be found under the rocks. They did not murmur while he led them another mile to another grove. Here he decided they'd camp for the rest of the day and night.

After dusk fell, and he had supervised Tutu's building of a fire, he sneaked away into the darkness. Not without some apprehension, for more carnivores prowled under the two small moons than in the light of the sun. Nevertheless, he walked without incident for a mile and there met Doctor Holmyard, waiting in a jeep.

After borrowing a cigarette from Holmyard, he described the events of the day more fully than he had been able to do over the transceiver. Holmyard gently squeezed the egg clinging to Carmody's chest, and he said, "How does it feel not only to give birth to a horowitz, but to give birth to speech among them? To become, in a sense, the father of all the horowitzes?"

"It makes me feel very odd," said Carmody. "And aware of a great burden on me. After all, what I teach these sentients will determine the course of their lives for thousands of years to come. Maybe even further.

"Then again, all my efforts may come to nothing."

"You must be careful. Oh, by the way, here's the stuff you asked for. A holster and belt. And, in a knapsack, ammo, a flashlight, more sugar, salt, paper, pen, a pint of whiskey."

"You don't expect me to give them firewater?" said Carmody.

"No," chuckled Holmyard. "This bottle is your private stock. I thought you might like a nip now and then. After all, you must need something to buck up your spirits, being without your own kind."

"I've been too busy to be lonely. But nine months is a long time. No, I don't really believe I'll get unbearably lonely. These people are strange. But I'm sure they have spirits kindred to mine, waiting to be developed."

They talked some more, planning their method of study for the year to come. Holmyard said that a man would always be in the ship and in contact with Carmody, if an emergency should come up. But everybody would be busy, for this expedition had many projects in the fire. They would be collecting and dissecting specimens of all sorts, making soil and air and water analyses, geological surveys, digging for fossils, etc. Quite often the ship would take a trip to other regions, even to the other side of the planet. But when that happened, two men and a jeep would be left behind.

"Listen, Doc," said Carmody. "Couldn't you take a trip to this valley and get some flint ore? Then leave it close to us, so my group could find it? I'd like to find out *now* if they're capable of using weapons and tools."

Holmyard nodded and said, "A good idea. Will do. We'll have the flint for you before the week's up."

Holmyard shook Carmody's hand, and the little monk left. He lit his way with the flashlight, for he hoped that, though it might attact some of the big carnivores, it might also make them wary of getting too close.

He had not gone more than a hundred yards when, feeling as if he were being stalked, and also feeling foolish because he was obeying an irrational impulse, he whirled. And his flashlight centered on the small figure of Tutu.

"What you do here?" he said. She approached slowly, as if fearing him, and he rephrased his question. There were so many words that she did not know that he could not, at this point, fully communicate with her.

"Why you here?"

Never before had he used *why*, but he thought that now, under the circumstances, she might understand it.

"Me . . ." she made a motion of following.

"Follow."

"Me follow . . . you. Me no . . . want you hurt. Big

meateaters in dark. Bite, claw, kill, eat you. You die;
me . . . how you say it?"

He saw what she meant, for tears were filling her large
brown eyes.

"Cry," he said. "Ah, Tutu, you cry for me?"

He was touched.

"Me cry," she said, her voice shaking, on the edge of
sobs. "Me . . ."

"Feel bad. Feel bad."

"John die after now . . . me want to die. Me . . ."

He realized that she had just coined a term for the
future, but he did not try to teach her the use of the future
tense. Instead, he held out his arms and embraced her. She
put her head against him, the sharp edge of her beak digging into the flesh between his ribs, and she burst into loud
weeping.

Stroking the plumage on top of her round head, he said,
"No feel bad, Tutu. John love you. You know . . . me love
you."

"Love. Love," she said between sobs. "Love, love. Tutu
love you!"

Suddenly, she pushed herself away from him, and he
released her. She began to wipe the tears from her eyes
with her fists and to say, "Me love. But . . . me 'fraid of
John."

" 'Fraid? Why you 'fraid of John?"

"Me see . . . uh . . . horowitz . . . by you. You look like
him, but not look like him. Him . . . how say . . . funny-
looking, that right? And him fly like vulture, but no wing
. . . on . . . me no able to say on what him fly. Very . . .
funny. You talk to him. Me understand some words . . . no
some."

Carmody sighed. "All me able to tell you now that him
no horowitz. Him man. Man. Him come from stars." He
pointed upwards.

Tutu also looked up, then her gaze returned to him, and
she said, "You come from . . . star?"

"Child, you understand that?"

"You no horowitz. You place on beak and feathers. But
. . . me understand you no horowitz."

"Me man," he said. "But enough of this, child. Some day
. . . after soon . . . me tell you about the stars."

And, despite her continued questioning, he refused to
say another word on the subject.

The days and then weeks and then months passed.

Steadily, walking about two and a half to three miles a day, progressing from grove to grove, the band followed Carmody northwards. They came across the flints left by the ship. And Carmody showed them how to fashion spearheads and arrowheads and scrapers and knives. He made bows for them and taught them to shoot. In a short time, every horowitz who had the manual skill was making weapons and tools for himself. Fingers and hands were banged and cut, and one male lost an eye from a flying chip. But the group began to eat better; they shot the cervinoid and equinoid animals and, in fact, anything that wasn't too big and looked as if it might be edible. They cooked the meat, and Carmody showed them how to smoke and dry the meat. They began to get very bold, and it was this that was the undoing of Whoot.

One day, while with two other males, he shot a leonoid that refused to move away from their approach. The arrow only enraged the beast, and it charged. Whoot stood his ground and sent two more arrows into it, while his companions threw their spears. But the dying animal got hold of Whoot and smashed him in his chest.

By the time the two had come for Carmody, and he had run to Whoot, Whoot was dead.

This was the first death among the group since Carmody had joined them. Now he saw that they did not regard death dumbly, as animals did, but as an event that caused outcries of protest. They wailed and wept and beat their chests and cast themselves down on the ground and rolled in the grass. Tutu wept as she stood by the corpse of her father. Carmody went to her and held her while she sobbed her heart out. He waited until their sorrow had spent itself, then he organized a burial party. This was a new thing to them; apparently, they had been in the custom of leaving their dead on the ground. But they understood him, and they dug a shallow hole in the ground with sharp-pointed sticks and piled rocks over the grave.

It was then that Tutu said to him, "Me father. Where him go now?"

Carmody was speechless for several seconds. Without one word from him, Tutu had thought of the possibility of afterlife. Or so he supposed, for it was easy to misinterpret her. She might just be unable to conceive of the discontinuity of the life of one she loved. But, no, she knew death well. She had seen others die before he had joined the group, and she had seen the death and dissolution of many large animals, not to mention the innumerable rodents and insects she had eaten.

"What think the others?" he said, gesturing at the rest of the group.

She looked at them. "Adults no think. Them no talk. Them like the animals.

"Me a child. Me think. You teached me to think. Me ask you where Whoot go because you understand."

As he had many times since he met her, Carmody sighed. He had a heavy and serious responsibility. He did not want to give her false hopes, yet he did not want to destroy her hopes—if she had any—of living after death. And he just did not know if Whoot had a soul or, if he did, what provision might be made for it. Neither did he know about Tutu. It seemed to him that a being who was sentient, who had self-consciousness, who could use verbal symbolism, must have a soul. Yet, he did not know.

Nor could he try to explain his dilemma to her. Her vocabulary, after only six months of contact with him, could not deal with the concepts of immortality. Neither could his, for even the sophisticated language at his command did not deal with reality but only with abstractions dimly comprehended, with vague hopes only stammered about. One could have faith and could try to translate that faith into effective action. But that was all.

Slowly, he said, "You understand that Whoot's body and the lion's body become earth?"

"Yes."

"And that seeds fall on this earth, and grass and trees grow there and feed from the earth, which Whoot and the lion becomed?"

Tutu nodded her beaked head. "Yes. And the birds and the jackals will eat the lion. Them will eat Whoot, too, if them able to drag the rocks from him."

"But at least a part of the lion and of Whoot become soil. And the grasses growing from them become partly them. And the grass in turn become eated by antelopes, and the lion and Whoot not only become grass but beast."

"And if me eat the antelope," interrupted Tutu excitedly, her beak clacking, her brown eyes shining, "then Whoot become part of me. And me of him."

Carmody realized he was treading on theologically dangerous ground.

"Me no mean that Whoot live in you," he said. "Me mean . . ."

"Why him no live in me? And in the antelopes that eat grass and in the grass? Oh, understand! Because Whoot then become breaked into many pieces! Him live in many different creatures. That what you mean, John?"

She wrinkled her brow. "But how him live if all teared apart? No, him no! Him body go so many places. What me mean, John, where Whoot go?"

She repeated fiercely, "Where *him* go?"

"Him go wherever the Creator send him," replied Carmody, desperately.

"Cre-a-tor?" she echoed, stressing each syllable.

"Yes. Me teached you the word *creature*, meaning any living being. Well, a creature must become created. And the Creator create him. Create mean to cause to live. Also mean to bring into becoming what no becomed before."

"Me mother me creator?"

She did not mention her father because she, like the other children and probably the adults, too, did not connect copulation with reproduction. And Carmody had not explained the connection to her because, as yet, she lacked the vocabulary.

Carmody sighed and said, "Worse and worse. No. You mother no you Creator. Her make the egg from her body and the food her eat. But her no create you. In the beginning . . ."

Here he boggled. And he wished that he had become a priest and had a priest's training. Instead, he was only a monk. Not a simple monk, for he had seen too much of the Galaxy and had lived too much. But he was not equipped to deal with this problem. For one thing, he just could not hand out a ready-made theology to her. The theology of this planet was in formation and would not even be born until Tutu and her kind had full speech.

"Me tell you more in the future," he said. "After many suns. For this time, you must become satisfied with the little me able to tell you. And that . . . well, the Creator make this whole world, stars, sky, water, animals, and the horowitzes. He make you mother and her mother and her mother's mother's mother. Many mothers many suns ago, he make . . ."

"*He?* That him name? *He?*"

Carmody realized he had slipped up in using the nominative case, but old habit had been too much for him.

"Yes. You can call him He."

"He the Mother of the first mother?" said Tutu. "He the Mother of all creatures' Mothers?"

"Here. Have some sugar. And run along and play. Me tell you more later."

After I have time to think, he said to himself.

He pretended to scratch his head and slid back the activating plate on the transceiver curved over his skull. And he asked the operator on duty to call Holmyard. In a minute, Holmyard's voice said, "What's up, John?"

"Doc, isn't a ship due in a few days to drop down and pick up the records and specimens you've collected so far? Will you have it take a message back to Earth? Notify my superior, the abbot of Fourth of July, Arizona, that I am in deep need of guidance."

And Carmody related his talk with Tutu and the questions that he had to answer in the future.

"I should have told him where I was going before I left," he said. "But I got the impression that he had put me on my own. However, I am now in a predicament which requires that wiser and better trained men help me."

Holmyard chuckled. He said, "I'll send on your message, John. Though I don't think you need any help. You're doing as well as anyone could. Anyone who tries to maintain objectivity, that is. Are you sure that your superiors will be able to do that? Or that it may not take them a hundred years to arrive at a decision? Your request might even cause a council of the Church heads. Or a dozen councils."

Carmody groaned, and then he said, "I don't know. I think I'll start teaching the kids how to read and write and do arithmetic. There, at least, I'll be navigating in safe waters."

He shut off the transceiver and called Tutu and the other young who seemed capable of literacy.

In the days and nights that followed, the young made exceptional progress, or so it seemed to Carmody. It was as if the young had been fallow, just waiting for the touch of somebody like Carmody. Without too much trouble, they learned the relation between the spoken and the written word. To keep them from being confused, Carmody modified the alphabet as it was used on Earth and made a truly phonetic system so that every phoneme would have a parallel notation. This was something that had been talked about for two hundred years among the English-speakers of Earth but had not, so far, been done. Orthography there, though it had changed, still lagged behind the spoken word and presented the same maddening and confusing picture to the foreigner who wished to learn English.

But reading and writing in short time led to Carmody's being forced to teach another art: drawing. Tutu, without any hint on his part that she should do so, one day began to make a sketch of him. Her efforts were crude, and he could have straightened her out very quickly. But, aside from later teaching her the principles of perspective, he made no effort to help her. He felt that if she, and the others who also began to draw, were influenced too much by Terrestrial ideas of art, they would not develop a truly Feral art. In this decision he was commended by Holmyard.

"Man has a fundamentally primate brain, and so he has worked out a primate's viewpoint through his art. So far, we've had no art produced by—forgive me—birdbrains. I'm with you, John, in allowing them to paint and sculpture in their own peculiar fashion. The world may some day be enriched by avian artistry. Maybe, maybe not."

Carmody was busy from the time he woke, which was dawn, until the time he went to sleep, about three hours after nightfall. He not only had to spend much time in his teaching, but he had to act as arbitrator—or rather dictator—of disputes. The disputes among the adults were much more trying than among the young, for he could communicate effectively with the latter.

The cleavage between the young and the adults was not as strong as he had expected. The adults were intelligent, and, though speechless, could learn to make flint tools and weapons and could shoot arrows and throw spears. They even learned to ride horses.

Halfway towards their destination, they began to encounter bands of animals that strongly resembled hairless horses. Carmody, as an experiment, caught one and broke it. He made reins from bone and a strong-fibered grass. He had no saddles at first but rode it bareback. Later, after the older children and the adults had caught their own horses and began to ride them, they were taught how to make saddles and reins from the thick skin of the tricorn.

Shortly after, he met his first resistance from the young. They came to a place where a lake was, where trees grew thickly, where a breeze blew most of the time from the nearby hills, and where the game was numerous. Tutu said that she and the others thought it would be a good idea if they built a walled village, such as Carmody had told them they would build when they got to the Valley.

"Many speechless ones live around here," she said. "Us able to take them young and raise them, make them us people. That way, us become stronger. Why travel every day? Us become tired of traveling, become footsore, saddlesore. Us able to make—barns?—for them horses, too. And us able to catch other animals, breed them, have plenty of meat to kill without hunting. Also, us able to plant seeds like you telled us and grow crops. Here a good place. Just as good as that Valley you speaked of, maybe gooder. Us children talked it over, decided to stay here."

"This a good place," said Carmody. "But not the goodest. Me have knowledge of the Valley, and me have knowledge that there many things this place no have. Such as flint, iron, which much gooder than flint, healthier climate, not so many big beasts that eat meat, gooder soil in which to grow crops, and other things."

"How you have knowledge of this Valley?" said Tutu. "You seed it? You goed there?"

"Me have knowledge of the Valley because someone who there once telled me of it," said Carmody. (And he wished that he had not avoided the use of the verb *know* to avoid confusion with the adjective and adverb *no*. So far he had not introduced any homonyms into the horowitz's vocabulary. But he determined at this moment to make use of know. He could, though, partially reinstate the original Old English pronunciation and have them pronounce the k. At the first chance, he would do that.)

"Who telled you of the Valley?" said Tutu. "No horowitz doed it, because none have speech until you teached them how to talk. Who telled you?"

"The man docd it," replied Carmody. "Him goed there."

"The man who comed from the stars? The man me seed you talking to that night?"

Carmody nodded, and she said, "Him have knowledge of where us go after death?"

He was caught by surprise and could only stare, open-mouthed, at her a few seconds. Holmyard was an agnostic and denied that there was any valid evidence for the immortality of man. Carmody, of course, agreed with him that there was no scientifically provable evidence, no facts. But there were enough indications of the survival of the dead to make any open-minded agnostic wonder about the possibility. And, of course, Carmody believed that every man would live forever because he had faith that man would do so. Moreover, he had a personal experience which had convinced him. (But that's another story.)

"No, the man no have knowledge of where us go after death. But me have knowledge."

"Him a man; you a man," said Tutu. "If you have knowledge, why no him?"

Again, Carmody was speechless. Then he said, "How you have knowledge that me a man?"

Tutu shrugged and said, "At first, you fool us. Later, everybody have knowledge. Easy to see that you put on beak and feathers."

Carmody began to remove the beak, which had chafed and irritated him for many months.

"Why no say so?" he said angrily. "You try to make fool of me?"

Tutu looked hurt. She said, "No. Nobody make fool of you, John. Us love you. Us just thinked you liked to put on beak and feathers. Us no have knowledge of why, but if you like to do so, O.K. with us. Anyway, no try to get off what we talk about. You say you have knowledge of where dead go. Where?"

"Me no supposed to tell you where. No just yet, anyway. Later."

"You no wish to scare us? Maybe that a bad place us no like? That why you no tell us?"

"Later, me tell. It like this, Tutu. When me first comed among you and teached you speech, me no able to teach you all the words. Just them you able to understand. Later, teach you harder words. So it now. You no able to understand even if me tell you. You become older, have knowledge of more words, become smarter. Then me tell. See?"

She nodded and also clicked her beak, an additional sign of agreement.

"Me tell the others," she said. "Many times, while you sleep, we talk about where us go after us die. What use of living only short time if us no keep on living? What good it do? Some say it do no good; us just live and die, and that that. So what? But most of us no able to think that. Become scared. Besides, no make sense to us. Everything else in this world make sense. Or seem to. But death no make sense. Death that last forever no do, anyway. Maybe us die to make room for others. Because if us no die, if ancestors no die, then soon this world become too crowded, and all starve to death, anyway. You tell us this world no flat but round like a ball and this force—what you call it, gravity?—keep us from falling off. So us see that soon no more room if us no die. But why no go to a place where plenty of room? Stars, maybe? You tell us there plenty of round worlds like this among the stars. Why us not go there?"

"Because them worlds also have plenty of creatures on them," said Carmody.

"Horowitzes?"

"No. Some have mans on them; other have creatures as different from both man and horowitz as me different from you. Or from a horse or a bug."

"Plenty to learn. Me glad me no have to find out all that by meself. Me wait until you tell me everything. But me become excited thinking about it."

Carmody had a council with the older children, and the upshot was that he agreed they should settle down for a short period at this site. He thought that, when they began to chop down trees for a stockade and houses, they would break and dull their flint axes and in a short time would run out of flint. Not to mention that his descriptions of the Valley would influence the more restless among them to push on.

Meanwhile, the egg on his chest grew larger and heavier, and he found it an increasing burden and irritation.

"I just wasn't cut out to be a mother," he told Holmyard over the transceiver. "I would like to become a Father, yes, in the clerical sense. And that demands certain maternal qualities. But, literally, and physically, I am beginning to be bothered."

"Come on in, and we'll take another sonoscope of the egg," said Holmyard. "It's time that we had another record of the embryo's growth, anyway. And we'll give you a complete physical to make sure that the egg isn't putting too much strain on you."

That night, Carmody met Holmyard, and they flew back in the jeep to the ship. This was now stationed about twenty miles from Carmody, because of the far-ranging of the horowitzes on their horses. In the ship's laboratory, the little monk was put through a series of tests. Holmyard said, "You've lost much weight, John. You're no longer fat. Do you eat well?"

"More than I ever did. I'm eating for two now, you know."

"Well, we've found nothing alarming or even mildly disturbing. You're healthier than you ever were, mainly because you've gotten rid of that flab. And the little devil you're carrying around is growing apace. From the studies we've made on horowitzes we've caught, the egg grows until it reaches a diameter of three inches and a weight of four pounds.

"This biological mechanism of attaching eggs to the bloodstream of hosts of another species is amazing enough. But what biological mechanism enables the foetus to do this? What keeps it from forming antibodies and killing itself? How can it accept the bloodstream of another totally different species? Of course, one thing that helps is that the blood cells are the same shape as a man's; no difference can be detected with microscopic examination. And the chemical composition is approximately the same. But even so . . . yes, we may be able to get another grant just to study this mechanism. If we could discover it, the benefit to mankind might be invaluable."

"I hope you do get another grant," said Carmody. "Unfortunately, I won't be able to help you. I must report to the abbot of the monastery of Wildenwooly."

"I didn't tell you when you came in," said Holmyard, "because I didn't want to upset you and thus bollix up your physical. But the supply ship landed yesterday. And we got a message for you."

He handed Carmody a long envelope covered with several official-looking seals. Carmody tore it open and read it. Then he looked up at Holmyard.

"Must be bad news, judging from your expression," said Holmyard.

"In one way, no. They inform me that I must live up to my contract and cannot leave here until the egg is hatched. But the day my contract expires, I must leave. And, furthermore, I am not to give the horowitzes any religious instruction at all. They must find out for themselves. Or rather, they must have their peculiar revelation —if any. At least, until a council of the Church has convened and a decision arrived at. By then, of course, I'll be gone."

"And I'll see to it that your successor has no religious affiliations," said Holmyard. "Forgive me, John, if I seem anticlerical to you. But I do believe that the horowitzes, if they develop a religion, should do it on their own."

"Then why not their speech and technology?"

"Because those are tools with which they may deal with their environment. They are things which, in time, they would have developed on lines similar to those of Earth."

"Do they not need a religion to ensure that they do not

misuse this speech and technology? Do they not need a code of ethics?"

Holmyard smiled and gave him a straight and long look. Carmody blushed and fidgeted.

"All right," said Carmody, finally. "I opened my big mouth and put both my feet in it. You don't need to recite the history of the various religions on Earth. And I know that a society may have a strong and workable code of ethics with no concept of a divinity who will punish transgressors temporally or eternally.

"But the point is, religions may change and evolve. The Christianity of the twelfth century is not exactly like that of the twentieth century, and the spirit of the religion of our time differs in more than one aspect from that of the twentieth. Besides, I wasn't intending to convert the horowitzes. My own Church wouldn't permit me to do so. All I have done so far is tell them that there is a Creator."

"And even that they misunderstood," said Holmyard, laughing. "They refer to God as He but classify Him as a female."

"The gender doesn't matter. What does is that I am in no position to reassure them of immortality."

Holmyard shrugged to indicate he couldn't see what difference it made. But he said, "I sympathize with your distress because it is causing you pain and anxiety. However, there is nothing I can do to help. And, apparently, your Church is not going to, either."

"I made a promise to Tutu," Carmody said, "and I don't want to break that. Then she would lose faith."

"Do you think they regard you as God?"

"Heaven forbid! But I must admit that I have worried about that happening. So far, there has been no indication on their part that they do so regard me."

"But what about after you leave them?" said Holmyard.

Carmody could not forget the zoologist's parting reply. He had no difficulty getting to sleep that night. For the first time since he had joined the group, he was allowed to sleep late. The sun had climbed halfway towards its zenith before he woke. And he found the partially constructed village in an uproar.

Not that of chaos but of purposeful action. The adults were standing around looking bewildered, but the young were very busy. Mounted on their horses, they were herding ahead of them, at the point of their spears, a group of strange horowitzes. There were some adults among these, but most were youngsters between the ages of seven and twelve.

"What mean what you do?" said Carmody indignantly to Tutu.

The smile-muscles around her beak wrinkled, and she laughed.

"You no here last night, so us no able to tell you what us planned to do. Anyway, nice surprise, heh? Us decide to raid them wild horowitzes that live near here. Us catch them sleeping; drive away adults, forced to kill some, too bad."

"And why you do this?" said Carmody, aware that he was about to lose his temper.

"You no understand? Me thinked you understand everything."

"Me no God," said Carmody. "Me telled you that often enough."

"Me forget sometimes," said Tutu, who had lost her smile. "You angry?"

"Me no angry until you tell me why you did this."

"Why? So us able to make us tribe bigger. Us teach the little ones how to talk. If them no learn, them grow up to become adults. And adults no learn how to talk. So them become like the beasts. You no want that, surely?"

"No. But you killed!"

Tutu shrugged. "What else to do? Them adults tried to kill us; us killed them, instead. Not many. Most runned off. Besides you say O.K. to kill animals. And adults same as animals because them no able to talk. Us no kill childs because them able to learn to talk. Us—what you say? adopt—yes, us adopt them. Them become us brothers and sisters. You telled me that every horowitz me brother and sister, even if me never see them."

She regained her smile and, bending eagerly towards him, she said, "Me haved a good thought while on raid. Instead of eating eggs that mothers hatch when no enough adults to attach eggs to, why not attach eggs to childs and to horses, and other animals, too? That way, us increase us tribe much faster. Become big fastly."

And so it was. Within a month's time, every horowitz large enough to carry the weight, and every horse, bore an egg on his/her chest.

Carmody reported this to Holmyard. "I see now the advantage of extra-uterine development of the embryo. If the unborn aren't as well protected from injury, it does furnish a means for a larger number to be born."

"And who's going to take care of all these young?" said Holmyard. "After all, the horowitz chick is as helpless as and requires as much care as the human infant."

"They're not going hog-wild. The number to be produced is strictly regulated. Tutu has it figured out how many chicks each mother can adequately care for. If the mothers can't furnish enough regurgitated food, they will prepare a paste of fruit and meat for the chicks. The mothers no longer have to spend a good part of their time hunting for food; the males are doing that now."

"This society of yours is not developing quite along the lines of those of Paleolithic Earth," said Holmyard. "I see an increase towards a communistic trend in the future. The children will be produced *en masse*, and their raising and education will have to be done collectively. However, at this stage, in order to gain a large enough population to be stable, it may be well for them to organize on an assembly-line basis.

"But there's one thing you've either not noticed or have purposely neglected to mention. You said attaching the eggs with be strictly regulated. Does that mean that any eggs for which there is no provision will be eaten? Isn't that a method of birth control?"

Carmody was silent for a moment, then he said, "Yes."

"Well?"

"Well, what? I'll admit I don't like the idea. But I don't have any justification for objecting to the horowitzes. These people don't have any Scriptural injunctions, you know. Not yet, anyway. Furthermore, under this system, many more will be given a chance for life."

"Cannibalism and birth control," said Holmyard. "I'd think you'd be glad to get out of this, John."

"Who's talking about the anthropocentric attitude now?" Carmody retorted.

Nevertheless, Carmody was troubled. He couldn't tell the horowitzes not to eat the surplus eggs, for they just would not have understood. Food wasn't so easy to get that they could pass up this source of supply. And he couldn't tell them that they were committing murder. Murder was the illegal slaying of a being with a soul. Did the horowitzes have souls? He didn't know. Terrestrial law maintained that the illegal killing of any member of a species capable of verbal symbolism was murder. But the Church, though it enjoined its members to obey that law or be punished by the secular government, had not admitted that that definition had a valid theological basis. The Church was still striving to formulate a rule which could be applied towards recognition of a soul in the extraterrestrial beings. At the same time, they admitted the possibility that sapients of other planets might not have souls, might not need them. Perhaps the Creator had made other provisions for assuring their immortality—if any.

"It's all right for *them* to sit around a table and discuss their theories," said Carmody to himself. "But I am in the field of action; I must work by rule of thumb. And God help me if my thumb slips!"

During the next month he did many things in the practical area. He arranged with Holmyard to send the ship to the Valley and there dig up and transport to the outskirts of the village several tons of iron ore. The following morning he took the children to the place where the ore lay. They gave cries of astonishment, cries which increased as he told them what they were to do with it.

"And where this iron ore come from?" asked Tutu.

"Mans bringed it from the Valley."

"On horses?"

"No. Them bringed it in a ship which comed from the stars. The same ship that carried me from the stars."

"Me able to see it some day?"

"No. You forbidden. No good for you to see it."

Tutu wrinkled her brow with disappointment and clacked her beak. But she made no further reference to it at that time. Instead, she and the others, with Carmody's help and some of the more cooperative adults, built furnances to smelt the ore. Afterwards, they built a furnace to add carbon from charcoal to the iron, and they made steel weapons, bridle braces and bits, and tools. Then they began to construct steel parts for wagons. Carmody had decided that it was time now to teach them to construct wagons.

"This fine," said Tutu, "But what us do when all the iron ore gone, and the steel us make rust and wear out?"

"There more in the Valley," said Carmody. "But us must go there. The starship bring no more."

Tutu cocked her head and laughed. "You shrewd man, John. You know how to get us to go to Valley."

"If us to go, us must get a move on soon," said Carmody. "Us must arrive before winter come and snow fall."

"Hard for any of us to imagine winter," she said. "This cold you talk about something us no able to understand."

Tutu knew what she was talking about. When Carmody

called another council and exhorted them to leave at once for the Valley, he met resistance. The majority did not want to go; they liked it too well where they were. And Carmody could see that, even among the horowitzes, and as young as they were, the conservative personality was the most numerous. Only Tutu and a few others backed Carmody; they were the radicals, the pioneers, pushers-ahead.

Carmody did not try to dictate to them. He knew he was held in high regard, was, in fact, looked upon almost as a god. But even gods may be resisted when they threaten creature comforts, and he did not want to test his authority. If he lost, all was lost. Moreover, he knew that if he became a dictator, these people would not learn the basics of democracy. And it seemed to him that democracy, despite its faults and vices, was the best form of secular government. Gentle coercion was to be the strongest weapon he would use.

Or so he thought. After another month of vainly trying to get them to make the exodus, he became desperate. By now the stick-in-the-muds had another argument. Under Carmody's tutelage, they had planted vegetable gardens and corn, the seeds of which came from seed brought by the supply ship on Carmody's request. If they moved now, they would not be able to profit by their hard work. All would go to waste. Why did Carmody have them break their backs digging and plowing and planting and watering and chasing off the wild life, if he intended them to move on?

"Because me wanted to show you *how* to grow things in the soil," he said. "Me no intend to remain with you forever. When us get to the Valley, me leave."

"No leave us, beloved John!" they cried. "Us need you. Besides, now us have another reason for no go to the Valley. If us no go, then you no leave us."

John had to smile at this childlike reasoning, but he became stern immediately thereafter. "Whether you go or no go, when this egg hatch, me go. In fact, me go now, anyway. You no go, me leave you behind. Me call on all of you who want to go with me to follow me."

And he gathered Tutu and eleven other adolescents, plus their horses, wagons, weapons, food, and twenty chicks and five adult females. He hoped that the sight of his leaving would cause the others to change their minds. But, though they wept and begged him to stay, they would not go with him.

It was then that he lost his temper and cried, "Very well! If you no do what me know the goodest for you to do, then me destroy you village! And you must come with me because you no have any place else to go!"

"What you mean?" they shouted.

"Me mean that tonight a monster from the stars come and burn up the village. You see!"

Immediately afterwards, he spoke to Holmyard. "You heard me, Doc! I suddenly realized I had to put pressure on them! It's the only way to get them off their fannies!"

"You should have done it long ago," replied Holmyard. "Even if all of you travel fast now, you'll be lucky to get to the Valley before winter."

That night, while Carmody and his followers stood on top of a high hill outside the village, they watched the spaceship suddenly appear in the dim light cast by the two small moons. The inhabitants of the village must all have been looking up for the promised destroyer, for a shriek from a hundred throats arose. Immediately, there was a mad rush through the narrow gates, and many were trampled. Before all the children, chicks, and adults could get out, the monster loosed a tongue of flame against the logwalls surrounding the village. The walls on the southern side burst into flame, and the fire spread quickly. Carmody had to run down the hill and reorganize the demoralized horowitzes. Only because he threatened them with death if they didn't obey him, would they go back into the enclosure and bring out the horses, wagons, food, and weapons. They then cast themselves at Carmody's feet and begged forgiveness, saying they would never again go against his wishes.

And Carmody, though he felt ashamed because he had scared them so, and also distressed because of the deaths caused by the panic, nevertheless was stern. He forgave them but told them that he was wiser than they, and he knew what was good for them.

From then on, he got very good behavior and obedience from the adolescents. But he had also lost his intimacy with them, even with Tutu. They were all respectful, but they found it difficult to relax around him. Gone were the jokes and smiles they had formerly traded.

"You have thrown the fear of God into them," said Holmyard.

"Now, Doc," said Carmody. "You're not suggesting that they think I am God. If I really believed that, I'd disabuse them."

"No, but they believe you're His representative. And maybe a demi-god. Unless you explain the whole affair from the beginning to end, they'll continue to think so. And I don't think the explanation will help much. You'd have to outline our society in all its ramifications, and you've neither the time nor ability to do that. No matter what you said, they'd misunderstand you."

Carmody attempted to regain his former cordial relations with them, but he found it impossible. So he devoted himself to teaching them all he could. He either wrote or else dicated to Tutu and other scribes as much science as he had time for. Though the country they had crossed so far was lacking in any sulfur or saltpeter deposits, Carmody knew that the Valley contained them. He wrote down rules for recognizing, mining, and purifying the two chemicals and also the recipe for making gunpowder from them. In addition, he described in great detail how to make rifles and pistols and mercury fulminate, how to find and mine and process lead.

These were only a few of the many technological crafts he recorded. In addition, he wrote down the principles of chemistry, physics, biology, and electricity. Furthermore, he drew diagrams of an automobile which was to be driven by electric motors and powered by hydrogen-air fuel cells. This necessitated a detailed procedure for making hydrogen by the reaction of heated steam with zinc or iron as a catalyst. This, in turn, demanded that he tell them how to identify copper ore and the processes for refining it and making it into wire, how to make magnets, and the mathematical formulae for winding motors.

To do this, he had to call frequently on Holmyard for help. One day, Holmyard said, "This has gone far enough, John. You're working yourself to a shadow, killing yourself. And you're attempting to do the impossible, to compress one hundred thousand years of scientific progress into one. What it took humanity a hundred millennia to develop, you're handing to the horowitzes on a silver platter. Stop it! You've done enough for them by giving them a speech and techniques in working flint and agriculture. Let them do it on their own from now on. Besides, later expeditions will probably get into contact with them and give them all the information you're trying to forcefeed them."

"You are probably right," groaned Carmody. "But what bothers me most of all is that, though I've done my best to give them all I can to enable them to deal with the material universe, I've done scarcely anything to give them an ethics. And that is what I should be most concerned with."

"Let them work out their own."

"I don't want to do that. Look at the many wrong, yes, evil, avenues they could take."

"They will take the wrong ones, anyway."

"Yes, but they will have a right one which they can take if they wish."

"Then, for Christ's sake, give it to them!" cried Holmyard. "Quit belly-aching! Do something, or shut up about it!"

"I suppose you're right," said Carmody humbly. "At any rate, I don't have much time left. In a month, I have to go to Wildenwooly. And this problem will be out of my hands."

During the next month, the party left the hot plains and began to travel over high hills and through passes between mountains. The air became cooler, the vegetation changed to that which superficially resembled the vegetation of the uplands of Earth. The nights were cool, and the horowitzes had to huddle around roaring fires. Carmody instructed them how to tan skins with which to clothe themselves, but he did not allow them to take time out to hunt and skin the animals and make furs from them. "You able to do that when you reach the Valley," he said.

And, two weeks before they were to reach the pass that would lead them to the Valley, Carmody was awakened one night. He felt a tap-tapping in the egg on his chest and knew that the sharp beak of the chick was tearing away at the double-walled leathery covering. By morning a hole appeared in the skin of the egg. Carmody did what he had observed the mothers do. He grabbed hold of the edges of the tear and ripped the skin apart. It felt as if he were ripping his own skin, so long had the egg been a part of him.

The chick was a fine healthy specimen, male, covered with a golden down. It looked at the world with large blue eyes which, as yet, were uncoordinated.

Tutu was delighted. "All of us have brown eyes! Him the first horowitz me ever see with blue eyes! Though me hear that the wild horowitzes in this area have blue eyes. You make him eyes blue so us know him you son?"

"Me have nothing to do with it," said Carmody. He did not say that the chick was a mutation, or else had carried recessive genes from mating by ancestors with a member of the blue-eyed race. That would have required too lengthy an explanation. But he did feel uncomfortable. Why had this happened to the chick that *he* was carrying?

By noon the tendrils holding the egg to his flesh had dried up and the empty skin fell to the ground. Within two days, the many little holes in his chest had closed; his skin was smooth.

He was cutting his ties to this world. That afternoon, Holmyard called him and said that his request for an extension of his stay on Feral had been denied. The day his contract ended, he was to leave.

"According to our contract, we have to furnish a ship to transport you to Wildenwooly," said Holmyard. "So, we're using our own. It'll take only a few hours to get you to your destination."

During the next two weeks, Carmody pushed the caravan, giving it only four hours sleep at night and stopping only when the horses had to have rest. Fortunately, the equine of Feral had more endurance, if less speed, than his counterpart on Earth. The evening of the day before he had to leave, they reached the mountain pass which would lead them to the promised Valley. They built fires and bedded down around the warmth. A chilly wind blew from the pass, and Carmody had trouble getting to sleep. It was not so much the cold air as it was his thoughts. They kept going around and around, like Indians circling a wagon train and shooting sharp arrows. He could not keep from worrying about what would happen to his charges after he left them. And he could not quit regretting that he had not given them any spiritual guidance. Tomorrow morning, he thought, tomorrow morning is my last chance. But my brain is numb, numb. If it were left up to me, if my superiors had not ordered me to be silent . . . but then they know best. I would probably do the wrong thing. Perhaps it is best to leave it up to divine revelation. Still, God works through man, and I am a man. . . .

He must have dozed away, for he suddenly awakened as he felt a small body snuggling next to his. It was his favorite, Tutu.

"Me cold," she said. "Also, many times, before the village burn, me sleep in your arms. Why you no ask me to do so tonight? You last night!" she said with a quavering voice, and she was crying. Her shoulders shook, and her beak raked across his chest as she pressed the side of her face against him. And, not for the first time, Carmody regretted that these creatures had hard beaks. They would never know the pleasure of soft lips meeting in a kiss.

"Me love you, John," she said. "But ever since the monster from the stars destroyed us village, me scared of you, too. But tonight, me forget me scared, and me must sleep in you arms once more. So me able to remember this last night the rest of me life."

Carmody felt tears welling in his own eyes, but he kept his voice firm. "Them who serve the Creator say me have work to do elsewhere. Among the stars. Me must go, even if no wish to. Me sad, like you. But maybe someday me return. No able to promise. But always hope."

"You no should leave. Us still childs, and us have adults work ahead of us. The adults like childs, and us like adults. Us need you."

"Me know that true," he said. "But me pray to He that He watch over and protect you."

"Me hope He have more brains than me mother. Me hope He smart as you."

Carmody laughed and said, "He is infinitely smarter than me. No worry. What come, come."

He talked some more to her, mainly advice on what to do during the coming winter and reassurances that he might possibly return. Or, if he did not, that other men would. Eventually, he drifted into sleep.

But he was awakened by her terrified voice, crying in his ear.

He sat up and said, "Why you cry, child?"

She clung to him, her eyes big in the reflected light of the dying fire. "Me father come to me, and him wake me up! Him say, 'Tutu, you wonder where us horowitzes go after death! Me know, because me go to the land of beyond death. It a beautiful land; you no cry because John must leave. Some day, you see him here. Me allowed to come see you and tell you. And you must tell John that us horowitzes like mans. Us have souls, us no just die and become dirt and never see each other again.'

"Me father told me that. And him reached out him hand to touch me. And me become scared, and me waked up crying!"

"There, there," said Carmody, hugging her. "You just dream. You know you father no able to talk when him alive. So how him able to talk now? You dreaming."

"No dream, no dream! Him not in me head like a dream! Him standing outside me head, between me and fire! Him throw a shadow! Dreams no have shadows! And why him no able to talk? If him can live after death, why him no talk, too? What you say, 'Why strain at a bug and swallow a horse?'"

"Out of the mouths of babes," muttered Carmody, and he spent the time until dawn talking to Tutu.

At noon of that same day, the horowitzes stood upon the rim of the pass. Below them lay the Valley, flashing with the greens, golds, yellows, and reds of the autumnal vegetation. In a few more days the bright colors would turn brown, but today the Valley glittered with beauty and promise.

"In a few minutes," said Carmody, "the mans from the skies come in the starwagon. No become frightened; it will not harm you. Me have a few words to say, words which me hope you and you descendants never forget.

"Last night, Tutu seed her father, who had died. Him telled her that all horowitzes have souls and go to another place after them die. The Creator have marked a place for you—so say Whoot—because you He's childs. He never forget you. And so you must become good childs to He, for He . . ."

Here he hesitated, for he had almost said Father. But, knowing that they had fixed in their minds the maternal image, he continued . . . "for He you Mother.

"Me have telled you the story of how the Creator maked the world from nothing. First, space. Then, atoms created in space. Atoms joined to become formless matter. Formless matter becomed suns, big suns with little suns circling around them. The little suns cooled and becomed planets, like the one you now live on. Seas and land formed.

"And He created life in the seas, life too small to see with the naked eye. But He see. And some day you, too, see. And out of the little creatures comed big creatures. Fish comed into being. And some fish crawled onto the land and becomed airbreathers with legs.

"And some animals climbed trees and lived there, and their forelimbs becomed wings, and they becomed birds and flyed.

"But one kind of tree-creature climbed down out of the trees before it becomed a bird. And it walked on two legs and what might have becomed wings becomed arms and hands.

"And this creature becomed you ancestor.

"You know this, for me have telled you many times. You know you past. Now, me tell you what you must do in the future, if you wish to become a good child of He. Me give you the law of the horowitz.

"This what He wish you to do every day of you lives.

"Love you Creator even gooder than you own parents.

"Love each other, even the one who hate you.

"Love the animals, too. You able to kill animals for food. But no cause them pain. Work the animals, but feed them and rest them well. Treat the animals as childs.

"Tell the truth. Also, seek hard for the truth.

"Do what society say you must do. Unless society say what He no wish you to do. Then, you may defy society.

"Kill only to keep from becoming killed. The Creator no love a murderer or a people who make war without good cause.

"No use evil means to reach a good goal.

"Remember that you horowitzes no alone in this universe. The universe filled with the childs of He. Them no horowitzes, but you must love them, too.

"No fear death, for you live again."

John Carmody looked at them for a moment, wondering upon what paths of good and of evil this speech would set them. Then he walked to a large flat-topped rock on which sat a bowl of water and a loaf of bread made from baked acorn flour.

"Each day at noon, when the sun highest, a male or female choosed by you must do this before you and for you."

He took a piece of bread and dipped it in the water and ate the piece, and then he said, "And the Choosen One must say so all able to hear,

"'With this water, from which life first comed, me thank me Creator for life. And with this bread, me thank me Creator for the blessings of this world and give me self strength against the evils of life. Thanks to He.'"

He paused. Tutu was the only one not looking at him, for she was busily writing down his words. Then, she looked up at him as if wondering if he meant to continue. And she gave a cry and dropped her pencil and tablet and ran to him and put her arms around him.

"Starship come!" she cried. "You no go!"

There was a moan of fear and astonishment from the beaks of the crowd as they saw the shining monster hurtle over the mountain towards them.

Gently, Carmody loosed her embrace and stepped away from her.

"Come a time when the parent must go, and the child must become adult. That time now. Me must go because me wanted elsewhere.

"Just remember, me love you, Tutu. Me love all of you, too. But me no able to stay here. However, He always with you. Me leave you in the care of He."

Carmody stood within the pilothouse and looked at the image of Feral on the screen. It was now no larger to him than a basketball. He spoke to Holmyard.

"I will probably have to explain that final scene to my superiors. I may even be severely rebuked and punished. I do not know. But I am convinced at this moment that I did rightly."

"You were not to tell them they had a soul," said Holmyard. "Not that I myself care one way or another. I think the idea of a soul is ridiculous."

"But you can think of the idea," said Carmody. "And so can the horowitzes. Can a creature capable of conceiving a soul be without one?"

"Interesting question. And unanswerable. Tell me, do you really believe that that little ceremony you instituted will keep them on the straight and narrow?"

"I'm not all fool," said Carmody. "Of course not. But they do have correct basic instruction. If they pervert it, then I am not to blame. I have done my best."

"Have you?" said Holmyard. "You have laid the foundations for a mythology in which you may become the god, or the son of the god. Don't you think that, as time blurs the memory of these events you initiated, and generations pass, that myth after myth and distortion after distortion will completely alter the truth?"

Carmody stared at the dwindling globe. "I do not know. But I have given them something to raise them from beasts to men."

"Ah, Prometheus!" breathed Holmyard. And they were silent for a long time.

The Blasphemers

I

Twelve thousand ancestors looked down on him.

Jagu stopped for a moment. Despite his skepticism, he could not help being impressed and even a little guilty. Twelve thousand! If there were such things as ghosts, what a might of phantoms was massed in this dark and holy chamber! How intense would be their assembled hatred, focused on him!

He was on the ground floor of the castle and in the Room of the Hero-Fathers. A hundred feet square, it was at this moment lit by a few electric flambeaux. A tremendous fireplace was at one end. In it, in the old days, the greatest enemy of the Wazaga, Ziitii of the Uruba clan, had been burned alive after the Battle of Taaluu. Above the mantel were the trophies of that battle: swords, shields, lances, maces and several flintlock blunderbusses.

Beyond this room, deeper in the castle, was a room decorated with the accumulated trophies of a thousand years. Beyond that was another in which the skulls and preserved heads of fallen enemies stared out from niches, above plates bearing their names and the date and place of death. Nowadays, the door to the room was kept locked out of deference to modern sensibilities. It was opened only to historians and anthropologists or during the clan Initiations, the Greeting of Ghosts.

Three nights ago, Jagu had been locked for twelve hours, all alone in that room.

That was the trouble, thought Jagu, as he turned away

and walked softly on four bare paws towards the dark anteroom. The Ghosts, the Hero-Fathers, had not greeted him. There had not been any.

He could not tell his four parents that. It was impossible to acknowledge that his ancestors had scorned him, that they thought him unworthy of the name of *joma*—"man." Not that he thought that the Heroes had scorned him.

What does not exist cannot scorn.

His parents did not know that. They had been elated because he had been one of the few to graduate from the space-navy Academy of Vaagii. They were happy to put their eldest son through the long-awaited initiation into adulthood. But they had not been so happy when he said that he was not yet ready to choose a group-mate from the eligible members of the clan. All four pleaded with him, threatened him, stormed. He must get married before he left for the stars. He must ensure the perpetuation of their line, leave many eggs in the hatchery before he assumed his duties as a spacer.

Jagu had said no.

Now, he was sneaking out late at night, and he had run the gauntlet of the twelve thousand. But . . . they were only squares of canvas or wood on which various colored oils had been arranged in different patterns. That was all.

He paused by a tall wallmirror. The lights behind him shone gloomily in it. He looked like a ghost stepping out of the dark past towards himself, and where his two selves met . . .

Six and a half feet tall he stood. His vertical torso was humanoid. At a distance, and in a dim light, if all but the forward breasts upwards had been hidden, he could have been mistaken for a human being. But his pinkish skin was hidden up to the neck with a golden pile of short curling hairs. The head was very broad and round and massively boned. The cheekbones bulged like bosses on a shield. The jawbone was very thick; the deeply cleft chin was a prow. (The latter was another sore point. His parents did not like it that he had shaved off the goatee.)

The nose was bulbous and covered with tiny bristling blackish hairs. The supraorbital ridges flared out Gothicly. The eyes beneath were large, hazel and rimmed with a half-inch wide circle of brown hair. The ears were shaped like a cat's, and the yellow hair on top of his head stood straight up.

At the base of the spine of his upper torso was a device of bone, a natural universal joint that permitted the upper torso a ninety-degree description forward. The lower torso was quadrupedal, as if he had only half evolved. The legs and paws were lion-shaped; his long tail was tufted at the end with black hair.

Jagu had the normal vanity of a youth. He thought he was rather good-looking, and he did not mind examining himself. The string of diamonds hanging from around his neck was magnificent, as was also the gold plate at its end. On the plate was a design formed of diamonds in the shape of a lightning streak, his totem.

Though he enjoyed the view, he could not stay there forever. He passed through a doublepointed arch into the anteroom. As he neared the door, he saw a big mound of fur rise and shake itself and slowly form into a six-legged animal with a long bushy tail, a sharp pointed nose, and great round scarlet ears. The rest of the *siygeygey* was, except for the black nose and round black eyes, a chocolate brown.

It rumbled in its massive chest. Then, recognizing Jagu with its nose, it whined a little and wagged its tail.

Jagu patted it and said, "Go back to sleep, Aa. I'm not taking you hunting tonight."

The animal slumped into amorphous shagginess. Jagu pointed the key at the lock and pressed on the end.

Just after dinner, he had deftly removed the key from its hook on the belt of Timo. Since another parent, Washagi, had locked the front door, Timo had not missed the key.

Jagu regretted having to do this, though he did get a thrill out of being a successful pickpocket. But he saw no sense in the custom of refusing a youth his own key until he had become married. He wanted to go out late that night. If he could not get permission, he would go without it.

The door swung open. He stepped quickly outside, and the door closed.

Ten years ago he would have had to bribe or sneak past the Watcher of the Door. Now doormen were of the past. They could make more money working in the factories. The last of the family retainers had died some years ago; his place was taken by an electronic device.

A full late-summer moon shone at zenith. It cast green-silver nets everywhere and caught shadows gaunt and grotesque. These were the towering diorite statues of the greatest Heroes on the broad lawn, the hundred-odd whose fighting fury had made the name of Wazaga famous.

He did not pause to look at them, for he feared that an awe and dread left over from childhood might influence him. Instead he looked upward, where a score of joma-made satellites raced brightly across the night sky. He thought of the hundreds he could not see, of the space-navy ships patrolling the reaches between the planets of the system, and of the few interstellar ships out there, probing the galaxy.

"What a contrast!" he murmured. "On this earth, dumb stone sculptures rule the minds of a people who can go to the stars!"

He walked into a dark spot at the foot of the castle wall, an opening to a tunnel that led at a sharp slope downward. Formerly this area had been the moat. Then the moat was filled in. Later the excavation was dug and lined with cement. At its end lay the underground garage.

Here Jagu used the key to open the door again, and he entered. He did not hesitate making a choice among the six vehicles. He wanted the long low sleek Firebird. This was last year's model, one electric motor per wheel, one hundred horsepower per motor, stick-controlled, with a bubble-top, holding four passengers. It was painted fiery red.

Jagu lifted the bubble-top and stepped over the low side onto the floor. He squatted down behind the instrument panel, his rump against a thick cushion attached to a vertical steel plate. Then he pulled the bubble down. This was secured by magnetic clamps to the chassis. A separate and small motor provided the power for the electro-magnets.

He flicked a toggle switch, and the *on* indicator lit up. The big hydrogen tank was full. He pulled out the sliding panel with its three small sticks and pushed forward on one.

Silently the Firebird rolled forward and up the ramp. As its rear cleared the garage, Jagu pressed a button and the iris of the garage door closed. The Firebird cruised down the driveway, past the stone ancestors and then turned to the right onto the private highway. This led him winding through the forest of *wexa* (scarlet pinoids) for about a mile. Only when he turned onto the public high-way, which inclined downwards at this point, did he push the speed-stick forward as far as it would go. The column of the velocity indicator, an instrument like a thermometer, showed 135 mph attained in twenty seconds.

II

He shot up and over the top of the hill and had to swerve violently to the left to pass a big cargo truck. But there were no approaching lights, and his horn, honking like a goose, answered the truckdriver's furious blasts.

He wished that these were the old days. Then when an aristocrat wanted to travel without obstacle he notified the police. They went ahead to clear the road. Now, to keep the ancient privilege in force would disrupt the heavy flow of commerce. Business came first; so he must take his chances like any one else. He was not, like his ancestors, immune from arrest if he ran over someone or forced somebody off the road. He was even supposed to obey the speed laws. Usually he did . . . but tonight he did not feel like it.

He passed a dozen other vehicles, several of them the old internal-combustion type. After traveling for several miles, he slowed enough to turn onto another private road with some screeching of tires and fishtailing.

He drove for a quarter of a mile, then stopped. Here he picked up Alaku. They gave each other a brief kiss. Alaku then jumped into the car beside Jagu and braced his rump against the plate; the bubble closed, the car turned around and they sped away.

Alaku unhooked a flask from his belt, unscrewed the top and offered Jagu a drink. Jagu stuck his tongue out, signifying a negative reply, so Alaku tipped the bottle to his own lips.

After gulping several times he said, "My parents were after me again to know why I didn't pick a mate-group."

"So?"

"So I suggested that I marry you and Fawani and Tuugee. You should have heard the gasping, the choking, seen the red faces, the bristling tails, the flying fingers. And heard the words! I calmed them down somewhat be telling them that I was only joking, of course. Nevertheless, I had to hear a long and hot lecture on the degeneracy of modern youth, its flippancy, its near-blasphemy. On how humor was a very good thing, but there were some things too sacred to joke about. And so on and on. If the lower classes wanted to forget about clan distinctions and marry just anybody, that was to be expected. What with increasing industrialization, and urbanization, mass migrations, modern mobility and so forth, the proletariat couldn't keep the clan lines straight. And it did not matter with them. But with us jorutama, the aristoi, it mattered very much. Where would society, religion, government, etc., be if the great clans let everything slide into chaos? Especially, if our clan, the Two-Fanged Eagles, set a bad example for the rest? You've heard the same thing."

Jagu sucked his breath inwards sharply with assent, and said, "A million times. Only I'm afraid I shocked my parents even more. Questioning marriage lines is bad enough. But to suggest that belief in ancestral ghosts just might—just barely might—*not* be true, might be a hang-over from the old superstitious days . . . well, you've no idea of outraged parenthood until you've hinted at that. I had to undergo a ceremonial purification—an expensive one for the family and a tiring one for me. Also I had to spend four hours locked up in a cell in the dungeon, and I had to listen to sermons and prayers piped into my cell. No way of turning the abominable stuff off. But the chanting did help me to sleep."

"Poor Jagu," said Alaku, and he patted Jagu's arm.

A few minutes later they hurtled over a hilltop and saw, a mile away at the bottom of the long hill, twin beams of light from a car parked by the roadside.

Jagu pulled up alongside the car. Two got out of it and walked into his Firebird: Fawani and Tuugee. Fawani of the Tree Lion clan and Tuugee of the Split-tongue Dragons. All gave each other a kiss. Then, Jagu drove back to the highway and, in a short time, had it whistling at full speed.

"Where are we meeting tonight?" said Tuugee. "I didn't get the message until late. Fawani phoned, but I had to make small talk and avoid saying anything about tonight. I think my parents are monitoring my calls. The Dragons have always had a reputation for excessive suspiciousness. In this case, they've good reason to be—though I hope they don't know it."

"We're going to the Siikii Monument tonight," said Jagu.

The others gasped. "You mean where the great battle was fought?" said Alaku. "Where our ancestors who fell in that battle are buried? Where . . ."

"Where the ghosts congregate every night and slay

those who dare walk among them?" said Jagu.

"But that's asking for it!" said Fawani.

"So we ask for it," said Jagu. "You don't really believe in all that tripe? Or do you? If so, you'd better get out now. Go home, ask at once for a ritual cleansing, take your beating. What we've done so far has been enough to stir up the ghosts—if any exist."

There was silence for a moment. Then Fawani said, "Pass the bottle, Alaku. I'll drink to defiance to the ghosts and to our everlasting love."

Jagu's laugh was hollow. He said, "A good toast, Fawani. But you'd better drink one to Waatii, the Hero of Speed. We're going to need his blessing, if he exists. Here comes a cop!"

The others turned to see what Jagu had detected in his rearview mirror. About a mile behind them, a yellow light was flashing off and on. Jagu flicked on a switch which brought in outside noises and turned the amplifier control. Now they could hear the barking of the highway patrolman's siren.

"One more ticket, and my parents will take the Firebird away from me," said Jagu. "Hang on."

He pressed a button. A light on the instrument panel lit up to indicate that shields were being lowered over the license plates.

He took the Firebird around a passenger vehicle, his horn blaring, while the approaching beams of another grew larger and larger. Just before collision seemed imminent, while the others in his car had broken into terrified calls to the ghosts of their ancestors to save them, he whipped in front of the car just passed. The cry of tires burning on the pavement came to them, and the gabble of the car they had just missed ramming keened away.

His passengers said nothing; they were too frightened to protest. Besides, they knew that Jagu would pay no attention to them. He would kill them and himself rather than allow them to be caught. And actually it was better to die than be exposed to a public scandal, the recriminations of their parents and the ritual cleansing.

Jagu drove for half a mile and overtook a lumbering semi-trailer. He could not pass on the left, for a string of twin beams, too near, told him that he would have to wait. If he did, the patrolman would be on them. So he passed on the right, on the shoulder of the road. Without slowing.

Fortunately the shoulder was comparatively smooth and wide. Just wide enough for the Firebird: an inch away from the right wheels, the shoulder fell off and began to slope ever more towards the perpendicular. At the bottom of the hill was a creek, silvery in the moonlight. It ran along a heavily wooded slope.

Alaku, looking out the bubble at the nearness of the hill, groaned. Then he lifted the bottle to his lips again. By the time he had taken a few deep swallows, Jagu had pulled around the truck.

Fawani, looking behind him, saw the patrol car pull up behind the truck. Then one beam appeared as the car began to make the same maneuver as Jagu's. But it disappeared; the cop had changed his mind and swung in behind the truck.

"He'll radio ahead," said Fawani. "Do you mean to crash a roadblock?"

"If I have to," said Jagu cheerily. "But the entrance to the Siikii Monument is only a half mile down the road."

"The cop'll know where we turned in," said Alaku.

Jagu switched off the lights, and they sped at 135 mph along the moonlit highway. He began to slow after a few seconds, but they were still traveling at 60 mph when he took the sideroad.

For a moment, all were sure that they were going to overturn—all except Jagu. He had practiced making this turn at least twenty times, and he knew exactly what he could do. He skidded, but he brought the Firebird out of it just in time to keep the rear from sideswiping a large tree. Then he was back on the road and building up speed on the narrow, treelined pavement.

This time he stopped accelerating at 90 mph and drove for a half mile, taking the twists and turns with the ease of much practice and familiarity with this road.

Suddenly he began slowing the car.

In another half mile, he had turned off the road and plunged into what looked to the others like a solid mass of trees. But there was a space between the trees, an aisle just wide enough for the Firebird to pass through without scraping the paint off the sides. And at the end of the dark aisle, another which turned at a forty-five degree angle. Jagu drove the car into the space there and turned off the power.

They sat there, breathing heavily, looking off through the trees.

From here they could not see the road itself, but they

could see the flashing yellow of the patrol car as it sped down the road toward the Siikii Monument.

"Isn't there danger he'll see the others there?" said Fawani.

"Not if they hid their cars like I told them to," said Jagu. He released the bubble, lifted it and jumped out of the car. Raising the trunk cover in the rear of the car, he said, "Give me a hand. I've got something to fool him when he comes back looking for our tracks on the roadside."

They climbed out and helped him lift a tightly rolled mass of green stuff. Under his orders, they carried it back to the point on the road at which they had turned off. After unrolling the stuff, they spread it out over the car tracks and smoothed it.

When they were done the area looked like smooth grass. There were even a few wild flowers—or what looked like wild flowers—sprouting up here and there among the grasses. Presently, from their hiding places behind trees, they saw the patrol car moving slowly back, its searchlight probing along the dirt and grass beside the pavement.

It passed, and soon they could see its lights no more.

Jagu gave the word, and they rolled the counterfeit grass into a tight bundle. Jagu had driven the car backward to the roadside while they were doing that. They placed the roll in the trunk, climbed back in, and Jagu drove off toward the Monument.

As they went along the twisting road, Fawani said, "If we hadn't been driving too fast, we could have avoided all this."

"And missed a lot of fun," said Jagu.

"The rest of you still don't understand," said Alaku. "Jagu doesn't care if we live or die. In fact, I sometimes think he'd just as soon die. Then his problems—and ours —would be over. Besides, he wants to make some sort of gesture at our parents and the society they represent— even if it's only outrunning a cop."

"Alaku's the cool, objective one," said Jagu. "He sits to one side and dissects the situation and the people involved. But, despite his often correct analysis, he never does anything about it. The Eternal Spectator."

"I'm not a leader," said Alaku somewhat coldly. "But I can take as much action as the next person. So far, I've participated quite fully. Have I ever failed to follow you?"

"No," said Jagu. "I apologize. I spoke from the back of my head. You know me; always too impulsive."

"No apology needed," said Alaku, his voice warming.

III

Then they were at the gateway to the Siikii Monument. Jagu drove the car past it and under some trees across the road. Other vehicles were parked there.

"All seven here," he said.

They recrossed the road to a point about forty yards south of the main gate. Jagu called softly. A voice replied softly; and a moment later a flexible plastic rope was thrown over the gate.

Jagu was pulled up the twenty-feet high stone wall first, with much difficulty because of the leocentauroid construction of his body. On the other side, he found Ponu of the Greentail Shrike clan waiting for him. They embraced.

After the others had descended and the rope was pulled back over the wall, they walked softly toward the assignation point. The stone statues of their great and glorious ancestors stared down at them. These were dedicated to the fallen of the Battle of Siikii, the last major conflict of the last civil war of their nation. That had occurred one hundred and twenty years before, and the ancestors of some of those assembled tonight had fought and slain each other then. It was this war that had killed off so many of the aristoi that the lower classes had been able to demand certain rights and privileges denied them. It was also this war that had accelerated the growth of the fledgling Industrial Age.

The youths walked past the frowning Heroes and the pillars that marked various heroic exploits during the battle. All but Jagu showed a restraint in the overwhelming presence of the heads. He chattered away in a low but confident voice. Before they had reached the center of the Monument, the others were also talking and even laughing.

Here, in the center, where the battle had been decided, was the most sacred of all sites in this area. Here was the colossal statue of *Joma*, the eponymous ancestor of the joma species.

The statue was carved out of a single mass of diorite and painted with colors that imitated those of the living joma. It had no upper torso nor arms, only the head and neck attached to the quadrupedal body. The holy scriptures of the joma, the Book of Mako, said that Joma had once been like his descendants. But in return for the power of sentience and for the privilege of seeing his young become the dominant species of this world, and eventually of the universe, he had surrendered his arms, become like a crippled beast. Pleased by this sacrifice, Tuu-God had allowed Joma to reproduce parthenogenetically, without the aid of the other three mates. (Since Joma was the surviving member of his kind after Tuu had, in a fit of righteous anger, killed most beings, Joma had no other partners.)

It was here that Jagu had decided to hold the love feast. He could not have picked a place more appropriate to show his contempt for the ghosts and for the beliefs that the entire population of the planet held sacred.

Jagu and his friends greeted those waiting for them. Drinks were passed around along with jests. Ponu was that night's administrator. He had spread the carpets and placed the food and drinks on them—eight carpets, and four joruma sat on each.

As the night passed, and the moon reached its zenith and began to sink, the talking and laughing became louder and thicker. Then Jagu took a large bottle from Ponu, unscrewed the cap and went among the group. He gave each one a large pill from the bottle. Each swallowed it under his watchful eye. They made faces of repulsion, and Fawani almost threw his up. But he managed to keep it down when Jagu threatened to ram it down with his paw if Fawani didn't do the job himself.

After that Jagu made a mock prayer to Mako, a parody of the one that newly married quartets made their particular household clan-Hero of Fertility. He ended by taking a swig from a bottle of wine and then smashing the bottle against the face of Joma.

An hour later the first round of the love feast had been completed. The participants were resting, getting ready for the next round, and discussing the beauty and the minor disappointments of the last congress.

A whistle blew shrilly.

Jagu sprang to his feet. "The cops!" he said. "All right, everybody, don't panic! Get your headpieces and breastplates. Don't bother to put them on yet. Leave the carpets here; they haven't got any clan insignias on them. Follow me!"

The statue of Joma stood on a small hill in the center

of the Monument. It was this advantage in viewing that had determined Jagu's choice of site, in addition to his purpose of making the greatest blasphemy of all. He could see that the main gateway was open, and several cars with beams burning had just come through it. There were three other gates; all but one was also open and cars coming through them. Probably, he thought, that gate had been left closed to lure them toward it. Once over it, they would find the police waiting for them beside the wall.

But if this were a trap, then the police would have observed them hide their cars in the brush. That meant that even if he and his friends eluded the cops, they would all have a long, long walk home. A useless walk, because the police would have no trouble determining and finding the owners.

There was a chance that this was not a prepared ambush. The patrolman who had chased them might have been suspicious and brought back other police. They could have climbed the walls, seen the group under Joma and decided to swoop in now. If so, it was also possible that they did not have enough personnel to come in through all the gates.

The unguarded fourth gate could be an escape route.

Almost he decided to make a run for the closed gate. But if he did so, and he was wrong, he would lead his friends to ruin. Whereas he had prepared some time ago a hiding place within the Monument grounds itself.

It would be foolish to take a chance on an unknown when he had something that was nearly one hundred per cent sure.

"Follow me to Ngiizaa!" he said. "Run, but don't panic. If anyone falls or gets into difficulty, call out. We'll stop to help you."

He began running; behind him was the thud of paws and the harsh breathing of stress.

They went down the hill on the side opposite the main gateway and toward the granite statue of the Hero Ngiizaa. Jagu looked around and noted that the other statues should hide them from the approaching policemen. He had chosen Ngiizaa because there was a ring of statues around it, marking where Ngiizaa had fallen inside a pile of his enemy's bodies. It took sixty seconds to get there from the center of the Monument, plenty of time to open the trapdoor at the base of Ngiizaa and for all of them to crowd into the hole beneath.

Over a year ago, Jagu and some of the others, working on moonless or cloudy nights, had dug out the hole. Then they had placed the beams which supported the trapdoor and put sod over it. The trapdoor was solid; he and five others had stood on it to test its weight and make sure that, on the days when crowds came to visit, the door would not betray its presence by bending.

Now he and three others began rolling the sod back. The strip was narrow; it did not take long to do the job. Then, while he held the door up, the others jumped into the hole beneath and went to the back of the hole to make room for those following.

By the time all except himself were in, the police cars had reached the center. Their searchlights began probing the Monument.

He had to drop down and lie motionless while several beams in turn sprayed the circle of statues. When they had passed he leaped up. Alaku, below, held the trapdoor up just far enough for him to squeeze through. He had replaced the sod on top of it.

This was the ticklish part of the whole procedure. No one could be left above to smooth the sod and make sure that the ragged edges did not show. But he did not think that the police could conceive of such a hiding place. When they started to make a search on paw, using their flashlights, they would expect to flush out the members of the party from behind individual statues. Their lights would play swiftly over the grass; they would be looking for youths lying flat on the grass, not for hidden trapdoors.

It was hot and crowded in the hole. Jagu hoped they would not have to wait too long. Zotu had a mild case of claustrophobia. If he started to panic, he'd have to be knocked out for the good of everybody.

The luminous face of his wrist watch showed 15:32. He'd give the cops an hour to search before deciding that the party had somehow gotten over the wall and away. After that, he would lead his friends out of the hole. If the police had not left somebody to watch the road, or if they did make a determined search of the woods nearby and found the hidden cars, then all would go well. Many ifs . . . but it was exciting.

A few minutes later, somebody stepped hard on the trapdoor.

Jagu suppressed a groan. If the cop heard the hollow

sound . . . but that was unlikely. They should be shouting at each other.

There was another rap as if somebody were stomping his feet on the trapdoor. Then, while he held his breath and hoped the others would not cough or make any other noise, he heard something grate against wood.

The next moment, the door swung up slowly. A harsh voice said. "All right, boys. The game's up. Come out. Don't try anything. We'll shoot you."

IV

Later, in the cell, when he had time to think, Jagu wished that he had resisted. How much better to have been killed than to go through this!

He was in a small cell and alone. He had been there for he did not know how long. There were no windows, his watch had been taken away and he had no one to talk to.

Three meals were given to him through a little swinging door at the bottom of the large door. The tray was bolted to the door, and the food was placed in depressions. There was no cutlery; he had to eat with his fingers. Fifteen minutes after the tray swung inwards, it began to withdraw. No amount of tugging on his part could keep it from moving.

The cell itself was furnished simply. The bed was bolted to the floor and without blankets or pillows. There was a washbowl and an airblower with which to dry himself, and a hole in the floor to receive refuse. The walls were padded. He could not commit suicide if he wished to.

Sometime after the third meal, while he paced back and forth and wondered what punishment he would have to endure, what his companions were going through, what his parents knew and felt, the door opened.

It did so silently; he was not aware of it until he turned to pace back toward it. Two soldiers—not police—entered. Silently they escorted him out of the cell.

Neither were armed, but he had the feeling that they knew all about bare-hand-and-pawfighting, that they were experienced and that he would get badly hurt if he tried to attack them. He had no such intention. Not until he saw his way clear, anyway. As long as he was inside a building new to him, one that must be equipped with closed-circuit TV and electronic beams, he would be quiet.

Meanwhile . . .

He was taken down a long corridor and into an elevator.

The elevator was some time rising, but he had no way of telling how many stories they had gone up. Then it stopped, and he was taken down another long hall and then another. Finally they stopped before a door on which was incised, in the florid syllabary of a century ago, *Tagimi Tiipaaroozuu*. Head of Criminal Detection. Arigi, the man responsible for detection and arrest of criminals of stature, conducted his business here. Jagu knew him, for Arigi had been among the elders present at his Initiation. He was a fellow clansman.

Though Jagu's knees shook, he swore he would show no fear. When he was marched in, he knew that he would have to remind himself constantly that he was not afraid. Arigi sat on his haunches behind a huge crescent shaped desk of polished *bini* wood. He had a cold hard face that was made even more unreadable by the dark glasses he wore. On his head was the four-cornered tall-crowned hat of the High Police. His arms were covered with bracelets, most of which had been awarded him by the government for various services. In his right hand was a stiletto with a jeweled handle.

"It may interest you, fledgling," he said in a dry voice, pointing the stiletto at Jagu, "that you are the first of your fellows to be interviewed. The rest are still in their cells, wondering when the trial will commence.

"Tell me," he said so sharply that Jagu could not help flinching, "when did you first decide that the ghosts of your ancestors did not exist? Except as a primitive superstition, figments in the minds of fools?"

Jagu had decided not to deny any accusation that was true. If he were to suffer, so much the worse. But he would not degrade himself by lying or pleading.

"I've always thought so," he said. "When I was a child I may have believed in the existence of the spirits of my ancestors. But I do not remember it."

"And you were intelligent enough not to proclaim this disbelief publicly," said Arigi. He seemed to relax a trifle. But Jagu was sure that Arigi was hoping he too, would relax so that he could spring at him, catch him off guard.

He wondered if his words were being recorded, his

image being shown on a screen to his judges. He doubted that his trial for blasphemy would be made public. It would reflect too much discredit and dishonor on his clan, and they were powerful enough to suppress these things. Perhaps they might even have him in here merely to scare him, to make him repent. Then he would be let off with a reprimand or, more likely, be assigned to a desk job. Forever earthbound.

But no, blasphemy was not merely a crime against the people of this planet. It was a spit in the face of his ancestors. Only pain and blood could wipe out that insult; the ghosts would crowd around him while he screamed over a fire and would lap at the blood flowing from his wounds.

Arigi smiled as if he now had Jagu where he wanted him. He said, "Well, at least you're a cool one. You act as a Wazaga should. So far, anyway. Tell me, do all your friends also deny the existence of an afterlife?"

"You will have to ask them that yourself."

"You mean you do not know what they believe?"

"I mean that I will not betray them."

"But you betrayed them the moment you led them to the Siikii Monument to defile the Heroes with your illicit lovemaking and your blasphemous prayers," said Arigi. "You betrayed them the moment you first confided to them your doubts and encouraged them to express theirs. You betrayed them when you bought an unlawful contraceptive from criminals and fed it to your comrades before the orgy."

Jagu stiffened. If no one had talked, how did Arigi know all this?

Arigi smiled again, and he said, "You betrayed them more than you know. For instance, the *weefee* pill you gave them tonight had no potency at all. I had already ordered your source of supply to give you a pill that looked like and tasted like *weefee*. But it had no effect. A fourth of your friends must be pregnant right now. Maybe you, too."

Jagu was shaken, but he tried to hide the effect of Arigi's words. He said, "If you've known about us for a long time, why didn't you arrest us before?"

Arigi leaned his upper torso back and placed his fingers behind his head. He looked at a point above Jagu, as if his thoughts were there. He said slowly, and it seemed irrelevantly, "So far, we joruma have discovered exactly fifty-one planets which can support our type of life. Fifty-one out of an estimated 300,000 in this galaxy alone. Of the ones discovered—all found in the last twenty-five years—twelve were inhabited by a centauroid type of sentient, similar to us, five by a bipedal type, six by very weird sentients indeed. All of these intelligent beings are bisexual or, I should say, have a sexual bipolarity.

"None of them have our quadrupolar sexual makeup. If we extrapolate on what we have so far found, we could say that the centauroid type of body is that most favored by Tuu or, if you prefer, the old pagan Four Parents of Nature. The bipedal form is second. And Tuu alone knows what other exotic beings are scattered throughout the Cosmos.

"We could also speculate that Tuu, for some reason, has favored us with a monopoly on the quadrupolar method of reproduction. At least, we joruma are the only ones encountered so far with that method. Now, what does that suggest to you?"

V

Jagu was puzzled. This inquisition was not going on the lines he had anticipated. He was not getting a thundering denunciation, a blistering lecture, threats of physical and mental punishment, of death.

What was Arigi leading up to? Perhaps this line of conversation was intended to make him think that he was going to escape. Then Arigi would attack savagely when his defenses were lowered.

"The Book of Mako says that a joma is unique in this universe. That the joruma are fashioned in the shape of Tuu. No other creature in all the world—so said Mako—is favored of Tuu. We are chosen by him to conquer the Cosmos."

"So said Mako," replied Arigi. "Or whoever wrote the book which is supposed to be written by Mako. But I want to know what you think."

Now Jagu thought he knew what Arigi was trying to do to him. He was talking thus, leading him, so he could get him to admit his disbelief. Then Arigi would spring.

But why should Arigi bother? He had all the evidence.

"What do I think?" said Jagu. "I think it rather strange

that Tuu should have made so many differing sentient beings—that is, those intelligent enough to have language and to have a word for God in their languages—but only make one in Tuu's image. If he wanted all the planets to be eventually populated by the joruma, why did he create other beings on these planets? All of whom, by the way, think they have been formed in their Maker's image."

The two pairs of Arigi's eyelids had moved inwards so that only a sliver of pale green showed between them. He said, "You know that what you have said is enough to condemn you? That if I submit the evidence to the judges, you could be slowly burned alive? It's true that most blasphemers are killed quickly by being thrown into an intense furnace. But the law still stands. I would be within legal rights if I had you toasted so slowly that it would take you twelve hours or more to die."

"I know," said Jagu. "I had my fun with my friends; I spat at the ghosts. Now I have to pay."

Again Arigi seemed to start talking without relevance to the issue.

"Before Mako died, he said that his ghost would go forth through the cosmos, and he would place on other worlds a sign that the world was to be the possession of the joruma. Now, this took place 2500 years before space travel. Such a thing was not even dreamed of in his time.

"Yet when we reached the first inhabitable world, we found the sign he promised to leave behind him: The stone statue of Joma, our ancestor. It was carved by Mako to show that he had been there and had staked out this world for the faithful, for the joruma; and five others of the fifty-five so far found have thereon a giant stone statue of Joma.

"Tell me, how do you account for that?"

Jagu said, slowly, "Either Mako's ghost carved the image of Joma out of the native stone, or . . ."

He paused.

"Or what?"

Jagu opened his mouth, but the words came hard. He swallowed and forced them out.

"Or our spacemen carved those statues themselves," he said.

Arigi's reaction was not what Jagu had expected. Arigi

laughed loudly until his face was red. Finally, wheezing, wiping his eyes with a handkerchief, he said, "So! You guessed it! I wonder how many others have? And like you are keeping silent because of fear?"

He blew his nose and then continued, "Not many, I suppose. There are not too many born skeptics such as yourself. Or many as intelligent."

He looked curiously at Jagu. "You aren't happy to find yourself right? What's the matter?"

"I don't know. Maybe, though I disbelieved, I'd always hoped that my faith could be re-established. How much easier for me if it could be! If our spaceships had found the statues of Mako waiting for them, I'd have no choice but to believe . . ."

"No, you wouldn't," said Arigi sharply.

Jagu stared. "I wouldn't?"

"No! If all the evidence pointed toward the reality of Mako as a ghost, if the evidence were overwhelming, you still would not have believed. You would have found some rationalization for your disbelief. You would have said that the correct explanation or interpretation just wasn't available. And you would have continued to reject the idea of the ghost."

"Why?" said Jagu. "I'm a reasonable person; I'm rational. I think scientifically."

"Oh, sure," said Arigi. "But you were born an agnostic, a skeptic. You had the temperament of the disbeliever in the womb. Only by a violent perversion of your innate character could you have accepted religion. Most people are born believers; some are not. It's that simple."

"You mean," said Jagu, "that reality doesn't have a thing to do with it? That I think as I do, not because I have reasoned my way through the dark labyrinth of religion, but because my temperament made me think so?"

"That's an accurate statement."

"But—but—" said Jagu, "what you're saying is that there is no Truth! That the most ignorant peasant and fervent believer of ghosts has as much basis to his claims as I have to mine."

"Truth? There are truths and truths. You fall off a high cliff, and you accelerate at such and such a velocity until you hit the ground. Water, if not dammed, flows, downward. These are truths no one argues about. Temperament does not matter in physical matters. But in the realm of metaphysics, truth is an affair of natal prejudice. That is all."

Jagu had not been shaken by the thought of the fire and the death that waited for him. Now he was trembling, and outraged. Later he would be depressed. Arigi's cynicism made his look like a child's.

Arigi said, "The enlightened members—pardon me— the born skeptics of the aristoi have not believed in the existence of ghosts for some time. In a land crowded with the granite images of their illustrious ancestors, and crowded with worshippers of these sculptured stones, we laugh. But silently. Or only among ourselves. Many of us even doubt the existence of God.

"But we aren't fools. We suppress any show of public skepticism. After all, the fabric of our society is woven from the threads of our religion. It's an excellent means for keeping the people in line or for justifying our rule over them.

"Now, haven't you detected a certain pattern in the finding of the statues of Mako on the interstellar planes? In the particular type of planet on which the statues are?"

Jagu spoke slowly to control the shakiness of his voice.

"The images are not found on those planets populated by sentients technologically equal to us. Only on those planets with no sentients or with sentients having an inferior technology."

"Very good!" said Arigi. "You can see that that is no coincidence. We aren't about to wage war on beings who are able to retaliate effectively. Not yet, anyway. Now, I'll tell you why I revealed this to you—rather, confirmed your suspicions. Ever since we have had a faster-than-light drive, our interstellar exploratory ships have been manned with crews of a certain type. All are aristocrats, and all are disbelievers. They have had no compunction about chiseling statues out of the native rock on the appropriate planets."

"Why do they have to do this?" said Jagu.

"To establish a principle. To justify us. Some day, another sentient of equal, maybe superior, technological development will try to claim one of our planets for its own. When that day comes, we want our warriors and the people at home to be fired with a religious frenzy."

"You want me and my comrades to do this work for you?"

"For yourselves, too," said Arigi. "You young ones will have to take the reins of government after we're dead. And there's another factor. We're recruiting you because we need replacements. This is dangerous work.

Every now and then, a ship is lost. Just lost. Leaves port and is never heard of again. We need new interstellar spacers. We need you and your friends now. What do you say?"

"Is there a choice?" asked Jagu. "If we turn down your offer, what happens to us?"

"An accident," said Arigi. "We can't have a trial and execution. Not even in secret. Too much chance of dishonoring ancient and honorable clans."

"Very well. I accept. I can't speak for my friends, but I'll speak to them."

"I'm sure they'll see the light," said Arigi dryly.

VI

A few days later, Jagu flew to the school for advanced space-navy officers.

He and his friends began to take numerous training trips on ships that operated within the confines of the solar system. A year passed, and then they made three trips to nearby planetary systems under the tutelage of veterans. On the final voyage and the combat exercises that went with it, the veterans acted only as observers.

There was another ceremony. A new interstellar destroyer was commissioned and christened the *Paajaa*, and Jagu was given a captain's redstone to wear on the brim of his hat. The rest of the group also got various insignias of lesser ranks, for the craft was to be manned entirely by them.

Before leaving on the maiden voyage of the *Paajaa*, Jagu was summoned for one more interview with Arigi. By now Jagu knew that Arigi held more power than the public guessed. He was not only head of the planetary police system, he also was responsible for all military security systems.

Arigi welcomed Jagu as a member of the inner circle. He asked him to sit down and gave him a glass of *kusuto*. It was vintage of the best, thirty years old.

"You have added honor and luster to our clan," said Arigi. "The Wazaga can be proud of you. You were not given the captainship merely because you are a Wazaga, you know. A stellar ship is too expensive and important to be entrusted to a youth whose main ability is affiliation with a ruling group. You are a captain because you deserve the rank."

He sniffed at the bouquet of the wine and took a small sip.

Then he put the glass down, squinted at Jagu and said, "In a few days you will receive official orders to make your first exploratory voyage. Your ship will have enough fuel and supplies for a four-year trip, but you will be ordered to return at the end of two and a half, circumstances permitting. During that one and a quarter year, you will try to locate inhabitable planets. If any planet has sentients with a technology with space travel restricted to its system and atomic power, you will note its present development and its potential resistance to future attack by us. If the sentients have interstellar travel, you will observe as much as possible but will not place your ship in danger of attack. And you will return, after making the observations, directly and at full speed to us.

"If the sentients have an inferior technology, you will locate a site easily observable from orbit and will erect or carve an image of Mako there.

"Now! By the time you will have returned, many more eggs will have been hatched here. There will be a larger proportion of natal disbelievers among them than in the few years previously. By the time you are my age, the number of disbelievers will be a great problem. There will be strife, changing mores, doubt, perhaps even bloodshed. Before this occurs, before the change of *Zeitgeist* is on the side of the disbelievers and the faith in the Heroes and in Mako declines, we will have settled colonies on various planets uninhabited by sentients. We will also have wiped out or reduced greatly in number those sentients inferior to us. We will have started populating these with our kind. Because of our method of reproduction, we can populate a planet faster than any other sentient. And that is well, since we will need these colonies to aid us in the wars that will come.

"It is inevitable that we will have to fight cultures equal or perhaps even superior to ours. When that comes, we will have established the pattern—that we have a spiritual right to take anything we want. By then the weakened belief in the religion of our fathers will not affect our fighting zeal. We will be replacing it with another belief. Our right to conquest.

"Meanwhile, of course, I will be doing my best to suppress any resistance to our official religion. Those infidels among the aristoi will be indoctrinated in the proper attitude: a conscious hypocrisy. Those who nobly refuse will be dealt with in one way or another. The disbelievers among the lower classes will also be eliminated. They will be branded as criminals.

"But, of course, they can only fight the *Zeitgeist* so long. Then it takes over. By that time, I will have joined my ancestors, and my work will be done."

He smiled wryly and said, "I will be a ghost, perhaps, with a statue erected to me. However, by then my descendants—except for the inevitable ultrareactionaries—will regard my shrine as a historical or anthropological curiosity. I will have to go hungry among the other hungry ghosts—unhonored, unfed, wailing with weakness and impotent anger."

Jagu wondered if Arigi did not more than half-mean those words. He also wondered if Arigi was not as self-deceiving as those he laughed at. He was making his own, personal mythology to replace the old.

After all, what evidence did he really have to support his thesis that believers were born, not made?

A week later, he was on the Paajaa and had given the order to take it off. Another week, and his natal star was only one among many, a tiny glow. He was headed for the faroff and the unknown.

A year later, thirty stars later, they found two inhabitable planets. The second, like the first, rotated around a star of the Ao-U type. Unlike the first, it was the third planet from the star and it had sentients.

The *Paajaa* went into orbit in the upper atmosphere, and the telescopes were turned on the surface. The powers of magnification of the telescopes were so great that the spacers could see as distinctly as if they had been poised only twenty feet above the ground.

The sentients were bipedal and comparatively hairless except for thick growths on their heads or, among the males, on the faces. The majority covered their bodies with a variety of garments. Like the joruma, their skin colors and hair types varied; the darker ones were mainly in the equatorial zone.

Thousands of photographs were made during the orbitings of the *Paajaa*. Those taken of the groups that wore little or no clothing made it evident that these bipedals had only two sexes.

Another fact was determined. These sentients had no technology to be compared to the joruma's. They did not even have aircraft, except for a few balloons. Their main propulsive power was the steam engine. Steam drove engines of iron on iron tracks and paddlewheels or screws on ships. There were many sailships, also. The most formidable weapons were cannons and simple breech-loading rifles.

The aborigines were roughly at about the same stage the joruma had been about a century and a half ago.

VII

On their three hundredth orbit, Alaku made a shattering discovery.

He was looking at the scene projected on a large screen by a telescope when he cried out loudly. Those nearby came running, and they stopped when they saw what he was staring at. They too cried out.

By the time Jagu arrived, the scene was out of the telescope's reach. But he listened to their descriptions, and he ordered that the photos made be brought to him at once.

He looked at the photos, and he said, keeping his face immobile so that the others could not understand how shocked he was, "We'll have to go down and see for ourselves."

Four of them went down on the launch while the ship, in stationary orbit, stayed overhead. Their destination was on a rocky plateau about five miles southeast of the nearest city. The city was on the west bank of a great river that created a ribbon of greenery in the middle of the desert that covered much of the northern half of the continent. It was night, but a full moon shone in a cloudless sky. It illuminated brightly the three huge pyramids of stone and the object that had upset the crew of the Paajaa so much.

This lay in the center of a large quarry.

After hiding their ship in a deep and narrow ravine, the four proceeded in a small halftrack. A minute later, Jagu halted it, and all got out to look.

There was silence for a while. Then Jagu, speaking slowly as if hesitant to commit himself, said, "It seems to be Joma."

"It's ancient," said Alaku. "Very ancient. If Mako

made this, he must have done so immediately after dying. He must have come straight here."

"Don't jump to conclusions," said Jagu. "I was going to say that another ship had gotten here before us. But we know no ship has been sent to this sector. However . . ."

"However what?" said Alaku.

"As you said, it's ancient. Look at the ripples in the stone. They must have been made by erosion from blowing sand. Look at the face. It's shattered. Still, the natives of long ago could have made this. It's very possible."

Silent again, they re-entered the halftrack and began to drive slowly around the enormous statue.

"It faces the east," said Alaku. "Just as Mako said the statues of Joma would."

"Many primitive sentients on many worlds face their gods, their temples and their dead towards the east," said Jagu. "It's natural to regard the rising sun as the recurrent symbol of immortality."

Fawani said, "This may be the biggest reproduction of Joma. But it's not the only one on this world. The photos showed others. They too must be ancient. Perhaps it's only coincidence. The natives themselves made them. They're figures, symbols of their religion."

"Or," said Alaku, "the natives founded a religion that was based on Joma after Mako came here and carved this statue out of the rock. He may even have given them our religion. So, as you saw, they set up a temple before Joma. I'm sure that's what the ruins in front of the breasts were. They made other smaller images of Joma. Then ages later they ceased to believe in Joma . . . just as we are ceasing to believe. Yet the testimony to the truth was before their mocking eyes . . ."

Jagu knew they could not determine the truth no matter how long they speculated among themselves. The thing to do was to locate somebody who did know.

He turned the halftrack towards the city.

There were isolated houses on its outskirts. Before he had gone a mile, he found what he was looking for. A party of natives were headed towards him. All were riding beasts that looked very much like the *gapo* of the deserts of his own planet, except that these had only four legs and one hump.

The gapoids scattered in a panic; some threw their riders. The joruma shot these with gasdriven darts, the tips of which were coated with a paralyzing drug. After tearing the robes from his victims to make sure he had a specimen of each sex (for he knew that the zoologists at home would want to examine them) the joruma chose a male and a female. These were loaded into the halftrack, which then returned to the launch. In a few minutes, the launch was rising towards the *Paajaa*.

Back on the ship, the sleepers were placed on beds within a locked room. Jagu inspected them and, for the thousandth time, wondered if the joruma were not designed by Tuu to be superior. Perhaps they were really made in Tuu's image. These bipedals seemed to be so scrawny and weak and so inefficient, sexually speaking. One sex could never hatch an egg or bear young. This fault halved the species' chances of reproducing. Moreover, he thought, preserving humor even in his semi-stunned condition, it cut out three-quarters of the fun.

Maybe the other sentients were, as some theologians had theorized, experiments on Tuu's part. Or maybe Tuu had meant for non-joruma to be inferior.

Let the theologians speculate. He had a far more important and immediate enigma to solve. Also he had Alaku to worry about.

Alaku, the cool one, he whose only permanent passion was intellectualism, the agnostic, was by far the most shaken.

Jagu remembered Arigi's words. You believe what you want to believe. The metaphysical cannot be denied or affirmed in terms of the physical.

"It's a judgment," said Alaku. "We thought we were so clever and our fathers so ignorant and superstitious. But Mako knew that some day we would come here and find the truth. He knew it before our great-great-great-great-grandfathers were born."

"We have two natives," said Jagu. "We'll learn their language. From them we may discover who did carve out Joma—I mean that statue that seems to resemble Joma."

"How will they know?" said Alaku, looking desperate. "They will have only the words of their ancestors as testimony, just as we have the words of ours."

This was the last time Jagu talked to Alaku.

Shortly thereafter, Alaku failed to appear for his turn of duty on the bridge. Jagu called him over the intercom. Receiving no answer, he went to Alaku's cabin. The door was locked, but it yielded to the master key. Alaku lay on the floor, his skin blue from cyanide.

He left no note behind. None was needed.

The entire crew was saddened and depressed. Alaku, despite a certain aloofness, had been loved. The many eggs he had fathered in them, and the eggs they had fathered in him, were in the cryogenic tank, waiting to be quick-thawed when they returned to their home.

A few hours later, the two natives killed each other. The bigger one strangled the other. But before that the veins of the strangler's wrists had been bitten into and opened by the other. After the smaller had died, the other had exercised violently to stimulate the bleeding.

Almost, Jagu decided to turn around and capture some more sentients from the same area. But he could not force himself to do that. To return and see Joma again, the awe-inspiring ancient being of stone . . . who knew but what more might go mad? He could be among them.

For several ship-days, he paced back and forth on the bridge. Or he lay in his bed in his cabin, staring at the bulkhead.

Finally, one third-watch, Jagu went onto the bridge. Fawani, the closest of all to him, was also on the bridge, carrying out his slight duties as pilot. He did not seem surprised to see Jagu; Jagu often came here when he was supposed to be sleeping.

"It has been a long time since we were together," said Fawani. "The statue on that Tuu-forsaken planet and Alaku's suicide . . . they have killed love. They have killed everything except wonder about one question."

"I don't wonder. I *know* that it was made by the natives. I know because that's the only way it could be."

"But there's no way of proving it, is there?" said Fawani.

"No," replied Jagu. "So before we get back home, long before, we must make up our minds to act."

"What do you mean?"

"We have several avenues of action. One, report exactly what we have seen. Let the authorities do the thinking for us, let them decide what to do. Two, forget about having discovered the second planet. Report only the first planet. Three, don't go home. Find a planet suitable for colonization, one so far away it may not be found by other joruma ships for hundreds of years, maybe longer.

"All three are dangerous," continued Jagu. "You don't know Arigi as I do. He will refuse to believe in the coincidence because the mathematical chances against it are too high. He will also refuse to believe that Mako did it. He will conclude that we made those statues to perpetrate a monstrous hoax."

"But how could he believe such a thing?"

"I couldn't blame him," said Jagu, "because he knows our past record. He might think that we did it just to raise hell. Or even that the long voyage unbalanced us, that we became converted, backslid to superstition, committed a pious fraud to convince him and others like him. It doesn't matter. He'll think we did it. He has to think that or admit his whole philosophy of life is wrong.

"If we try to get rid of all evidence, the photos, the logbook, we run a risk of someone talking. I think it'd be a certainty. We belong to the species that can't keep its mouth shut. Or somebody else may go mad and babble the truth.

"Personally I think that we should try the third alternative. Go far out into an unknown sector, so far that we can't return. This will put us beyond the range of any ships now built. If, in the future, one should find us, we can always say we had an accident, that the ship couldn't return."

"But what if we reach the end of our fuel, and we still have found no suitable planet?" said Fawani.

"It's a long chance, but the best we have," said Jagu.

He pointed at the lower lefthand corner of a starmap on a bulkhead. "There are quite a few Ao-U stars there," he said. "If I gave the order to you now, at this moment, to head the ship toward them—would you obey my order?"

"I don't know what to think," said Fawani. "I do know that we could spend the rest of our long voyage home arguing about the best course of action. And still be undecided by the time we let down on earth. I trust you, Jagu, because I believe in you."

"Believe?" said Jagu. He smiled. "Are there also born believers in others? And those men born to be believed in? Perhaps. But what about the rest of the crew? Will they as unhesitatingly follow me?"

"Talk to them," said Fawani. "Tell them what you

told me. They will do as I did. I won't even wait for the outcome. I'll turn the ship now. They won't need to know that until after they've decided to do so—provided you talk to them before I'm relieved."

"Very well. Turn it around. Head it in that general direction. We'll pick out a particular star later. We'll find one or die trying. We'll begin life anew. And we don't teach our children anything about the ghosts of long-dead heroes."

"Turn about it is," said Fawani. He busied himself with the controls and with inserting various cards in the computer.

Then, he said, "But can man exist in a religious vacuum? What will we tell them to replace the old beliefs?"

"They'll believe what they want to believe," said Jagu wearily. "Anyway, we've a long time to think about that."

He was silent while he looked out at the stars. He thought about the planet they had just left. The sentients there would never know what gratitude they owed to him, Jagu.

If he had returned to base and told his story, the Navy— no matter what happened to Jagu and his crew—would go to that planet. And they would proceed to capture specimens and would determine their reaction to a number of laboratory-created diseases. Within a few years only the naturally resistant of the natives would be left alive. Their planet would be open to colonization by the joruma.

Now the bipedals had a period of grace. If they developed space travel and atomic power soon enough, the next joruma ship would declare them off-limits.

Who knew? His own descendants might regret this decision. Some day, the sons of those sentients who had been spared by his action might come to the very planet on which his, Jagu's, sons would be living. They might even attack and destroy or enslave the joruma.

That was another chance he and his descendants would have to take.

He pressed the button that would awaken the sleepers and summon those on watch. Now he must begin talking.

He knew that they all would be troubled until the day they died. Yet, he swore to himself, their sons would not know of it. They would be free of the past and its doubts and its fears.

They would be free.

How Deep The Grooves

Always in control of himself, Doctor James Carroad lowered his voice.

He said, "You will submit to this test. We must impress the Secretary. The fact that we're willing to use our own unborn baby in the experiment will make that impression a deeper one."

Doctor Jane Carroad, his wife, looked up from the chair in which she sat. Her gaze swept over the tall lean figure in the white scientist's uniform and the two rows of resplendent ribbons and medals on his left chest. She glared into the eyes of her husband.

Scornfully, she said, "You did not want this baby. I did, though now I wonder why. Perhaps, because I wanted to be a mother, no matter what the price. Not to give the State another citizen. But, now we're going to have it, you want to exploit it even before it's born, just as . . ."

Harshly, he said, "Don't you know what such talk can lead to?"

"Don't worry! I won't tell anyone you didn't desire to add to the State. Nor will I tell anybody how I induced you to have it!"

His face became red, and he said, "You will never again mention that to me! Never again! Understand?"

Jane's neck muscles trembled, but her face was composed. She said, "I'll speak of that, to you, whenever I feel like it. Though, God knows, I'm thoroughly ashamed of it. But I do get a certain sour satisfaction out of knowing that, once in my life, I managed to break down that rigid self-control. I made you act like a normal man, one able to forget himself in his passion for a woman. Doctor Carroad, the great scientist of the State, really forgot himself then."

She gave a short brittle laugh and then settled back in the chair as if she would no longer discuss the matter.

But he would not, could not, let her have the last word. He said, "I only wanted to see how it felt to throw off all restraints. That was all—an experiment. I didn't care for it; it was disgusting. It'll never happen again."

He looked at his wristwatch and said, "Let's go. We must not make the Secretary wait."

She rose slowly, as if the eight months' burden was at last beginning to drain her strength.

"All right. But I'm submitting our baby to this experiment only under protest. If anything happens to it, a potential citizen . . ."

He spun around. "A written protest?"

"I've already sent it in."

"You little fool! Do you want to wreck everything I've worked for?"

Tears filled her eyes.

"James! Does the possible harm to our baby mean nothing to you? Only the medals, the promotions, the power?"

"Nonsense! There's no danger! If there were, wouldn't I know it? Come along now!"

But she did not follow him through the door. Instead, she stood with her face against the wall, her shoulders shaking.

A moment later, Jason Cramer entered. The young man closed the door behind him and put his arm around her. Without protest, she turned and buried her face in his chest. For a while, she could not talk but could only weep.

Finally, she released herself from his embrace and said, "Why is it, Jason, that every time I need a man to cry against, James is not with me but you are?"

"Because he is the one who makes you cry," he said. "And I love you."

"And James," she said, "loves only himself."

"You didn't give me the proper response, Jane. I said I loved you."

She kissed him, though lightly, and murmured, "I think I love you. But I'm not allowed to. Please forget what I said. I mean it."

She walked away from him. Jason Cramer, after making sure that he had no lipstick on his face or uniform, followed her.

Entering the laboratory, Jane Carroad ignored her husband's glare and sat down in the chair in the middle of the room. Immediately thereafter, the Secretary of Science and two Security bodyguards entered.

The Secretary was a stocky dark man of about fifty. He had very thick black eyebrows that looked like pieces of fur pasted above his eyes. He radiated the assurance that he was master, in control of all in the room. Yet, he did not, as was nervously expected by James Carroad and Jason Cramer, take offense because Jane did not rise from the chair to greet him. He gave her a smile, patted her hand, and said, "Is it true you will bear a male baby?"

"That is what the tests indicate," she said.

"Good. Another valuable citizen. A scientist, perhaps. With its genetic background . . ."

Annoyed because his wife had occupied the center of the stage for too long, Doctor James Carroad loudly cleared his throat. He said, "Citizens, honored Secretary, I've asked you here for a demonstration because I believe that what I have to show you is of utmost importance to the State's future. I have here the secret of what constitutes a good, or bad, citizen of the State."

He paused for effect, which he was getting, and then continued, "As you know, I—and my associates, of course—have perfected an infallible and swift method whereby an enemy spy or deviationist citizen may be unmasked. This method has been in use for three years. During that time, it has exposed many thousands as espionage agents, as traitors, as potential traitors."

The Secretary looked interested. He also looked at his wristwatch. Doctor Carroad refused to notice; he talked on at the same pace. He could justify any amount of time he took, and he intended to use as much as possible.

"My Department of Electroencephalographic Research first produced the devices delicate enough to detect the so-called rho waves emanated by the human brain. The rho or semantic waves. After ten years of hard work, I correlated the action of the rho waves in a particular human brain with the action of the individual's voice mechanisms. That meant, of course, that we had a device which mankind has long dreamed of. A—pardon the term—mind-reading machine."

Carroad purposely avoided scientific terminology. The

Secretary did have a Ph.D. in political science, but he knew very little of any biological science.

Jason Cramer, at a snap of the fingers by Carroad, wheeled a large round shining machine to a spot about two feet in front of Jane. It resembled a weird metallic antelope, for it had a long flexible neck at the end of which was an oval and eyeless head with two prongs like horns. These pointed at Jane's skull. On the side of the machine—Cervus III—was a round glass tube. The oscilloscope.

Carroad said, "We no longer have to attach electrodes to the subject's head. We've made that method obsolete. Cervus' prongs pick up rho waves without direct contact. It is also able to cut out 99.99 percent of the 'noise' that had hampered us in previous research."

Yes, thought Jane, and why don't you tell them that it was Jason Cramer who made that possible, instead of allowing them to think it was you?

At that moment, she reached the peak of her hate for him. She wished that the swelling sleeper within her was not Carroad's but Cramer's. And, wishing that, she knew that she must be falling in love with Cramer.

Carroad's voice slashed into her thoughts.

"And so, using the detected rho waves, which can be matched against definite objective words, we get a verbal picture of what is going in the subject's mind at the conscious level."

He gave an order to Cramer, and Cramer twisted a dial on the small control board on the side of Cervus.

"The machine is now set for semantic relations," Carroad said.

"Jane!" he added so sharply that she was startled. "Repeat this sentence after me! Silently!"

He then gave her a much-quoted phrase from one of the speeches of the Secretary himself. She repressed her scorn of him because of his flattery and dutifully concentrated on thinking the phrase. At the same time, she was aware that her tongue was moving in a noiseless lockstep with the thoughts.

The round tube on the side of Cervus glowed and then began flashing with many twisting threads of light.

"The trained eye," said Carroad, "can interpret those waveforms. But we have a surprise for you to whom the patterns are meaningless. We have perfected a means whereby a technician with a minimum of training may operate Cervus."

He snapped his fingers. Cramer shot him a look; his face was expressionless, but Jane knew that Cramer resented Carroad's arrogance.

Nevertheless, Cramer obeyed; he adjusted a dial, pushed down on a toggle switch, rotated another dial.

A voice, tonelessly and tinnily mechanical, issued from a loudspeaker beneath the tube. It repeated the phrase that Carroad had given and that Jane was thinking. It continued the repetition until Cramer, at another finger-snap from Carroad, flicked the toggle switch upward.

"As you have just heard," said Carroad triumphantly, "we have converted the waveforms into audible representations of what the subject is thinking."

The Secretary's brows' rose like two caterpillars facing each other, and he said, "Very impressive."

But he managed to give the impression that he was thinking, Is that all?

Carroad smiled. He said, "I have much more. Something that, I'm sure, will please you very much. Now, as you know, this machine—my Cervus—is exposing hundreds of deviationists and enemy agents every year.

"Yet, this is *nothing!*"

He stared fiercely at them, but he had a slight smile on the corners of his lips. Jane, knowing him so well, could feel the radiance of his pride at the fact that the Secretary was leaning forward and his mouth was open.

"I say this is nothing! Catching traitors after they have become deviationist is locking the garage after the car has been stolen. What if we had a system of control whereby our citizens would be *unable* to be anything but unquestioningly loyal to the State?"

The Secretary said, "Aah!"

"I knew you would be far from indifferent," said Carroad.

Carroad pointed a finger downwards. Cramer, slowly, his jaws set, twisted the flexible neck of Cervus so that the pronged head pointed directly at Jane's distended stomach. He adjusted controls on the board. Immediately the oscilloscope danced with many intricate figures that were so different from the previous forms that even the untutored eyes of the Secretary could perceive the change.

"Citizens," said Carroad, "for some time after we'd discovered the rho waves in the adult and infant, we searched for their presence in the brain of the unborn child. We had no success for a long time. But that was not because the rho waves did not exist in the embryo. No, it was because we did not have delicate enough instruments. However, a few weeks ago, we succeeded in building one. I experimented upon my unborn child, and I detected weak traces of the rho waves. Thus, I demonstrated that the ability to form words is present, though in undeveloped form, even in the eight month embryo.

"You're probably wondering what this means. This knowledge does not enable us to make the infant or the unborn speak any sooner. True. But what it does allow us to do is . . ."

Jane, who had been getting more tense with every word, became rigid. Would he allow this to be done to his own son, his own flesh and blood? Would he permit his child to become a half-robot, an obedient slave to the State, incapable in certain fields of wielding the power of free will? The factor that most marked men from the beasts and the machine?

Numbly, she knew he would.

". . . to probe well-defined areas in the undeveloped mind and there to stamp into it certain inhibitory paths. These inhibitions, preconditioned reflexes, as it were, will not, of course, take effect until the child has learned a language. And developed the concepts of citizen and State.

"But, once that is done, the correlation between the semantic waves and the inhibitions is such that the subject is unable to harbor any doubts about the teachings of the State. Or those who interpret the will of the State for its citizens.

"It is not necessary to perform any direct or physical surgery upon the unborn. The reflexes will be installed by Cervus III within a few minutes. As you see, Cervus cannot only receive; it can also transmit. Place a recording inside that receptacle beneath the speaker, actuate it, and, in a short time, you have traced in the grooves of the brain—if you will pardon an unscientific comparison—the voice of the State."

There was a silence. Jane and Cramer were unsuccessful in hiding their revulsion, but the others did not notice them. The Secretary and his bodyguards were staring at Carroad.

After several minutes, the Secretary broke the silence. "Doctor Carroad, are you sure that this treatment will not harm the creative abilities of the child? After all, we might make a first-class citizen, in the political sense, out of your child. Yet, we might wreck his potentialities as a first-class scientist. If we do that to our children, we lose out in the technological race. Not to mention the military. We need great generals, too."

"Absolutely not!" replied Carroad, so loudly and flatly that the Secretary was taken aback. "My computations, rechecked at least a dozen times, show there is no danger whatsoever. The only part of the brain affected, a very small area, has nothing to do with the creative functions. To convince you, I am going to perform the first operation upon my own son. Surely, I could do nothing more persuasive than that."

"Yes," said the Secretary, stroking his massive chin. "By the way, can this be done also to the adult?"

"Unfortunately, no," said Carroad.

"Then, we will have to wait a number of years to determine if your theory is correct. And, if we go ahead on the assumption that the theory is correct, and treat every unborn child in the country, we will have spent a tremendous amount of money and time. If you are not correct . . ."

"I can't be wrong!" said Carroad. His face began to flush, and he shook. Then, suddenly, his face was its normal color, and he was smiling.

Always in control, thought Jane. *Of himself and, if circumstances would allow, of everybody.*

"We don't have to build any extra machines," said Carroad. "A certain amount will be built, anyway, to detect traitors and enemies. These can be used in hospitals, when not in use elsewhere, to condition the unborn. Wait. I will show you how simple, inexpensive, and swift the operation is."

He gestured to Cramer. Cramer, the muscles twitching at the corners of his mouth, looked at Jane. His eyes tried desperately to tell her that he had to obey Carroad's orders. But, if he did, would he be understood, would he be forgiven?

Jane could only sit in the chair with a face as smooth and unmoving as a robot's and allow him to decide for himself without one sign of dissent or consent from her. What, after all, could either do unless they wished to die?

Cramer adjusted the controls.

Even though Jane knew she would feel nothing, she trembled as if a fist were poised to strike.

Bright peaks and valleys danced on the face of the oscilloscope. Carroad, watching them, gave orders to Cramer to move the prongs in minute spirals. When he had located the area he wished, he told Cramer to stop.

"We have just located the exact chain of neurones which are to be altered. You will hear nothing from the speaker because the embryo, of course, has no language. However, to show you some slight portion of Cervus' capabilities, Cramer will stimulate the area responsible for the rho waves before we begin the so-called inhibiting. Watch the 'scope. You'll see the waves go from a regular pulse into a wild dance."

The cyclopean eye of the oscilloscope became a field of crazed lines, leaping like a horde of barefooted and wire-thin fakirs on a bed of hot coals.

And a voice boomed out, *"Nu'sey! Nu'sey! Wanna d'ink!"*

Jane cried out, "God, what was that?"

The Secretary was startled; Cramer's face paled; Carroad was frozen.

But he recovered quickly, and he spoke sharply. "Cramer, you must have shifted the prongs so they picked up Jane's thoughts."

"I—I never touched them."

"Those were not my thoughts," said Jane.

"Something's wrong," said Carroad, needlessly. "Here. I'll do the adjusting."

He bent the prongs a fraction, checked the controls, and then turned the power on again.

The mechanical voice of Cervus spoke again.

"What do you mean? What're you saying? My father is not crazy! He's a great scientist, a hero of the State. What do you mean? Not any more?"

The Secretary leaped up from the chair and shouted above Cervus' voice, "What is this?"

Carroad turned the machine off and said, "I—I don't know."

Jane had never seen him so shaken.

"Well, find out! That's your business!"

Carroad's hand shook; one eye began to twitch. But he bent again to the adjustment of the dials. He directed the exceedingly narrow beam along the area from which the semantic waves originated. Only a high-pitched gabble emerged from the speaker, for Carroad had increased the speed. It was as if he were afraid to hear the normal rate of speech.

Jane's eyes began to widen. A thought was dawning palely, but horribly, on the horizon of her mind. If, by some intuition, she was just beginning to see the truth . . . But no, that could not be.

But, as Carroad worked, as the beam moved, as the power was raised or lowered, so did the voice, though always the same in tone and speed, change in phrase. Carroad had slowed the speed of detection, and individual words could be heard. And it was obvious that the age level of the speaker was fluctuating. Yet, throughout the swiftly leaping sentences, there was a sameness, an identity of personality. Sometimes, it was a baby just learning the language. At other times, it was an adolescent or young boy.

"Well, man, what is it?" bellowed the Secretary.

The mysterious voice had struck sparks off even his iron nerves.

Jane answered for her husband.

"I'll tell you what it is. It's the voice of my unborn son."

"Jane, you're insane!" said Carroad.

"No, I'm not, though I wish I were."

"*God, he's at the window!*" boomed the voice. "*And he has a knife! What can I do? What can I do?*"

"Turn that off until I get through talking," said Jane. "Then, you can listen again and see if what I'm saying isn't true."

Carroad stood like a statue, his hand extended towards the toggle switch but not reaching it. Cramer reached past him and flicked the switch.

"James," she said, speaking slowly and with difficulty. "You want to make robots out of everyone. Except, of course, yourself and the State's leaders. But what if I told you that you don't have to do that? That Nature or God or whatever you care to call the Creator, has anticipated you? And done so by several billion years?

"No, don't look at me that way. You'll see what I mean. Now, look. The only one whose thoughts you could possible have tapped is our son. Yet, it's impossible for an unborn baby to have a knowledge of speech. Nevertheless, you heard thoughts, originated by a boy, seeming to run from the first years of speech up to those of an adolescent. You have to admit that, even if you don't know what it means.

"Well, I do."

Tears running down her cheeks, choking, she said, "Maybe I see the truth where you don't because I'm closer to my baby. It's part of me. Oh, I know you'll say I'm talking like a silly woman. Maybe. Anyway, I think that what we've heard means that we—all of humanity without exception—*are* machines. Not steel and electrical robots, no, but still machines of flesh, engines whose behavior, motives, and very thoughts, conscious or unconscious, spring from the playing of protein tapes in our brains."

"What the hell are you talking about?" said Carroad.

"If I'm right, we are in hell," she said. "Through no fault or choice of ours. Listen to me before you shut your ears because you don't want to hear, can't hear.

"Memories are not recordings of what has happened in our past. Nor do we act as we will. We speak and behave according to our 'memories,' which are not recorded *after* the fact. They're recorded *before* the fact. Our actions are such because our memories tell us to do such. Each of us is set like a clockwork doll. Oh, not independently, but intermeshed, working together, synchronized as a masterclock or masterplan decrees.

"And, all this time, we think we are creatures of free will and chance. But we do not know there isn't such a thing as chance, that all is plotted and foretold, and we are sliding over the world, through time, in predetermined grooves. We, body and mind, are walking recordings. Deep within our cells, a molecular needle follows the grooves, and we follow the needle.

"Somehow, this experiment has ripped the cover from the machine, showed us the tape, stimulated it into working long before it was supposed to."

Suddenly, she began laughing. And, between laughing and gasping, she said, "What am I saying? It can't be an accident. If we have discovered that we're puppets, it's because we're supposed to do so."

"Jane, Jane!" said Carroad. "You're wild, wild! Foolish woman's intuition! You're supposed to be a scientist! Stop talking! Control yourself!"

The Secretary bellowed for silence, and, after a minute, succeeded. He said, "Mrs. Carroad, please continue. We'll get to the bottom of this."

He, too, was pale and wide-eyed. But he had not gotten to his position by refusing to attack.

She ordered Cramer to run the beam again over the previous areas. He was to speed up the process and slow down only when she so directed.

The result was a stream of unintelligibilities. Occasionally, when Cramer slowed Cervus at a gesture from Jane, it broke into a rate of speech they could understand. And, when it did, they trembled. They could not deny that they were speeding over the life thoughts of a growing male named James Carroad, Junior. Even at the velocity at which they traveled and the great jumps in time that the machine had to make in order to cover the track quickly, they could tell that.

After an hour, Jane had Cramer cut off the voice. In the silence, looking at the white and sweating men, she said, "We are getting close to the end? Should we go on?"

Hoarsely, the Secretary shouted, "This is a hoax! I can prove it must be! It's impossible! If we carry the seeds of predeterminism within us, and yet, as now, we discover how to foresee what we shall do, why can't we change the future?"

"I don't know, Mr. Secretary," said Jane. "We'll find out—in time. I can tell you this. If anyone is preset to foretell the future, he'll do so. If no one is, then the problem will go begging. It all depends on Whoever wound us up."

"That's blasphemy!" howled the Secretary, a man noted for his belligerent atheism. But he did not order the voice to stop after Jane told Cramer to start the machine up again.

Cramer ran Cervus at full speed. The words became a staccato of incomprehensibility; the oscilloscope, an almost solid blur. Flickers of blackness told of broad jumps forward, and then the wild intertwined lightning resumed.

Suddenly, the oscilloscope went blank, and the voice was silent.

Jane Carroad said, "Backtrack a little, Jason. And then run it forward at normal speed."

James Carroad had been standing before her, rigid, a figure seemingly made of white metal, his face almost as white as his uniform. Abruptly, he broke into fluidity and lurched out of the laboratory. His motions were broken; his shouts, broken also.

"Won't stay to listen . . . rot . . . mysticism . . . believe

this . . . go insane! Mean . . . no control . . . no control . . ."
And his voice was lost as the door closed behind him.

Jane said, "I don't want to hear this, Jason. But . . ."

Instantly, the voice boomed, *"God, he's at the window! And he has a knife! What can I do? What can I do? Father, father, I'm your son! He knows it, he knows it, yet he's going to kill me. The window! He's breaking it! Oh, Lord, he's been locked up for nineteen years, ever since he shot and killed my mother and all those men and I was born a Caesarean and I didn't know he'd escape and still want to kill me, though they told me that's all he talked about, raving mad, and . . ."*